Goldie Bird

Written by Patty Ihm

ISBN (paperback): 979-8-218-53496-7

ISBN (hardcover): 979-8-218-53498-1

Cover Art by Patricia Kirk

For my sister Kera, who unwittingly taught me about sunsets, birch bending, bravery, and the magic inside.

Part One: Birch Bending

August 2018
Charlotte, IL

I woke in the darkness. The shadows looked different from Elise's side of the room. I thought sleeping in her bed, where her peppery, flowery smell still lingered, would make me miss her just a little bit less. I held Clover, my stuffed fox, tightly and closed my eyes again. Then, I heard Mama's voice.

"Sorry, yes, this is Florence Martell." I could tell Mama was in the kitchen, right outside my bedroom that I had always shared with my sister. I wondered why she would be talking on the phone in the middle of the night.

"Oh, no…" Her voice was shaky. "Was she, did she…let me get something to write with." I heard Mama shuffling around a bit. "Okay, well, thank you. It will take me a day or so to get myself together and get down there. Yes, by Tuesday, I think I can."

It was especially lonely in the night without Elise. I wondered if she was able to sleep in her room at the university, or if she was awake, too. I just kept thinking that I would have to walk alone to the Candy Counter, swing by myself in the park, even on the double swing, and sit only with Myles the cat while I waited for Mama to return from working at Mr. Quinns' shop each evening. I tried thinking of some of the good things I did with my sister, like balancing on the backs of the park benches when we thought nobody was watching, going with her to watch her boyfriend Teddy's baseball games, and—best of all—falling asleep back-to-back in her bed.

The darkness was just beginning to turn to light when Mama opened my door.

"Oh, Goldie, you're in your sister's bed!" Mama said, as she came to sit beside me. "You miss her, too, I know." Her voice sounded thick.

"Aunt Aida's gone," Mama managed to say, before her tears came. She reached for me, then, and hugged me tightly. I felt sorry for Mama. Her two favorite people had gone away on the same day: one to college and one to heaven.

We left a few hours later that morning to make the long drive to the Courtyard Apartments in Heritage where Aunt Aida had lived and died. I had been staring out the window as the miles passed. My knees were still stiff from driving the day before, when Mama and I had taken Elise to the university. My head was full of thoughts about so many things that there was not much room left for trees, wild grasses, city buildings, or street signs.

I thought about my sister, about her good smell when she hugged me by the elevator before we left her. I had tried breathing in as much of her as I could because Mama said we might not see her again until Christmas.

"Goldie, why don't you ride in Elise's spot on the way to Aida's?" Mama had suggested as we got into the car that morning. I felt hot, sticky, and a little bit sick as I rode in my sister's spot. For the first time, I was in the front seat, and I wondered if I even belonged there.

I also thought about sixth grade. Junior high seemed so scary with locker combinations and room numbers to remember and such long hallways with so many people and so much noise. My summer would be over by the time we got back from Aunt Aida's apartment, and I would have to be brave and grown up and take the bus to Mason Hill Junior High every day. I didn't want this trip to end. I wasn't ready for the things that would happen in junior high.

I thought, too, about Aunt Aida.

Mama was fourteen when she went to live with Great Aunt Aida in the apartment at the Courtyard after her own mother, Grandma Lizzie, had died. Aunt Aida never married, and besides Mama, she had only ever shared her home with three parakeets, one after the other. I remember visiting Aunt Aida one of the last times, and the bird, which had been a vibrant green, was a dusty lilac blue.

"What happened to Murphy? His feathers look different." I hadn't considered that this could have been a different bird entirely.

"Goldie, dear, parakeets don't live forever, and they don't change colors. That's Smiley," offered Aunt Aida, who then went back to her business of knitting a few rows on her sixth cotton kitchen dishcloth of the day.

I never really thought much about birds, or at least about ones that stayed inside the house, unless we were at Aunt Aida's place at the Courtyard. I did like watching the birds that would come to the feeders outside Mr. Quinns' shop. He knew just what kind of bird would eat what type of food, and during which seasons they would visit. "Goldie, birds are like people," he often told me. I was never sure what he meant by this. I thought about Aunt Aida's little parakeet, though, and it struck me that Smiley may have been a little bit lonely. Maybe he was a little like me.

Aunt Aida fascinated me with her simplicity. For a very long time, she had walked to her work at the library in town where she served as a desk clerk. Even in her retirement, she was always very busy, and though I could never figure out just what she did all day, she always seemed content. In many ways, I hoped to be just like her when I was old.

We visited only about once every year—and some years not at all—because it was hard for Mama to take time away from her work and because it was an eleven-hour car ride to the Courtyard.

Aunt Aida had never made the trip to Charlotte. She knew about the secret lilac cave at the edge of the parking lot behind the Warehouse Apartments, but she had never hidden inside, though I know she would have wanted to.

The train station was just down the road from the Courtyard. Mama would tell me about when she rode the train to Aunt Aida's home where she would stay for three weeks each summer. Aunt Aida loved Mama like Mama loved Elise. And I think she loved me like that, too. Then, when Mama's mother died, Mama rode the train to Heritage to live with Aunt Aida.

One of the best things I remember about Aunt Aida was when she helped me and Elise bake our very own apple pies. There was just enough space on the windowsill for two pies to sit for cooling with just a tiny bit of room left between the two tins, so the crusts did not touch. When we could wait no longer for our pies to cool, Aunt Aida gave us each a spoon and a cup of milk in her special milk mugs that had little animals making up the handles and said "Always Drink Milk" in upper case letters. She set two places at the round metal table, which looked as if it had been bright blue at one point in time. She let us eat our entire pies all at once right out of the tins. When we had finished our pies, Elise accidentally knocked her mug off the table. It smashed to pieces, but Aunt Aida didn't get mad at all.

It was late when we arrived at the Courtyard. I slept after dinner until just a few miles outside of Heritage. The warm late summer air pushed through the open car windows and filled me with a dreamy sort of feeling. Mama had been listening to music while I was sleeping. She would only sing if she thought I was asleep. I could tell she was crying, too, by how her voice sounded. When I looked over at her, I could see the tears.

Aunt Aida was the last grownup that meant something to Mama. That's what she told me, anyway. I was sure, though, that Mr. Quinn meant something to her. I figured that she was crying for Aunt Aida, but I wondered if she was crying for more reasons, too.

Mama never wanted me to see her cry. "I'm okay, Goldie," is what she always said when she didn't really seem okay at all. I don't think she wanted me to know when something was bothering her. Really, though, I did know. I could feel it from her heart to mine.

On this night, she put her hand on my knee for a little second.

"We're almost there. We'll have to be super quiet." I just looked straight ahead as Mama spoke to me. I never made much noise, mostly because I never knew what to say.

Mama parked the car in front of Aunt Aida's garage. I could smell the flower blossoms on the plantings that lined the sidewalks leading up to the Courtyard. We didn't have much to carry in. Mama had a small suitcase with what we would need for the next few days, and a bag of groceries. I brought my backpack and, of course, Clover, because even though I was getting older, she still helped me fall asleep at night. Together, Mama and I, without Elise, were going to take care of Aunt Aida's things and, as Mama said, to "carry out her last wishes." Whatever that meant.

Mama still kept a key to Aunt Aida's apartment on her key ring. The Courtyard was a big rectangle with eighteen apartments surrounding an area of green space. Every apartment had a back entrance with a garage. We had to go through the main entrance to get to Aunt Aida's front door because Mama had forgotten the code for her garage.

A little creaking noise came from the gate as we made our way through. I saw a light go on in one of the apartments. When we came to the entrance of Apartment #4, which was also the number for our apartment in Charlotte, Mama set down her bags on Aunt Aida's metal table, the same one where Elise and I had eaten our pies so many years before. Mama fumbled with the key, and I could see her hand shaking a little bit. I heard the sound of something falling from the other side of the courtyard. At the apartment directly across from Aunt Aida's, there was a boy who looked to be about my age, though I couldn't tell for sure in the darkness of the late night...or early morning...whichever it was. He was sitting in a rocking chair. He leaned to pick up a flashlight that had fallen to the ground. He shone the light directly at me and Mama, which startled me, and him as well, before sheepishly raising a hand to greet us. My first instinct was to look away, but I nodded to acknowledge him and also to try to get a better look at this boy. He must have been reading a book outside because he pulled it from his lap and pointed the light at the pages. I wondered what he was reading and why he would be out there alone so late at night.

"Goldie!" Mama had the door open by then and was struggling to get our belongings inside. I turned away from the boy, took a last deep breath of the night air, and walked through the front door into the place where I had had many of my best days.

I was going to be sleeping in Mama's old room. Almost everything was still the same as it had been the last time I had been there with Elise, except of course, Aunt Aida was not there. This time I would get the whole bed to myself. I secretly liked sleeping with Elise because she would let me sleep right up against her with our backs touching. I would try to make my breathing match hers. It wasn't a very big bed for two people, but I loved having Elise to myself for the whole night. I wondered if she had gone to sleep yet, in her new bed at the university.

Mama made herself a cup of tea before tucking me in

with the quilt that one of Aunt Aida's friends had made for her when Grandma Lizzie (Mama's mother) had died. Mama turned off the light in her old room, closed the door, and went down the hallway. After a few minutes, I could hear the bath water running. Aunt Aida had the best bathtub. It was deeper than ours at home and the tiles around it were black with little white streaks in them. The rest of the wall tiles were light pink, like the color of the cotton candy at the summer fair. Aunt Aida always had the same kind of green soap in the little soap holder, also pink, that was built right into the wall. When I was a little girl, I would bring the babies from Aunt Aida's dollhouse into the bathtub with me, and the little soap holder would be where they slept while I had my bath. I hoped I would be able to find those babies while we were at the Courtyard for the last time.

I wondered if the boy was still outside reading his book. Since the bedroom had a window that faced the courtyard, I could find out. I wrapped myself in Mama's quilt and shuffled to the rocking chair. I had to be very careful when I lifted the shade just a tiny bit because sometimes it snapped and rolled all the way to the top. I didn't want the boy to see me, and I didn't want Mama to know that I was out of bed.

The boy was still in the chair. His face was soft in the brightness of the flashlight. I really wanted to know what he was reading and why he was out there. I watched him for a while until I fell asleep in the rocker.

My neck was stiff when I woke to the light of the sun coming through the small opening in the shade. It must have been morning, and I hadn't even slept in Mama's old bed. Across the courtyard, the boy's chair was now empty. I wondered if I would see him again.

Still wrapped in the quilt, I curled up in the middle of the bed and fell asleep, wishing Elise were there with me. At least I still had Clover.

The buzzer to Aunt Aida's door startled me as I woke for the second time. I listened from under the quilt as Mama pulled the chain and opened the door.

"Florence!" I heard a woman's voice.

"Good morning, Nina. Thank you for coming." Nina was Aunt Aida's friend who had worked with her at the library. She drove her places and played cards with her. I remember meeting her for the first time, riding in the back seat of her car with Elise when Nina and Aunt Aida took us to the zoo for my fifth birthday. Mama stayed behind because she didn't feel well, and we got to eat fried calamari at the snack bar after we saw the dolphin show. The dolphins did a special birthday song just for me where they splashed high up out of the water. Aunt Aida told me that it was Nina's idea.

"I'm so sorry, dear," said Nina.

"Me, too," said Mama, and I could hear her voice break. Then, they hugged.

Nina had come to help Mama go through Aunt Aida's things and also to go with her to "make the arrangements." Aunt Aida was not having a funeral. She was being cremated, and Mama was going to get her ashes in a container. Mama said we were going to take Aunt Aida's ashes to the Knotty River by the fairgrounds where Aunt Aida worked when she was younger. Mama said that was the happiest place for Aunt Aida and that's where she would have spent all her days if she could have.

Mama sat with Nina at the kitchen table. They were having tea and jelly donuts, the kind with sugar on the outside. I couldn't wait any longer to use the bathroom, and I had to walk past them to get there.

"Goldie! How you've grown!" exclaimed Nina.

I hurried down the hall and closed the bathroom door behind me without saying a thing.

When I came out, Mama and Nina were already going through Aunt Aida's things. Nina had a key to the apartment, and it had been decided that people from Nina's church would come to take the leftover belongings for their ministries. Mama said I could have anything that I wanted from the apartment. She wanted me to help her pick things for Elise because she wasn't there to choose for herself. They were going to set up a sale with some of the things, too. I took a spot at the table to watch them work.

Nina gave me a jelly donut cut in half. I could see all the dark red jelly even before I took the first bite. I wished I could have had the other half, too. I took my half-donut and the cold milk that Mama had poured into Aunt Aida's special milk mug, the one that was left after Elise had broken the other on the day that we made our pies. Mama said that she remembered drinking from one of the mugs when she and Grandma Lizzie would come to the Courtyard. I knew I wanted to take the milk mug back home to Charlotte.

The front stoop seemed like a good place to eat the last few bites of my donut. The cold milk mixed with the sugary sweetness of the donut tasted so good. There was nobody else outside except for a quiet little dog sitting on the porch of the apartment next to Aida's.

I picked up the empty milk mug and turned to go back inside.

"Goldie!" I spun all the way around to see the boy from the night before walking towards me. "Hello, Goldie. I'm Kip. I hope I didn't scare you last night, shining my flashlight at you." His voice was soft and strong at the same time. He was a good bit taller than me with sandy hair and eyes that reflected colors from the sun.

"But...how did you know my name?" I was confused

and intrigued at the same time.

"Your mom called you 'Goldie' last night. My grandpa said you must be Aida's granddaughter. I heard she died, and I'm sorry."

"Thanks, yeah...Aida was my great aunt. She never had any kids."

"Okay, well, Goldie, it's good to meet you," he said, as he held out his hand.

"So, what were you reading last night?" I had been wondering, so I just asked.

"*The Little Prince*. It's for school, required reading for the summer. I have to finish it by the end of next week, and I've barely started."

"My sister read that book for French class in high school. She was supposed to read the French version, but she mostly read her English copy. Then, she read it to me because she liked it so much. Anyway, how old are you?" I asked.

"I'm twelve. I start seventh grade the week after next here in Heritage. I'm staying with my grandpa for a while, so this is going to be a new school for me," he said.

"I'm starting at a new school, too, back in Charlotte, Illinois, where I live. I'm going to junior high. I don't want to go."

"You don't like school?" He sounded surprised.

"It's not that I don't like school, I mean the work part. Reading and math are pretty okay, and I love doing art.

It's just all the people...so many...and everything is so fast. I'm just afraid."

"I think you are going to be surprised, Goldie. You are going to be just fine." I was trying hard to figure out what color his eyes really were. His cheeks were a pinkish red, from the sun, and he had a splash of freckles. I liked Kip already.

"I should go now. I have to go somewhere with Mama and Aunt Aida's friend," I said.

"So nice to meet you, Goldie. Maybe I'll see you later." I stood still, watching him as he walked toward his grandpa's apartment. Kip turned around as he reached the door and saw me, still staring in his direction. He smiled, waved, and let the door close behind him.

When I went back inside Aunt Aida's place, Mama and Nina were in the middle of piles of Aunt Aida's things. There were two medium-sized boxes, one marked "Elise" and one marked "Goldie," and a few bigger boxes with no markings. Elise's box was full. On top were some of the dishcloths that Aunt Aida had crocheted. My box had only two things: an embroidery kit and a bag of bird seed.

"Goldie, I think Aunt Aida would want you to have Smiley. What do you think?" Mama's face looked a little like she had been crying again. I felt bad for wishing I was still outside with Kip.

"I guess so, if you think he would like to live with us."
I wasn't sure about having a pet bird.

Mama drove to town, and Nina sat with her in the
front seat. My stomach pounded with worry for what we
were about to do. The sun was already hot, but I could see
some darkness in the clouds in the distance, as if there
might be some rain. Elise said that her Grandpa David
once told her that the rain washed away all the hard stuff
to make us feel better. I loved the rain for that reason.

I only got to meet Grandpa David and Granny Boots
one time when they drove halfway to Charlotte to pick up
Elise one summer. She got to stay with them for ten days.
They went fishing, shopping, and to a carnival where the
spinning rides made Elise sick. They lived far away from
Charlotte. Mama and Elise had lived with Elise's daddy,
Davy, in a little yellow cottage house behind a fancy
Victorian home in downtown Charlotte. Both houses
were owned by Grandpa David and Granny Boots, who
had planned to move to the big house at some point. A lot
of things happened, and they never moved to Charlotte.
I hadn't seen Elise's grandparents since that time they
came for Elise, but I always remembered what Grandpa
David said about the rain. Also, when it rained and I wore
my boots outside, I would think about Grandpa David
and Granny Boots, and I would wonder if they had ever

thought about me.

Mama and Nina were having a meeting about getting Aunt Aida's ashes and some other things. The funeral home smelled like flowers and barbecued pork. There was a wide room with a thick carpet that had red and maroon swirls and gold on the edges. Most of the doors were closed, but there was one open door at the end of the wide room. We went in there and met with a tall, thin man named Barry, who had absolutely no hair. He shook Mama's and Nina's hands before turning to shake mine. I liked how he looked when he smiled, and I was grateful that he thought to include me in the handshaking.

There was more handshaking after talking about Aunt Aida's "remains," and Barry told Mama that he would call in a few days. It still looked like it might rain when we left the funeral home. Nina took me and Mama to the diner in town. She told us that every Thursday she would eat there with Aunt Aida. This day was Tuesday. Maybe she was thinking about that and about how Thursdays were never going to be the same again.

I ordered a grilled cheese sandwich and a Monkey Milkshake, which was chocolate ice cream and bananas all blended up. There was a tiny plastic purple monkey that hung from the straw. The sandwich came with green beans, the long string-type. They were even better than the milkshake or the grilled cheese.

Nina ate a salad with chopped-up eggs and Mama

had barley soup with at least four pieces of bread. They talked for a long time, mostly about Aunt Aida and Elise. I didn't say a single thing the whole time we were eating. They didn't seem to notice.

I had been thinking about Kip and whether I might see him again. I certainly hoped so; we were going to be at the Courtyard until Barry was done with whatever he had to do with Aunt Aida and then we were going to take her ashes to the fair, which made me feel very weird to even think about.

The sun was shining when we left the diner. I could tell it had been raining by the little puddles at the edge of the sidewalk and the way the flower petals sparkled in the brightness of the early afternoon. I walked ahead of Nina and Mama, neither of whom told me to stop balancing along the backs of the city benches as we returned to Mama's car. I thought of Elise, how she had taught me to do that many summers ago, and how she still did it when we were together.

Mama and Nina went back to the boxes when we returned to the Courtyard. Aunt Aida had a lot of stuff. Mama asked me to go to the Courtyard office to pick up Aunt Aida's mail.

I had to ring the bell two times before a little hunched

man appeared behind the counter. He took a long time trying to put Aida's big pile of mail into a brown box. After a while, he dumped it all back onto the table in front of him and disappeared again. When he returned a few minutes later, he had a grocery bag. At about the same speed that he had used to fill the box, he loaded Aunt Aida's mail into the bag. He slid the full bag across the counter to me, offered a half smile, and went back to where he came from before I could thank him. I left the office carrying the bag from beneath and thinking the whole time how much better the box would have been.

"Hey!" Kip seemed to have appeared out of nowhere. He was standing on the bench outside of the office, holding his book in one hand. His hair was a little messy, sort of windy-looking. Maybe that was just how it always was.

"You know," I said, "You're kind of like the Little Prince, just showing up in random places."

"Huh?" He looked confused. "Oh, the book. I still haven't read enough to really know what you mean. Anyway, hello, Goldie Bird!"

"Goldie Bird? Where did you get that?" The only person that had really ever called me anything except "Goldie" was Elise, and only once in a while, when she called me "Goldie Girl."

"I think you're kind of like one of those birds. You know, they're little and yellow and mighty, and they dart around really fast from place to place. You're like that,

Goldie. Like a goldfinch, that's what they're called. I watched you balancing along the backs of those benches when you were going to the office, and I just thought of that for some reason, probably because your name is Goldie."

He waited for me to say something.

"Well, my name is actually Jane Golden Martell. The Jane part is after my Great Aunt Aida, but my sister's name is Elise Aida, so I got Aunt Aida's middle name, Jane." Kip's smile was quiet and sweet as he listened to what I had to say.

"I'm still going to call you Goldie Bird, okay?" he asked.

"Elise first called me Goldie, actually. It was from a book she liked about a golden bear," I began. "Mama was going to choose Jane Golden Martell because Golden was her maiden name. Elise really wanted the Golden part to be my first name, because she wanted to call me Goldie, but Mama didn't think that Golden would be a very good first name."

"Well, I like it, Goldie Bird." Kip had been listening to my story. I wasn't really used to that.

Aunt Aida liked birds for sure, so I think she would have liked it, too... and Mr. Quinn.

"You can call me Goldie Bird if you like," I answered in a hesitant voice, though my insides were dancing with happiness that someone—not just any someone, but

Kip—would make a special name for me.

"Hey, Goldie Bird, are you doing anything this afternoon? I mean, do you want to meet my grandpa?" I was a little afraid to seem too excited about the invitation.

We walked together back to #4 where Mama and Nina were drinking coffee from Aunt Aida's mugs and, from the looks of it, not working on loading the boxes very quickly. They were talking about setting up a sale, which would be Thursday and Friday.

I went through the door first, and Kip followed behind.

"Mama...Nina...this is Kip," I said. Mama looked surprised, and Nina looked confused.

"Hello. I'm Charlie Weller's grandson. He lives across the courtyard. I'm staying with him for a while." Kip was such a gentleman.

"Oh, Charlie Weller," said Nina, "Aida often spoke of Charlie and his wife. I met your grandfather one time, some years ago. My youngest daughter got her wedding dress from his shop. Lovely man. The dress was lovely, too. Sorry about your grandmother, son. What did you say your name was?"

"Patrick, but most everyone calls me Kip. Yeah, thank you. We miss her...especially Grandpa does."

Mama said it would be fine if I went with Kip for a while that afternoon. We would be going to Nina's house in the country for dinner, though, so I would need to be back for that.

Across the Courtyard, I could see Kip's grandpa watching us through his front window. His face was kind. We walked past the chair where I had seen Kip for the first time. It seemed strange to me that it had only been the day before because I somehow felt that we had known each other much longer.

Kip pushed open the door, and my feet felt heavy under my body as I followed behind. There was music coming from down the hall. The apartment smelled of tomatoes and spices. Kip's grandpa turned around as we entered and spoke softly. "You must be Goldie! I'm so happy to meet you!"

Kip's Grandpa Charlie poured iced tea into three glasses that were all different, all old-looking. Mine had a red rim and a red bottom, and the rest was clear glass with a bubble pattern all over. It was beautiful, and I liked how it felt in my hands and how the bubbles reflected all of the colors in the room.

"The glasses are cool, huh?" said Kip.

I nodded, "They came from your shop, right, Grandpa?" asked Kip. "You should tell Goldie about Secondhand Charlie's."

"Years ago, Ellen—that's my wife--and I opened a shop called, Secondhand Charlie's." Grandpa Charlie's eyes brightened as he spoke. "It's a collector's and vintage shop. Ellen loved old things; treasures, as we liked to call them."

"The shop was close to downtown in a building that had been a barn for many years before," he continued, "and we were able to buy it with help from the city when the old farm was sold."

I could see the sparkle in Grandpa Charlie's eyes as he talked about his beloved shop. I hoped I would get to see it sometime.

"That's so cool," I said. "I like old stuff, too." I told him about the old harmonica Gabriella, my school friend, and I had found in the secret spot inside my and Elise's bedroom closet.

He talked for a long time, for a couple of hours. He just kept on going, and I kept on listening. I loved hearing his stories and learning what his life was about. Grandpa Charlie talked about Mary, his only child, and how she was the best thing in his life next to Ellen, who was his sweetheart when he was a young man. They hadn't even known each other for very long when they got married. Her family wasn't happy about this. Grandpa Charlie vowed to love her like no one had loved another before, and that's just what he did. They had Mary about five years after they were married. He said she was the perfect little girl, just a blessing every single day.

His eyes were misty, but it didn't make me uncomfortable. I wondered if he needed to say all this stuff, all this stuff that I needed to hear. At one point, Kip got up, went to the kitchen, and brought back a silver metal pitcher filled with iced tea. He topped off the glasses: first his grandpa's, then mine, and finally, his own.

"You know, Pat, he doesn't treat her right. He never did, not as I saw it." As Grandpa Charlie spoke, I looked at Kip, who moved his eyes from mine as soon as they met. He looked down to the floor, specifically, I thought, at my bare toes with the almost-worn-off purple glittery nail polish.

"Pat. That's my dad. That's why my name is Patrick."

Then, neither of them said anything for a long time.

"Mom wanted me to stay with Grandpa for a while, so when we came for our summer visit, I just stayed. I wanted to. It wasn't just Mom."

"Where is she now?" I asked.

"Mary's back at their house in Ohio with the girls." Grandpa Charlie had a long sigh. I could tell he missed her, and I could tell he missed his wife, Ellen. Loving someone so much for so long and then losing them...I really couldn't think of anything sadder.

Then, Kip spoke up. "My parents are having a hard time. They argue about stuff that doesn't make sense. Not to me, anyway. Mom thought it would be a good idea for me to keep Grandpa company, but I sort of think she wants me away from what's going on at home. The girls are little, but I know there's a lot that she doesn't want me to hear."

"Oh, Goldie, I have kept you too long! You kids were going to go out and have fun for the afternoon." I wished Grandpa Charlie hadn't seen it that way.

"Grandpa Charlie. Can I call you Grandpa Charlie? I loved your stories, your iced tea, and just sitting here in your house." I meant every word, and I didn't want to leave, but I knew I had to go with Mama to Nina's place that night.

"Of course, Goldie. I would love for you to call me Grandpa Charlie." I saw the spark returning to his eyes.

"I have to go now," I said, as I stood up. I hadn't noticed that I had been sitting on a couch that looked like something from the space-age, rust-colored and on wheels. Kip skipped over the back of the couch and beat me to the door.

"I wish you both could come with us," I said, as I stepped into my sandals.

"I wish, too," said Kip. He put his hand gently on my shoulder as he opened the door. "But Goldie Bird, I've got reading to do!"

"Yes, you do! Maybe I'll see you later." I waved to Kip and Grandpa Charlie, and as I heard the door close behind me, I felt as though my heart might explode.

Nina's house was a few miles in the opposite direction from town, high up on a hill that was bursting with wildflowers. There were five wooden boxes with lids that looked like tiny houses in a row at the edge of the property. Mama said those were Nina's beehives. I wondered why anyone would want to have beehives on their property until Nina gave me my own jar of honey from her bees.

She also sent me back to Aunt Aida's place with a plate of brownies, vanilla frosted with sprinkles, because after eating chicken and broccoli and applesauce, I had no room left in my stomach for dessert. Also, I had taken Nina's cat for a ride on the big tree swing while Mama and Nina finished eating in the kitchen, so I was feeling just a little weird inside.

The dark stretch of country road on the way back to the Courtyard made wonder what it was like for Nina to live alone on that big property. Mama said Nina had two daughters and two sons who were already grown by the time Nina and her husband inherited the farm. Nina talked about the bees and the flowers and working with Aunt Aida at the library, and how after her husband had died, she was so grateful to have Aida to do things with like walking around town, eating at restaurants, and reading books on the benches at the park, because she was otherwise alone.

Since Aunt Aida died, it didn't seem like Nina had anyone left, except the cats, and unless her children or grandchildren came for a visit, which it seemed like they hardly ever did. I thought she must have been happy to have Mama, and even me, too, even if it was for a sad reason.

I picked at the frosting on the brownies as we got closer to town. I had thought of sharing them with Kip and Grandpa Charlie, so I didn't want to make a mess of them. I was going to ask Mama if she wanted one, but I didn't want to interrupt her from whatever she had been thinking about. I felt sad for Mama because a lot of things were happening to her, like Aunt Aida dying and Elise going away. I was sad for me, too, but I guess it didn't matter as much because...well, because it just didn't.

Mama parked her car in the driveway. The office man had given us Aunt Aida's garage code along with her mail, so we went into #4 through the back door. There was so much stuff in Aunt Aida's garage, probably because she never had a car to keep in there. There were books, tools, a rack with fancy old-looking coats and hats (far too many for one person, I thought), a big, thick, old television, a chair with an old-fashioned hair dryer mounted at the back of it, a wooden table with the chairs stacked all on top, and so many other things. I thought there would be no possible way they could be ready to have a sale that started anytime soon.

Mama changed her shoes and went back out through the garage.

"See you soon, Goldie. Remember, stay close!" She didn't really say where she was going or when she would be back.

I watched her from the little window in Aunt Aida's bathroom. Her hair was a bit lighter than Elise's, but a little darker than mine, and twisted back into a sort of bun at the back of her head. Mama was pretty, like Elise. From behind, it seemed like she was a teenager. She walked up the road toward town and soon disappeared over the hill.

I took the brownies that Nina had made and went to sit at the little table in front of the apartment just in case Kip might be out there—in case he wanted a brownie.

Kip was, indeed, outside. He sat with his legs over one side of the rocking chair in front of his grandpa's apartment. His flashlight was on the ground beside his chair, as if he were anticipating reading long into the night. I waited for what seemed like an hour for him to notice me.

"Goldie Bird! What are you eating?" I took that as my invitation to join him.

"Did you ever notice? The Little Prince doesn't

really eat food. I thought you were kind of like him, but I guess you're not, because you just ate like five of Nina's brownies." Kip was looking at me as I spoke, but I didn't think he really heard what I had said.

"Oh, yeah, I still haven't gotten very far in the book. I keep trying, but it's just really distracting, being here and trying to get this done."

"It's a great book," I promised, because it really was. "Do you even know what it's about?"

Kip shrugged.

"Hey, how about if we read it together? We can take turns reading, and it will go lots faster," I suggested.

"Hold on," said Kip. He sprang from one side of the rocker without knocking it over, handed me his copy of *The Little Prince* and disappeared inside his grandpa's apartment.

He had folded the page where the Little Prince asked the pilot to draw him a sheep. Indeed, Kip had not gotten very far.

He came back out a few minutes later with two cream-colored diner mugs full of cocoa. He put them down next to the flashlight, which I suspected we might need very soon because the sun had nearly set. "Grandpa Charlie said to ask if you would swap a brownie for some cocoa? And he said to tell you goodnight. I know he misses my grandma's good baking."

Kip was back right away to find that I had taken over

his rocking chair. He said nothing about it, taking a spot on the sidewalk next to the mugs of cocoa. He pulled his knees to his chest. Kip handed me the flashlight as he smiled up at me. I could still see the sunshine in his eyes, even in the darkness. "I think this is a great idea, Goldie," he said.

He listened as I read aloud. It almost seemed like I was Elise and Kip was me. For a little while, I wasn't even lonely for my sister.

"The Little Prince visits so many random people," he said when I had come to the end of another chapter. "Do you ever think about what all of these people here are doing inside their apartments? I mean, it's like each of us has a little planet. Everyone is so different, but how is it that two people get the chance to meet?"

From Kip's question, it was clear that he had been listening. We looked at each other then, and I thought inside that I was so happy to be in the same place as Kip on this planet.

"And sometimes," he went on, "Grandpa Charlie's home feels like a completely different planet than my home in Ohio. A better one, I think, where people are just happier, even though sad things still happen. Do you get what I mean, Goldie Bird?"

"I think I do," I said in a quiet voice. And really, I did.

A light went on in #4. I handed the book back to Kip. "You can read next time," I said, as I turned to go back to Aunt Aida's place. I had no idea how much time had passed, but the day had been long, and I knew it was time to get some sleep.

"Goodnight, Goldie!" Kip called to me as I crossed the courtyard.

Even with the combination of brownies, hot cocoa, and thoughts of a full day's adventures, sleep came easily under the quilt in Mama's old bed.

"What's his name again, Goldie? Charlie Weller's grandson?" I had been watching cartoons on Aunt Aida's television and hadn't heard Mama come down the hallway until she spoke. She was already dressed, ready to pick up where she had left off the day before.

"His name's Kip, Mama," I answered.

"Do you think you two could help me with some stuff a little later this morning? I need help moving some boxes and setting up tables for Aunt Aida's sale," she said.

"I can ask him, Mama. And I really like him. He's different from anyone I know in Charlotte."

Mama smiled and went to the kitchen to make coffee. I hoped she would let me have some. It always depended on her mood, not how late it was or anything like that.

I brought my buttered toast with me to Kip's place.

When I got to his porch, I noticed the empty brownie pan that I had left the night before. The flashlight and the book were still outside, too.

The door opened before I even knocked.

"I didn't read anymore. After you left, I mean," Kip offered, apologetically. He still had his clothes on from the night before.

"That's not why I'm here," I said. "Mama wanted me to ask for your help with something to get ready for my Aunt Aida's sale."

"Really? Kip's face brightened as he spoke. "Let me make sure it's okay with my grandpa. I was going to go to work with him today, but he might let me stay back to help."

"There she is!" Grandpa Charlie came out from around the corner. His mood was much lighter than it had been when we were last together. "What are you up to today, Goldie Bird?" he asked. Kip must have told him about the name he had given me.

I told both of them how we were preparing to sell Aunt Aida's things. Grandpa Charlie seemed interested in knowing if there would be anything that he could use for his shop. He thought he would come around after he closed his shop for the night. Kip was able to stay to help as long as he promised to make himself useful and to take good care of me. I knew he would.

We worked hard for Mama, lifting, and arranging

tables, chairs, boxes, random things, and so many books. It was hard to think that one little lady could have so much stuff.

Mama said we had helped as much as she needed until Nina would come back, so she gave us money to walk to town and get some lunch. I was a little surprised that she didn't want to go along with us. Maybe she wasn't hungry. Maybe she was going to eat some of the chicken that she had brought back from Nina's from the night before. Maybe she was tired of being around me all the time, and she was glad that Kip could keep me company.

On the way to town, I walked along the backs of as many benches as I could possibly find. Kip was good at keeping my pace. The red geraniums in the planter boxes along the sidewalks downtown made me think of Mr. Quinns' shop and how he must have been missing Mama's help while we were gone.

We decided to have lunch at the same diner where I had eaten the day before with Mama and Nina. Kip ordered grilled cheese with tomato soup, and that sounded good to me, so I ordered the same. We both got Monkey Milkshakes.

We ate our lunch and talked about what we might do later that afternoon. Mama didn't need any more help, and I thought iht it might be best if I just stayed out of her way. Kip said he wanted to show me the lagoon down beyond the Courtyard. He said we could pick the wild blueberries that grew there, and nobody would care at all. To me, that sounded perfect.

"Maybe we can read some more of your book, too," I suggested. I didn't want to be a bad influence, or Grandpa Charlie might not have wanted me to spend my time with Kip.

"Maybe. But let's go to the lagoon first. I have to show you something!" Kip ran a few steps ahead of me.

Behind the Courtyard on Grandpa Charlie's side was a grassy area that sloped down into a grove of trees. Some were tall, slim trees with bark that seemed to be shedding. And there were so many blueberry bushes just bursting with blue-black fruit.

We stopped at Kip's place to get a bucket for our harvest.

"Is this what you wanted to show me, Kip?" I asked eagerly.

"Oh, this is just the beginning!" He reached for my arm, holding firmly between my shoulder and my elbow. "Come this way," he said. "Be careful. It might still be slippery down here from yesterday's rain." Kip pulled me along next to him, past the blueberry bushes, onto a well-worn path of rocks and stone, near where the trees with the loose bark grew. We came to a clearing.

"The lagoon! What do you think?" His eyes sparkled.

I wasn't sure what I should say. It was like a secret tiny lake of some sort with nobody near except me and Kip.

"Come around here." He had let go of my arm, but he grabbed it again and pulled me a little further along the edge of the water. He stopped before what looked like a little cave about as high as my shoulders, made of stones and earth. It was set back from the water by about ten feet and tucked beneath a few of the trees.

"What...what is that?" I asked.

"It's my secret cave. Grandpa Charlie helped me build it a few summers ago when my family was visiting. Nothing has bothered it, and every summer when I come, I add a little more dirt, so it stays really solid." I could tell Kip was proud of his little cave.

Inside Kip's cave toward the front was a cross section of a tree, a foot and a half high, with three logs surrounding it, just like chairs around a table. Across the back of the cave were all sorts of thin branches that must have come from the trees with the loose bark, but if they were from those trees, all of the bark had been peeled off to make them smooth. The branches were tied—more like woven—together with twine.

"See that?" Kip pointed to where I had been looking. "That's my birch tree bed."

"Oh. Those are the trees with the loose bark?" I asked. "So, do you stay in here? Like, sleep in here? By yourself?"

"I have, but no one ever found out, except now you know. I did it two times this summer when Grandpa Charlie was sleeping. I climbed out the window in the room where I was staying. I knew Grandpa would be leaving for work early on those mornings, and I always close the door when I go to bed. He goes to work before I get up, unless I am going with him, so he never found out either of those times."

My eyes were wide with disbelief. "Why would you do that? And weren't you afraid? Afraid of getting caught or of something coming after you in the night?"

"Nah, I didn't think about that stuff. Sometimes I just want to be in charge of myself and do stuff that feels right, no matter what anyone else thinks. Do you know what I mean?" he asked.

I did. I knew just what he meant. I wasn't sure, though, that I was brave enough to be like Kip.

"Goldie, do you like climbing trees?" Kip asked.

"I love to climb trees! Once when I was mad," I told him, "I climbed up super high into a tree behind the warehouse. That's part of the shop where Mama works. Mama, my sister Elise, Mr. Quinn—that's Mama's boss— and all the workers from the store were searching for me, calling my name, and getting all worried about me while I sat up on the highest branches and watched them."

"Oh, you are funny!" Kip said. "What were you mad about, anyway?"

"I have no idea. I just know I was mad. I was so mad but being up far above everything made me feel so much better. And when they finally found me, Mama was so relieved that she hugged me and didn't let go for a long time. She didn't get angry or yell or anything. She was too happy to see me, I guess."

"So come over here with me," he said, this time taking my hand in his and heading toward the water with long, quick steps so I had to nearly run to keep pace. We stopped just before a gathering of tall, thin trees with the peeling bark.

"This is going to be better than climbing a tree, Goldie. Trust me. Watch this!" Kip stood between two of the birch trees and flashed a little smile of adventure.

He made his way up to about the middle of one of the trees, using a second tree to hold onto to help him keep his balance. Then, he let go of the second tree and continued to scoot higher, slowly, and cautiously, up the birch tree.

I don't remember how far up he was in the tree when it started to sway. My eyes widened. He climbed further still and then suddenly let go with his feet, keeping hold with his hands. The tree bent from his weight and gently lowered Kip all the way to the ground. He let go of the birch tree, and it sprung back to its original straight position in the grove. We laughed and laughed so hard that our bellies hurt, and we both fell to the ground.

"You have to try it! It's the best feeling, like you're

floating!"

I chose a tree near to the one that Kip had climbed. I thought of that day when I had hidden from everyone and how different I felt on this day as I made my way high up into the late afternoon air. Nobody was looking for me or worried about me at all. Just me and Kip having fun doing something that Mama might have been angry with me for doing, but I didn't care one bit. It was magical, like I was an actual bird or fairy for those seconds when the birch tree carried me to the ground. I couldn't wait to tell Elise!

"We should try doing it together," suggested Kip. "Maybe we would go extra fast."

I climbed first, and Kip followed. I went higher and higher, as quickly as I could move. My arms burned and my legs were so tired, almost shaking. The sun was bright and blinding through the tops of some of the trees. Kip was just a few feet below me when the tree began to sway. Before I could even let go with my feet, the tree shifted harshly toward the ground and, like a giant slingshot, launched me and Kip right into the water. We learned that day that real birch bending was a one-person activity.

We laughed as we sat in the murky lagoon water up to our necks. It had been the very best afternoon that I had ever remembered. I had a feeling Kip felt the same.

And we had forgotten all about the blueberries.

Mama and Nina would have been in the garage organizing all of Aunt Aida's things, so I thought it would be best to try to sneak in through the front door to clean myself up. I left my soaked, muddy shoes outside and turned the doorknob as carefully and quietly as I could. Smiley noticed me and cocked his head sideways, but he didn't chirp.

The green soap bar was quite a bit smaller once I had finished washing all of the lagoon dirt from my entire body. It felt good to get so clean, and the smell of the soap reminded me of when I used to play with Aunt Aida's dollhouse babies. Wrapped in a soft lilac towel and wearing nothing else, I crept down the hall toward the bedroom to get dressed. I had almost reached the door when I heard Mama's voice.

"Goldie! What on earth have you done?" I turned to see not only Mama with an angry face, but a trail of dirty footprints leading from the front door to the bathroom, along Aunt Aida's soft pink carpet. My cheeks burned and tears welled up in my eyes. I felt sick inside.

"Mama, I'll clean it, I promise. I'm sorry."

"Yes, you will. We're in here working so hard to get ready for tomorrow, and you are running around outside in the mud making more work for us?" Mama was mad!

"What were you doing to get that dirty, anyway?"

"I'm sorry, Mama," I said again. "We...I fell in the lagoon, in the shallow water."

"Well, I don't know about that boy, that Kip, if you are falling in the lagoon or whatever."

Mama would never have understood Kip, and she would definitely never have understood birch bending. I wasn't ever going to tell her.

"So, can I..." I started to ask if I could go to get dressed when Nina came through the door and startled me. The lilac towel dropped from my hands and fell to my feet. There I stood, completely naked and humiliated, in front of Mama and Nina.

Mama let out an uncomfortable laugh and just then I hated her for it. Nina turned so as not to embarrass me further. I collected my towel, which was hardly worth wrapping around me anymore, and hurried the rest of the way into the bedroom where I tucked myself under the quilt. Then came the tears, so hard that they shook my whole body.

I had cried myself to sleep and woke to a sharp knock on the bedroom door.

"Goldie, the stuff to clean your mess from the rug is outside your door. Are you coming to dinner with us?" It was Mama, and she didn't sound as mad as before. Still, I didn't want to see her, even though I was so hungry that my stomach hurt.

"I'm not hungry," I lied. I hadn't gotten dressed, and I really didn't want to get out of bed. I missed Elise, and I didn't want to be with Mama, but I didn't want to go home, either.

"Okay, well, we will bring something back for you then. I love you," she said as I heard her voice trail away.

I didn't answer. After a few minutes, I put some new clothes on and got busy cleaning the rug. My footprints came out pretty easily; it just took a little bit of scrubbing. I thought about Mama, and how she had laughed at me. I felt a little sad for her. I figured that she didn't have much to laugh about these days, with all the sad things that had happened. I didn't think she would have laughed if it had been Elise, though.

Just as I was on my way to the kitchen to get some water, someone knocked at the front door. It was Kip. He, too, had gotten cleaned up after our birch-bending adventure.

"Hey, Goldie Bird, what are you doing tonight? Grandpa Charlie said that you could come with us to go school shopping, if you want to." Kip smelled fresh and clean, like a pine tree and candy. His hair had been combed with the front slicked to mostly one side, and it was long enough to curl up in a few places to frame his face, a lot like the Little Prince's hair looked in the book.

School shopping! I still needed to get all of my supplies for junior high. The list had come in the mail, but with everything that happened, we hadn't had a chance to get anything.

"Mama's at dinner with Nina," I told him. "I shouldn't go anywhere without her permission."

"You okay?" Kip asked.

I shrugged my shoulders just a little bit, wondering how he had known. He told me they could wait, that he was going to get his book, and that he would stay with me until Mama came back, so I wouldn't have to be alone.

We sat outside, this time on Aunt Aida's front porch, in the same place where Elise and I had eaten those pies. I wished for pie like the ones we had made, one for me and one for Kip this time.

Kip helped me clean up my shoes with Grandpa Charlie's hose, and we left them in the sun to dry. He then began reading *The Little Prince* from the place where I had left off the night before, when the Little Prince visited the planet of a lamplighter. He continued, and I thought of how I had loved listening to Elise as she read about the Little Prince's travels, his appreciation of sunsets, and how dearly he loved and missed his flower. I thought a little bit about Rosa, Mr. Quinns' daughter, too. She liked everything about flowers.

Mama had come in through the garage; I hadn't heard the car pull in. She opened the front door and set a pizza box in front of me and Kip. "Here's something for you two to eat. And Goldie, the rug looks great," she said. Nina wasn't with her.

"Mrs. Martell? Is it okay if Goldie comes along with me and my grandpa to get my supplies for school?" He addressed Mama before I even had the chance. Mama had a faraway look on her face for a few seconds. She must have remembered that I, too, would need some supplies for school.

Mama asked Kip to call her "Florence." She said she had some arranging to do to finish getting ready for the sale anyway. She gave me two ten-dollar bills to get what I needed for school. We each took one more piece of pizza from the box as we headed back to Kip's place.

It was close to sunset when we finally left for the store. We rode in the front seat of Grandpa Charlie's old blue truck, with me between Kip and his grandpa. I wished that Elise was with us, but then there would have been no room for her to sit.

I wasn't expecting Grandpa Charlie to pull the truck to the side of the road so suddenly. He pushed open his door and stepped out onto the side of the road. Fear rose suddenly in my throat. I could feel my chin quiver as I looked, wide-eyed, to Kip.

"Oh, Goldie, don't be afraid! He always does this for the good sunsets!" Kip said.

Grandpa Charlie looked back at us from his spot at the side of the road. "Always remember, the sunset sky will be there for you when you think you have nothing left," he said.

"Don't forget that, Goldie, and I won't either," said Kip in a voice that seemed a little far away.

The sunset! It was so beautiful, with waves of orange and pink that looked like sherbet and little bursts of yellow-white light. Kip opened the passenger-side door, and I followed him out of the truck. There we stood, staring at the late summer sky for what seemed like a pretty long time to me, and nobody said a word. I just thought about how the Little Prince loved watching the sunsets, and I was no longer afraid.

We shopped for pencils, notebooks, pink erasers, folders, loose leaf paper (we both liked the college rule kind best), index cards, and a few other things that seemed important to starting a new school year. I figured I would have enough money left to get some Sugar Babies. Grandpa Charlie insisted on paying for everything, including my candy. He said it was his way of thanking me for being such a good friend to Kip. I thought, then, that he must have been glad that I came to Heritage with Mama, and I knew that I was.

Grandpa Charlie stopped again on the way back to the Courtyard, but this time it was too dark to watch the sunset. He was taking us for ice cream. A milkshake, birch-bending, and ice cream all in the same day!

We sat under pineapple-shaped string lights which hung from a few trees planted at the edges of the patio bricks. Nobody else was out there; just me, Kip, and his grandpa. Kip had a chocolate cone that dripped down his arm and onto the patio. He hadn't seemed to notice; he was lost in his thoughts.

"What's your mom really like, Goldie? And what about your dad?" he asked. Grandpa Charlie looked up from his marshmallow sundae as if he, too, had been wondering.

I wondered if it would be a good thing to talk about some of the things that usually stayed inside of me.

"Mama," I began, "well, it's just me, and Mama, and Elise. Or actually not really Elise anymore because she just went to the university. She left last week. Sometimes I wonder where I'm going to fit in now. It's different with Elise gone." My voice trailed off as I realized I wasn't really answering what had been asked of me. I continued, "I don't have a dad. Well, I did, or I do, but he has never been around or in my life. Mama doesn't like when I ask about him." I could feel my cheeks getting hot again. I didn't know much about my dad, except that he only stayed with Mama for a short while and then he went away. There were so many things that I wondered about him. Mostly, I wondered why he left and if I even mattered to him. Sometimes I would ask Mama questions about him even though I knew she didn't want me to. She would pull me close, but she would mostly just tell me it wasn't the right time to talk about him. I wondered if it ever would be.

Grandpa Charlie put his arm around me. The pineapple lights made his face sparkle a little bit.

"Goldie, dear, sometimes adults are hard to understand. I think a lot of times grown-ups do not even understand themselves. You need to know, though, that you are a magnificent girl, and it makes no difference how you got here. Your mom must be pretty great, too, because you came from her." I could tell how much he meant the words that he had said.

"My family is mixed up, too," offered Kip. "I guess I don't mean to say that your family is mixed up, but I mean..."

"No, Kip, it's fine. I know what you mean," I said.

"But your dad," Kip went on, "...don't you think it's fair that you get to know about your dad? I mean, your mom does...know about him, right?"

"It's hard for Mama. She was married to my sister Elise's dad, Davy. They were high school sweethearts. He died in a car accident, and everything was different after that. I came along, and I think sometimes it would have been easier for her if she just had Elise. I know Mama loves me. I just don't know what really makes her happy besides Elise."

"Goldie Bird, you make her happy, and you will

continue to make her happy. You will look back some day and realize just how much you have meant to her. And when the time is right, I bet she will tell you a bit more about your dad." Grandpa Charlie, like Kip, always seemed to say the right things.

Kip sprung from his spot under the pineapple lights. "We forgot about the blueberries," he cried. "After that crazy time we spent birch-bending, we completely forgot about picking blueberries!" Grandpa Charlie had a quiet laugh and looked at me as he shook his head.

"Kip!" I was so surprised. "You told him? Grandpa Charlie knows what we did?"

"Of course, Goldie. Kip tells me everything…at least I think he does. Besides, I showed him how to do that in the first place. That's what I did for fun, too, when I was somewhere around your age. I don't remember landing in the lagoon, but I think it would have been a good time!" Grandpa Charlie was like a kid, but better. He had taught Kip to do something that I could not even tell Mama about.

It was dark when we got back to the Courtyard. Nina's car was gone. I used the back door code to get in the apartment. Walking through the garage with the tables full of Aunt Aida's possessions made me a little sad, with so many things that must have been important to her at one time or another, marked with little price stickers.

Mama had fallen asleep on the couch with the television and living room light still on. She must have been waiting for me. Poor Mama. She had done so much that day, and I had made her angry. I went to Aunt Aida's room and got the soft yellow blanket that Mama always liked using. I spread it over her on the couch. As I hugged Clover tightly that night, I felt some kind of feeling, but I wasn't really sure what it was.

"Goldie! Get up, Goldie!" Mama's voice was urgent. I sat straight up in the bed as Clover fell onto the hardwood floor. "I need you to make some signs for me! I forgot all about the signs!"

I just stared at Mama. I wanted to hide under the quilt, and I wanted Mama to leave me alone.

"For the sale, Goldie! Signs for the sale! Now, hurry and get dressed. We have only an hour." I had nearly forgotten about the sale, after all the things that had happened the day before.

By the time I was dressed, Mama had already gone out to the garage. She had left three big pieces of cardboard on the kitchen table along with a thick black marker. I went to the garage to look for her.

"Mama, what did you want me to write..." I stopped short as I opened the door to the garage. There was a man, a tall, thin man that I had not seen before, and he was standing really close to Mama.

"Oh, Goldie! Good. You are up. This...this is..." I didn't remember the man's name, probably on purpose. "...a friend of mine from high school from when we were growing up here in Heritage. This is my youngest daughter, Goldie," said Mama.

"Hello, Goldie. Florence has told me a lot about you, and I am very pleased to meet you." The man shook my hand, which I didn't like.

I didn't say anything to him, but I did ask Mama what I should write on the signs.

SALE
COURTYARD #4
THURSDAY 9-4
FRIDAY 9-?

That was all that she wanted me to write on them, but she wanted me to tack them onto sticks and put them in the ground, one coming from each side of town, and one right in front of Aunt Aida's garage. Once I had the writing done, I went to find Kip.

Grandpa Charlie let me into his apartment. Kip was sleeping on the couch, but Grandpa Charlie said that he should be getting up anyway because they had to leave pretty soon for the shop.

With Grandpa Charlie's help, I tacked the signs onto three sticks that I had gathered from the grove near the lagoon. By that time, Kip was dressed and ready for the day. His hair went in different directions on the top of his head, and I remember thinking that, as he pushed a few of the curls away from his face, they were looser than they had been the day before. Kip looked nice…handsome, really. I wondered, then, if he would have paid attention to me if he had grown up, like me, in Charlotte.

"Let's get those signs in the ground before the customers show up for your sale!" I liked how Grandpa Charlie was taking charge of this project. We loaded ourselves and the three signs into the cab of the truck, and Grandpa Charlie took off down the street. We drove first to the end of the street that led to downtown, and we used a baseball bat from the back of the truck to drive one of the signs into the ground, which was still soft from Tuesday afternoon's rain.

We placed the other sign about as far from the Courtyard as the first, at the base of the hill on the road that led to Nina's farm. Grandpa Charlie pulled up to the back entry of Aunt Aida's place, and we all got out. We had just finished with the signs when the garage door lifted. It must have been time for the sale to begin, and the man from Mama's high school was still in the garage. Something about him bothered me.

"See ya, Goldie!" he said, as he waved in my direction and set off down the sidewalk toward town. I stared at him but did not say anything at all.

Grandpa Charlie and Kip were going to look around in Aunt Aida's garage before they left for the shop. Kip had told me that whenever they were out, Grandpa Charlie stopped at any sale that they passed. "You just never know what treasures you might find," he would tell Kip. That seemed true for more than just sales.

Mama was on her phone, talking to Elise. She had a worried look on her face. She asked if she was drinking enough water and suggested she try taking a nap. "Here," continued Mama, passing her phone to me, "talk to Goldie."

"Elise!" I was so happy to hear Elise's voice, but she sounded different when she spoke.

"Oh, I miss you, my little Goldie Girl!" So, she had missed me! She told me that she and Meredith, her roommate, had stayed out very late the night before, and she woke up feeling sick. I felt sorry for Elise, so far away and without Mama or me to help her when she wasn't feeling well. Then, she said she thought she had better go because she really needed to lay down for a while before her classes started for the day. I would have to wait until the next time that we talked to tell her about Kip.

Grandpa Charlie was in one corner of the garage looking at the vintage hats and coats that I doubted Aunt Aida had ever had a reason to wear. He was making a pile for himself on the table where Mama had put the money box.

A few people were coming into the garage to look at Aunt Aida's things. Mama thanked Grandpa Charlie for helping with the signs and for taking me shopping for my school supplies. He said that he wished we could stay at Aunt Aida's place. I wished that, too, but I knew that we had to get back to Charlotte soon.

Mama put the things Grandpa Charlie had chosen into a big box. She tried to get him to put his money away, but he insisted that she take it. He said he was going to be able to use Aunt Aida's things in his shop, and he wouldn't have felt right just taking them. Kip looked back at me with his sunny eyes as he followed his grandpa to the truck.

"I've got some reading to do," he said, as he held up a copy of *The Little Prince* which he had found in Aunt Aida's pile. "I'll bring it back to you tonight. See you later, Goldie Bird."

Nina showed up shortly after they left. She had brought a box of donuts, cups of coffee for her and for Mama, and cocoa for me. I liked Nina. Mama had lost her aunt, but it was sad for Nina, too, that Aida was gone. I thought about how we would still have to go to see Barry at the funeral home and pick up the ashes and take them to that park. And soon after we did that, it would be time to make the long trip back home. I was hoping that somehow, something would happen so we wouldn't have to go.

People had been coming to the sale all day, and lots of Aunt Aida's possessions had been sold. It was nearly closing time, and Mama and Nina were condensing things on the tables. It was going to be another warm day on Friday. Mama thought it might be a good idea to sell lemonade for the second day of the sale.

Mama said it would be okay for Kip to help with the sale and the lemonade stand. Nina volunteered to make some of her frosted brownies, to sell along with the lemonade.

"So, I have another job for you and your friend," said Mama. "You can walk to town and buy some cups for tomorrow's lemonade sale." I couldn't wait for Kip to get back.

Mama made me a frozen chicken pie, which was kind of soggy at the edges. When I asked why she hadn't made one for herself, she said that she was planning to go out with the man from the garage for a while, and they would be going to dinner.

I didn't like hearing about this man. Mama had never mentioned him before we came to Heritage, and I really thought that if she had extra time, we could have done something together, like watch a movie or anything, really. I knew that if Elise had been with us, Mama would not have been spending this much time with the man from the garage.

She must have sensed what I was feeling. "Goldie, you know how you like doing things with Kip? Well, I like to see my friends, too. It has been a long time since I have seen anyone from Heritage. I spent a lot of time here, and..."

Mama's phone rang. It was Barry from the funeral home, calling about Aunt Aida's "arrangements." He spoke so loudly that I could hear what he said through the phone. He told Mama that the "cremation had been completed," and that we could pick up the "urn" tomorrow in the late afternoon. That made me nervous because we were going to have to bring Aunt Aida's burned up remains in Mama's car and also because I knew that our time in Heritage was nearing its end.

Kip and I went to the market in town to get what we needed for the lemonade sale. Kip said that Grandpa Charlie made the best blueberry lemonade, and he figured that we could pick some blueberries down by the lagoon that evening. We could add them to Aunt Aida's lemonade powder. I walked on the back of every bench along the way, and Kip followed.

"It's a little hard to keep up with you, Goldie Bird," said Kip, as he tried to catch his breath. "You are so much like one of those little goldfinches."

As we left the market, we could hear music. A street musician was playing around the corner from the diner. The sound of the fiddle matched how I felt inside as I looked forward to what was ahead, but not too far ahead.

"Hey, I was reading so much today," offered Kip. "I read all the way to the part where the Little Prince meets a snake. It's kind of sad."

"It's really sad," I said. "You know, the Little Prince has to leave soon. He has to go back to his planet."

Neither of us said anything for a little while after that.

As I was hopping down from the back of the last bench on our walk home, I noticed something sparkly on the sidewalk in front of me. It was some sort of stone. When I stopped to pick it up, Kip nearly knocked me over, as he bumped into me from behind.

"Oh, sorry!" I could feel my face flushing. "Look! Look at this little thing!" I showed him the tiny stone. It looked like a small piece of magic, glittery and milky and speckled with iridescent colors. He said that Grandpa Charlie would know about it for sure, and he might like to have it for his shop. I wanted to keep it but giving it to Grandpa Charlie seemed like the second-best idea.

As we walked further away from town, I could still hear the music, but just barely.

Mama's car was not in the driveway when we got back to Aida's place. I knew she had gone somewhere with the man from the garage. I didn't mind because I had something to do with Kip. Mama deserved to have a good time. I just didn't like the man from the garage. And sometimes I wanted it to be just her and me, if it couldn't be her, me, and Elise anymore.

The buckets that we had taken to the lagoon were still down there, near Kip's secret cave where we had left them the day before. The bushes were loaded with berries, and nobody else seemed interested in picking them, or maybe nobody else had even known about them.

We may have eaten as much as we picked, but we managed to fill the buckets to the top by dusk.

Mama still wasn't back when we had finished picking the blueberries. Kip got his book, the copy that he had found in Aunt Aida's garage. The sky was, once again, remarkable, and Kip thought it would be a good idea to watch the sunset from the hill behind the Courtyard.

We couldn't see Nina's farm, but I knew it was out there somewhere in that direction. I could tell Nina was a good person, always helping people and never asking for anything in return. I wondered if she would miss us when we were gone.

It was nearly dark when we finished the book, this time with Kip reading aloud. He turned off his flashlight.

The lights from the neighboring town mixed with all the stars and sparkled like a million fireflies. As we stretched out on the grassy hill, I wondered how different the ends of our summers would have been had Aunt Aida not died, had Mama not taken me to Heritage, and had Kip not stayed back when his mom and sisters returned to their home in Ohio.

"The Little Prince had to leave to go home to his planet," Kip began. "You have to leave soon, too. I get what the book meant when the Little Prince tamed the fox, and the fox became his friend. It's a little like us: before we met, we didn't mean anything to each other. But now that we are friends, I guess we are responsible for each other, right?"

That made me smile. He really had been listening. Kip and I had tamed each other, and we both knew it.

"The Little Prince leaves his planet because he's frustrated with his rose. Even though he meets other people, he's lonely for her while he's gone," Kip said. "I think the book is about being with others—about finding out what's really important, you know?"

I smiled again. I nodded. I did know.

"I should walk you back to your place soon," Kip said. "I don't want to get you in trouble."

"Yeah, I don't always know what to expect from Mama. Sometimes she doesn't care what I do. Other times, she gets mad when I don't even think I did anything. It seems like she doesn't know how she feels some days." I wasn't even sure what I was saying, but it still felt good to get it out.

"Maybe you're right. Maybe she doesn't always know how she feels or what to say," said Kip. "But I think you should talk to her about that sometime. She would want to know how you feel."

He was so smart. I never thought about it that way; I just always did my own thing to try to stay out of trouble. It was hard for me to talk sometimes, and it was that way for Mama, too. We were a little bit alike.

"I was thinking, too," he went on, "that if you wonder about something, you should ask. Like about your dad. Don't you think you have the right to know? I mean, she knows. You know she does."

I used the bottom of my shirt to wipe my tears, the unexpected, hot tears that fell.

"Oh, I'm sorry, Goldie! I made you cry. I didn't mean to make you cry." He pulled me close to him then and hugged me tightly. I cried a little more, but it was a great comfort to be held so tightly, so honestly. "Come on, Goldie Bird. Time to get you home. We've got a big day of lemonade sales tomorrow." He took my hand then, holding it gently in his until we reached Aunt Aida's apartment.

I slipped right into the bed in Mama's old room, under the quilt that I had shared with Elise, where I found Clover waiting for me. I thought about the stars, the Little

Prince's fox, and Kip...mostly Kip... as I drifted off.

On Friday, it was Kip, not Mama, who woke me up. I heard a knock at the front door, and it jarred me out of a dream where I was sitting on a hill with the actual Little Prince. The sun shone through my window from a higher place in the sky than the previous morning, which made me believe that Mama had let me sleep.

The knock came again, and I went to the door, still sleepy and wrapped in the quilt.

"Goldie, you better hurry! We might be missing out on some lemonade sales." Kip had a freezer container full of blueberries, and he didn't seem to care that he woke me up from a good dream.

"Alright, well, you can get started with the lemonade. The stuff is in the kitchen," I said.

I stopped first in my bedroom to get my clothes for the day and then I left Kip to do the work while I got dressed. Mostly because I didn't have many clean outfits left, I wore a yellow cotton sundress with a tiny birds-and-flowers pattern. It was going to be hot; I could already tell. I tied my hair up high on my head to keep it from bothering me while we were busy at work, and I was finally ready for the morning. To my image in Aunt Aida's bathroom mirror, I gave a half smile, uneven as it always was, with one side going higher than the other.

"Okay, sorry. What can I help you with, Kip?" He was busy stirring his creation in the one pitcher of Aunt Aida's that didn't get tagged for the sale. It was iridescent pink plastic—something Grandpa Charlie would have liked.

"Goldie!" He stared at me as I approached. "You look… you are so…so pretty!" His face flushed. He looked at the floor as soon as he was done speaking. Nobody had ever said that I was pretty before.

"I mean, I don't want you to think that I didn't already think you were pretty, but I hadn't really thought of you in that way before…" Kip's voice trailed off. He stopped talking completely and went back to stirring the lemonade.

I didn't care at all, though, because Kip had said that I was pretty.

Aunt Aida's kitchen was almost completely empty. The milk mug, though, was still on the counter. I filled it with milk because there was still a bit left from the day Nina had brought the jelly donuts. I asked Kip if he wanted some, but he said he had eaten breakfast with Grandpa Charlie before he left.

"We're going out 'treasure hunting' today, looking for yard sales and that sort of thing," Kip announced. "Grandpa Charlie is going to close the shop for a while so we can go."

"Anyway," he continued, "He wanted to know if you

wanted to go along with us? Maybe after the lemonade runs out or something. Maybe you can see his shop?"

"That sounds fun! I hope I can go," I replied. "I guess we should get out there. I don't want Mama to be mad at me."

The man from the garage was out there again when we went out to set up the lemonade sale. Nina was there, too, and she had a little table ready for us. A thick white paper plate full of Nina's brownies was already on the table.

I handed Nina the first cup of lemonade. She smiled, thanked me, and said that she would be back in a little while.

Mama said I could have a brownie for breakfast. She told me to hurry in and put the milk mug on the counter just as soon as I had finished eating.

"I want to put that in Elise's box, so I don't want you to break it before it makes it to her," said Mama, who went off right away to talk to someone that wanted to buy Aunt Aida's blue table and chairs, which I had also kind of wished for. That mug was what I wanted most from Aunt Aida's things, and she wanted to put it in Elise's box.

Lots of people came for lemonade, which kept me and Kip busy, and which was also good because it kept me from thinking about the milk mug and being angry with Mama. It was still morning, but the brownies were gone, and we were on the last pitcher of lemonade.

Grandpa Charlie pulled up in his truck and beeped his

horn. I told Kip that I thought he should ask Mama if I could leave with them because I really didn't want to talk to her.

"Mrs. Mar—Florence," began Kip, "would you let Goldie come along with me and my grandpa on a little trip to some junk sales?"

"No, Goldie can't go with you, and she knows that," snapped Mama. "Goldie will be going with me to do something important as soon as the sale is over." She turned her back to us and made herself look extra busy straightening some of Aunt Aida's stuff on the tables. She didn't seem to care that going with Kip would have been important to me.

I didn't want to meet with Barry to get Aunt Aida's ashes. Mama said that we would be going by the fairgrounds, but it sounded scary, and I wished that I could have gone with Kip and Grandpa Charlie instead. I watched the truck pull away. I was so mad I could barely breathe.

The time seemed to drag without Kip. When the sale was finally closing, the man from the garage and two boys that seemed a little younger than me came to help move Aunt Aida's things around and pack what was left into boxes. I wondered why Mama wanted them to come, why we couldn't just do it without them. There was already a pretty tall stack of boxes that were taped and ready to go—somewhere—when I saw Grandpa Charlie's truck coming from up the road.

"Goldie, go and get yourself cleaned up. We need to leave in half an hour," said Mama, who waved to Grandpa Charlie as his truck passed the Courtyard. I didn't see Nina anywhere.

Then, I remembered about "the arrangements."

"Mama," I began, as I felt a little hot in my belly, "can Kip come along to the fairgrounds, you know, to do the stuff with Aunt Aida's ashes or whatever?"

"No, he cannot," she said sharply. "We are not going somewhere to have fun. We are going to honor your great aunt's last wishes, and l do not think your little friend needs to be part of it." I could almost feel my head spin with anger as I turned to go inside.

As I passed through the kitchen on the way to the room where I had been staying, I saw the milk mug. I was so upset with Mama. The hot feeling inside of me grew bigger. I felt as if I would burst. I ran back to the door to the garage, pushed hard until it opened, and shouted to Mama and whoever else was out there, "I want the milk mug! You said I could have whatever I wanted, but you want to give it to Elise! I want it. It's mine! Elise broke the other one! I want the milk mug!" I slammed the door shut and went back inside.

Mama was waiting in the car when I came back out. I didn't look at her. This time, I took my place in the back seat. Nobody had told me if Nina was coming along, but even if she wasn't, I didn't want to sit by Mama. We didn't speak to one another on the short drive to the funeral home. Barry was waiting for us at the door. He shook hands first with Mama and then with me. Then, he led us to the same room where we had first started the "arrangements" three days earlier. That seemed like a lifetime ago.

Barry brought a small bag made of burlap, the kind of material that Mr. Quinn tied around the root balls of the trees and bushes that he was taking to his jobs. There was some white tissue paper inside the bag, and the bag also held a box: a fancy goldish-brown box. Inside that box was another container, also brown. That's what held Aunt Aida's ashes. Barry said that the container, which he called an "urn," was biodegradable. He said we wouldn't open it, but that it could just be placed like that in the Knotty River as Aunt Aida had wished. The ashes would be dispersed over time. All of this made me very uncomfortable.

I tried tuning Barry out as he went on to talk about how there were no regulations around there to keep us from doing that and whatever else he was going on about. I was still thinking about the milk mug, and I was also thinking about Aunt Aida and how all of those eighty-something years of living, reading, making pies, and playing cards were all burned up and put in this "biodegradable urn." At least she got to spend the rest of her days—whatever that really meant—in the place that she loved best. I decided right then that I was never going to go swimming in the Knotty River, and probably not any river, just in case.

Mama gave Barry some money that I thought was from Aunt Aida's sale. Barry shook hands with Mama and with me, one last time. I didn't feel quite as mad at Mama anymore after thinking about the ashes and poor Aunt Aida being in that urn. I wondered if Kip's Grandma Ellen was in an urn somewhere. Or Davy, Elise's daddy, or my dad, even. I wondered if my dad was dead.

The afternoon sun had gone behind the clouds, and it was beginning to look a bit like it might rain. Mama held the burlap bag close to her chest as we left the funeral home. Once I was buckled in the car, Mama lifted the bag over the back of the seat and asked me to hold it. My eyes widened. I had no choice but to take it from her. There I sat in the back of Mama's hot car, holding the ashes of my great aunt and feeling a whole bunch of things. I missed Elise more than ever.

We took the road out of town that led to Nina's farm. I was relieved when Mama pulled into the long driveway; it would not just be me and Mama taking care of the ashes.

Nina was waiting for us by the bee boxes at the edge of her property. She was carrying her umbrella and a small basket of tomatoes.

"Hello Florence," she said, as she got into the front seat of Mama's car. She turned around to look at me in the back seat, "And Miss Goldie, how lovely you look today!" Her words made me feel better right away, and I was so grateful that she had been with us through all of the things that had happened that week.

"How are you ladies holding up?" Nina asked.

Mama told Nina that most of the things were cleaned up from the sale and that we had finished the arrangements with Barry. Once Nina noticed the bag that held what was left of Aunt Aida, she didn't say anything else until we reached the old fairgrounds by the Knotty River.

Mama parked the car in an old lot at the edge of the road. It looked like a place where boats would have been tied. There were some small docks but no boats at all, at least not that I could see. Across the road from the river, there was an old, lonely-looking carousel. It wasn't operating on that day, but Nina said that people were able to ride on it when the fairgrounds were open. She told me that there used to be more carnival rides. That's where Aunt Aida had worked when she was much younger.

A soft rain was falling. Mama and Nina were already out of the car, so I figured that I was supposed to carry the bag. I tried not to think about it. I wondered what Elise was doing on this early Friday evening. I thought that if she had been with us, I would not have had to do this alone. I could never be mad at Elise, though, even if Mama did want her to have the milk mug.

A path of dirt, gravel, and leaves ran between the old parking lot and the edge of the Knotty River. Nina reached for my hand, "so she wouldn't lose her footing if it was slippery," but I was grateful that I had someone to hold onto for more than just that reason. Mama walked a few steps ahead of us. She kept going for a little while once we got close to the river. A few times, she stopped and looked around but then walked further.

"Nina, why would Aunt Aida want to go to the river? I mean, why would she wish for that?" I asked.

"Well, dear, when Aida was a young girl, about the same age as your sister, she worked at the old fairgrounds, helping with the carnival rides. She met a man there that she loved for many years. He went away after a time, and she never understood quite why. She said that she had never really loved anyone again after that, not in a romantic way, anyway. She loved your mother dearly, of course, and you girls. But she looked back on those years as, really, the best times of her life. And that's where she wanted her final stop to be," said Nina, who let go of my hand briefly to wipe a tear that had slipped down her cheek.

"Well, that seems sad to me," I said, "to really love

someone like that but to never see him again." I thought of Kip for a moment, and though I was really still a little girl, I wondered if I would ever meet anyone that meant as much to me as he did. "So maybe," I continued, "she always lived with the hope that she might see him again, and maybe that was enough for her."

Nina squeezed my hand. "I sure am going to miss you, sweetie," she said.

Mama stopped once again, this time right next to a birch tree and a few good-sized rocks. She turned around. "Okay. Goldie, can I have the urn, please?" I held out the bag and its contents. I wasn't about to open the box to give it to her. Nina must have sensed that because she took it from me, slipped the box from the tissue paper, and opened it carefully. She lifted the urn, ran her hand along it for a second, bowed her head, and passed it to Mama.

"So, I guess this is it," Mama said, as she stepped forward and gently lowered the urn into the Knotty River. It bounced around for a bit until it was caught up in a swirl of the current. We watched as it floated downstream, sinking deeper into the body of the river. Pretty soon, we lost sight of the urn that held what was left of Great Aunt Aida.

The rain fell harder, and no one said a word as we walked back up the footpath and through the parking lot. This time, Mama and Nina walked arm-in-arm, and I followed behind. Nina had forgotten her umbrella, so we were all dripping by the time we made it to the car.

Mama stopped outside a pizza restaurant before we reached Nina's farm. The three of us were going to dinner. We had pizza so many times during that week; that was Elise's favorite thing, except for the kind from Gas Mart, so that meant Mama must have missed her. That was okay with me, though, to have a lot of pizza.

The conversation that I had been dreading began once we had ordered our food. Mama told Nina that the man from the garage and his sons had helped her pack most of the leftovers from the sale, and she would be able to finish when we got back that night. She didn't tell Nina that I had helped, too.

"I want to leave pretty early in the morning," Mama said. "It's such a long drive, and Goldie starts school on Monday. We will both be so tired when we get in, and Goldie will have lots to do to be ready for her first day of junior high."

"Junior high! Goldie, how exciting!" Nina had no idea how much I was dreading going to Mason Hill, or that I didn't like being in crowds of people, or that I really just wanted to stay here in Heritage and never go back, at least not until Elise came home. I excused myself to go to the bathroom where I stayed until a lady and two little girls came in. I didn't think we would have to leave Heritage in such a rush. It just didn't seem fair.

Mama and Nina were already eating when I got back to the table. They were talking about something that didn't involve me. Nina asked if there was something wrong and if I was feeling okay. I thought of telling her that I didn't want to leave Heritage, that I had found the best friend I would ever have here, that Elise wasn't going to be home anyway and I didn't want to go back to live with just Mama, that I was afraid to start school, and that I never really felt like I mattered to anyone. Instead, I just offered a quiet, "I'm okay," and took a piece of pizza, but only one, because I didn't feel very much like eating anymore—not even pizza.

The skies were clearing by the time we left the restaurant. The hard rain had left puddles in the parking lot. I didn't walk through them or even try to balance on the back of the bench near the corner where Mama had parked the car. I wanted to get back to the Courtyard to tell Kip that we would be leaving but also, I didn't. It didn't seem like the rain had washed the hard stuff away, at least not this time.

We stopped to take Nina back to her farm. I wondered if I would ever see her again. Mama thanked her for everything and assured her that she would leave Aunt Aida's keys on the kitchen counter. Nina told her not to worry, that she would finish taking care of what needed to be done, and that she would leave the apartment very clean. They hugged but neither cried. I figured they must have had enough of that this week.

"Goldie," Nina began, "you take care of your mama. You're the big girl now. And who knows, maybe one day I will make it to Illinois to see you ladies." She reached for me then, and I hugged her back for a very long time.

"Nina? Will you check on Grandpa Charlie and Kip for me once in a while? To make sure they are okay?" I pleaded.

She even promised to make them some brownies with sprinkles.

The sun was already beginning to set as we drove the few miles back to town. The sky was striped, and the colors were somehow bright and dark at the same time, much different from the ice cream skies that we had seen. I watched a line of birds flying just above the deepest blue.

The apartment was mostly cleared out, except for the boxes, of course, and a bit of leftover furniture that Nina would be collecting for her church. I watched as Mama pulled the last few things from the kitchen cabinets. "Here, Goldie," she said, as she handed me an unopened bag of marshmallows. "Why don't you take these to your friend? It's nice enough now; maybe you two can have a campfire in the ring behind the Courtyard." She surprised me with this idea. We had barely spoken a word to each other that day. I felt mad and sad at the same time, but I wanted to see Kip before we had to leave, so I was grateful for the bag of marshmallows.

Kip and Grandpa Charlie were eating salad when I got to their apartment.

"Goldie! I was afraid you might have left. When I stopped by your place a while ago and nobody answered, I thought you were on your way back home," said Kip.

"Tomorrow," I said. "We have to leave in the morning."

"It's going to be different here without you. I'm not going to have anybody to do cool stuff with or just to talk to," Kip said.

"Hey..." started Grandpa Charlie, "don't forget about me!"

"Of course, Grandpa Charlie, but you know what I mean. There's just something about Goldie. I mean, do you really think you would have climbed up one of those birch trees with me?" asked Kip.

"Well, I would have, had I been your age. I know what you mean, Kip. I am sorry to see Goldie go, too." Grandpa Charlie looked away, as if he, too, was a little bit sad. He went back to eating his salad.

Kip and Grandpa Charlie both thought marshmallows would make a fine ending for a salad dinner, so off to the fire pit we went. There was a tiny woodshed at the back of the Courtyard, directly behind Grandpa Charlie's apartment. He said it was there because he had built it years ago for the common use of all of the Courtyard residents. It was really just him, though, who stocked the wood and made fires.

Kip ran down to the lagoon to get roasting sticks for the marshmallows. Grandpa Charlie spoke as soon as Kip was on his way down the hill.

"This has been hard on Kip, you know, Goldie, the struggle between his mom and dad. He hasn't talked much about it, but I know he is having a tough time. You came to Heritage just when he needed you most. I wish his mother could know you. Mary lost her mother, and now she and Patrick are not getting along..." He got that misty look again. "I'm just...I'm so glad you came when you did, Goldie." He reached for my hand and held it between both of his, just for a second. I didn't say anything. I didn't think I needed to.

Kip held three long sticks in one hand as he came up the hill. I noticed that they were from the birch trees.

Grandpa Charlie sat next to me on the grass. Kip was across the fire pit. The sky had a mysterious glow that evening, from the rain that had fallen earlier. It somehow seemed brighter than most other nights, though the stars were few. I looked at Kip when he did not know I was watching. The light of the fire reflected his sunny brownish hair, which looked tangled from the wind, like he had been surfing or something, but which also looked like it did every other day. I remembered the first time that I had really looked at him, that morning in the Courtyard when I noticed how his eyes held all the colors of the sun.

I could see the fire reflected in his eyes. I wondered if this was what it was like to love someone.

"Goldie." Kip's voice interrupted my thoughts.

I looked up at him.

"Come on. Let's go down to the secret spot. We can play cards or read or something for a little while until you have to go back." I could still taste the sweetness of the marshmallows. I wanted the few short hours that I had left in Heritage to last forever.

Grandpa Charlie was going to sit by the fire for just a bit longer, so I said goodbye before Kip and I headed down the hill.

The little cave looked just as it had on our day of birch-bending. Kip had brought a lantern to the secret spot at some point, or I hadn't noticed it before. He gestured toward the logs that surrounded the little table. "Want to play cards or something?" We decided on *Slapjack* because it was easy to talk while playing the game.

He told me that he had always loved visiting his grandparents in the summer, but that this summer was different for so many reasons. He really missed his grandma, but he knew that she was still with him, in his spirit, especially when he was here. The only thing that he couldn't do in Heritage that he had loved doing at home was play on his baseball team. He had missed the second half of his season this year because he ended up staying for a longer time. I told him about Teddy and about how he had given me a baseball mitt. If only I had known to bring it; Kip and I could have been playing catch.

"Isn't there a baseball team in Heritage?" I asked.

"There is. I know there is, Goldie, but I've grown up playing with the same guys, and we all know each other's game so well. It just wouldn't be the same," he said.

"Of course, it wouldn't be the same. But did you ever think it might be better?" I asked.

"Listen to you!" Kip brightened. "Think about what you're saying. You, who doesn't want to go to junior high. Goldie, what if it's better? Did you ever think of that?"

I hadn't, but I suppose there was a chance—just a little one—that it could be.

"Kip, do you miss your mom and dad?" I asked.

He looked at me for a bit. "I miss how they used to be," he said. "I miss playing catch with my dad and getting a day off from school to go to his office with him. I miss the long talks I had with my mom and the times that we would take the girls to daycare and then stop at the coffee shop before I had to go to school. We always got the same kind of donut, chocolate glazed. I miss the girls, too, how silly they always are, and how sweet they look when they are asleep, all curled up together in the same little bed." Kip kept talking, "That stuff, though, hadn't been happening so much lately. Everything was an argument. Mom would cry, and my dad spent so much time at his office that he missed most of my games this summer. It's better for me to be here with Grandpa Charlie, at least for now."

"Kip, I'm sorry," I offered. I didn't know what else to say.

"Goldie?" he asked.

I looked at him, at those sunny eyes which did a pretty good job of covering up some sadness.

"Thanks for being my friend. You're the best." He had gotten up from the stump seat and sprawled on his birch branch bed. "So, you know, you're going to be okay. We all are. I promise."

I really wanted to believe him. He always meant what he said.

"But you're not afraid?" I asked. "About seventh grade, being away from your family, or anything else?"

"I don't know, Goldie. But I am going to get up every day and do the best I can. For Grandpa Charlie, for me, for everyone. And when I feel unsure, I guess I can look at the stars or the sunset, right?"

Kip was so wise.

"Kip?"

"What is it, Goldie?"

"I don't want to go." Once again, the tears fell. I knew I had to go back to #4. I had no idea what time it was, but I knew it was past when I should have been in bed.

It was Kip's idea to exchange addresses. Since neither of us had our own phones, he suggested that we take turns writing letters. He said he would go first and then I could answer him. It wouldn't be the same as talking or being together, but at least we could still know one another was out there. He walked back alongside me with his arm over my shoulder, like Teddy sometimes did with Elise.

"Goodbye, Goldie Bird. Remember me, will you?" He pulled me close and held me tight, but just for a little while.

"See ya, Kip." I turned to watch him go, one last time.

Mama had left a note outside my bedroom door. She had gone out for a while with the man from the garage. She said that I should be ready to go by eight the next morning.

It was warm in Aunt Aida's apartment. I opened the window in the bedroom just enough to feel the thick night-time air, which had the same perfumed smell that I remembered so clearly from the first evening of the trip. I was tired, but I couldn't sleep. There were too many thoughts streaming through my head. I didn't know how to quiet my racing mind.

I woke with a sick feeling inside of me. In my dream, I had been riding on the carousel from the parking lot. Aunt Aida was riding, too, only she was on the other side from where I was, and she didn't notice me. Barry from the funeral home was sitting on the horse right next to mine. He had a giant grin on his face, and he kept trying to shake my hand. He kept saying "biodegradable urn... biodegradable urn..." as he held out his hand for another shake. The man from the garage was there, too, moving from one carousel animal to the next. He wasn't saying anything; he just looked very busy. The carousel was moving more quickly until it spun so fast that it seemed to fly up into the sky...and then I was startled awake.

It was still dark outside. Soon it would be morning, and soon it would be time to leave Heritage. I couldn't stand that thought. I took the quilt and wrapped it tightly around my shoulders. I thought of how Kip had put his arm on my shoulder. I felt a terrible, heavy loneliness inside of me. As quietly as I could, I gathered Clover the fox and slipped out of my room. I didn't know if Mama was still gone with the man from the garage. I turned the knob to the front door and stepped outside.

I was grateful for the darkness. The Courtyard was very quiet. I hadn't bothered to put on any shoes, and I still wore my yellow sundress from the day before. As I crossed the Courtyard, I noticed the empty rocking chair on Grandpa Charlie's front porch, the one where Kip had been reading when I saw him for the first time.

The slope at the back of the Courtyard seemed much steeper at night. There was an eerie glow in the sky, just enough to help me find my way to the lagoon. I stopped at the grove of trees where Kip and I had our birch-bending adventure and ran my hands along the birch bark.

The quilt kept slipping from my shoulders as I found my way to the secret cave. I laid Clover on the birch branch bed at the back of the cave and curled up beside her under the quilt. There I felt safe, comfortable, and peaceful as I drifted off to sleep once again.

Clover rode alongside me on the carousel this time. Our horses moved up and down, alternating. At least I thought it was Clover, but she looked exactly like the Little Prince's fox. There was nothing scary about this ride. I could hear the fiddle music that had been played by the street musicians in town. The only other person in the dream was Nina. She stood at the edge of the carousel and offered a brownie to me and to Clover each time we passed by.

I slept until the filtered light came into the cave through the birch trees. It must have been morning, but very early morning. Slowly, I peeked my head outside to see that the sun was just beginning to rise. The sound of a voice echoed among the birch trees before fading into the distance. I remembered that Mama wanted me to be ready to leave for Charlotte, but I didn't care at all about what Mama wanted just then. Instead, I returned to my spot on the birch branch bed and closed my eyes. I thought of Kip, and Grandpa Charlie, and how I had learned so much about friendship and sunsets and blueberry lemonade.

I thought of Nina, her farm, her beehives, what a good companion she had been to Aunt Aida, and also a lot about those brownies. I even thought about Barry, and about the man from the garage. I thought the most about Kip and about how I wished I could stay.

A rustling sound woke me for the second time. At first, I thought it must be a squirrel or a little animal of some sort. It got louder and louder, and soon I could hear footsteps. They were coming toward the secret cave. My heart raced, and I pulled the quilt over my head, trying not to make any noise.

"Goldie! Goldie, are you here?" It was Kip's voice. I knew that he would find me. "Goldie Bird. It's me, Kip." He waited before kneeling beside me on the birch branch bed. "Hey, can I come in there?" he asked.

I didn't say anything at all. Very gently and slowly, Kip pulled the quilt down from over my head.

"Hey," he spoke softly, as he moved onto the mat and under the blanket with me, "your mom is looking for you. She came to our door and said she couldn't find you anywhere. I guess she's been looking around for a while. She's really worried about you, Goldie."

"She's not worried about me. She doesn't care about me. She never did," I cried. "Really, Kip...just Elise and you. You are the only ones that want me around," I continued. "I can't stay here, and I can't be with Elise. What am I going to do?" I sobbed as Kip held me tightly under the blanket.

"Goldie, we have to go to her. She needs to know that you are okay. Your mom does care about you, and she loves you. My mom loves me, too, though she sometimes has a weird way of showing it. She worries about me. All moms worry about their kids." He pulled the quilt down. "It was getting hot under there. Come on, Goldie Bird, you know we have to," he said.

Kip stood up then, holding Clover. He tried pulling me up by my arm, but I pulled away.

"You're going to tell her where I am, aren't you?" My eyes flashed with hopeless, desperate anger.

"I told her I thought I knew," he said. "She wanted to come with me. I told her I thought I should go alone, and I'm glad I did. But I've kept her waiting."

"Well, I'm staying here," I insisted.

"Goldie, please...please don't make me go back there alone," Kip pleaded.

"I'm not going with you," I cried, as he tucked Clover under the blanket where I had returned.

As he left the cave, I knew he was going to tell Mama, and I called to him: "Kip, how could you? How could you do this to me?!"

I didn't know that Kip had cried, too, as he climbed the hill.

I heard the rustling noises again, but this time I knew it wasn't a squirrel. Kip had brought Mama to the cave. He had betrayed me. Still under the blanket, I knew that we had lost, Clover and me. It was time to go home.

"Goldie, I'm so sorry," said Kip in a broken, shaky voice. He was first in the cave, followed by Mama, whose face was dirt-stained and red.

Mama said some words that she had told me never to say. She pulled the quilt from me. I reached for it and tried to hide under it again, but Mama was much stronger. She rolled the quilt, held it under one of her arms, and tried to yank me to my feet. She told me to say goodbye to my friend.

From my place on the birch-branch bed, I screamed out that nobody really ever loved me or cared what I wanted. I didn't even look at Kip, much less say goodbye to him. Once on my feet, I ran out of the cave, up the hill, through the main Courtyard gate, and straight into Aunt Aida's apartment. My heart was pounding. I splashed water on my face in the pink and black tiled bathroom, gathered the rest of my belongings, and buckled myself into the back seat of Mama's car. I had to move a box and Smiley, cage, and all, to the front seat, but there was no way I was going to sit by Mama.

The car was full of Aunt Aida's leftover belongings. A whole life stuffed into a hot car, which smelled mostly like tomatoes because the basket that Nina had brought for us the day before was still in there somewhere. I had a terrible feeling that we were leaving Heritage for the last time. I was already sorry for how I had yelled at Kip and for not even saying goodbye. I knew I had messed up.

After about half an hour, Mama came with one last box, the bag she had brought, and a carafe of coffee. She started the car, and we were on our way.

I had fallen asleep a few times, but the bumps along the road kept jostling me awake. My head hurt, and my stomach hurt. I wondered how far we had gone. Mama must have known that I couldn't sleep.

"Are you hungry?" she asked. I was surprised by the calm in her voice. She said that she needed to stop for gas and that there was a pancake restaurant just a few miles ahead. I told her that I wasn't hungry. Mama stopped anyway. I got out of the car and followed her inside, making sure to stay a few steps behind.

It turned out that I was really hungry. I ate a stack of pancakes and bacon, and Mama didn't say anything when I asked the waitress for some coffee with cream.

"Goldie, I'm sorry. I am really sorry for everything. I

know this has been a very hard week," said Mama.

I thought for a minute. "Well, it was a good week. It was the best week, actually, until this morning. Why are you making me go back, Mama? Can't I just stay with Kip and Grandpa Charlie?" I pleaded.

"You know you can't do that. I know you like Kip and his grandpa, but we belong in Charlotte. Our lives are there," said Mama.

"Maybe your life is there, but I don't have anything good left, not even Elise." I tried to make her understand, but I knew I couldn't. "So, why did you keep seeing that man from the garage, if you wanted to leave so badly?"

"I know you are not going to understand, Goldie. Heritage is where I spent a lot of time when I was growing up. He was my closest friend in high school. We were always together until I met Davy. They never got along, so our friendship suffered. We lost touch once Davy and I left town. When you and I came back for Aunt Aida's arrangements, I looked him up. Turns out, he never left Heritage. He lives here with his partner and their two boys," Mama spoke quietly, sincerely. She had never really talked to me like that before.

"So, why did you want to see him after all these years?" It didn't make much sense to me.

"I wish I could tell you that, Goldie. Maybe because he knew who I used to be. I think that's it. There's a connection to people that have meant something to you, and though you might not be with them or even see them, you still know that they are there. They remind you of yourself again, even when you are lost. I guess seeing him makes me miss Davy just a little less."

Elise had just turned seven when her daddy, Davy, died. He was riding in the passenger seat of a car with his best buddy, Marc, who had been his college roommate. Marc was visiting Mama, Davy, and Elise in Charlotte when the accident happened. Marc was not badly injured. Mama said she saw Marc a few times after the accident but that it was too painful to spend time with him because of what had happened. I never understood much about that, though, because everyone said the crash was an accident.

"I can look up to the sky and know that somewhere, there are people out there that mean something. Do you understand, Goldie?" asked Mama. That time, I really did.

When we got back to the car, Mama asked if I would sit in the front seat with her. I moved the box and the bird cage to where they had been in the back. She hugged me then, and as I got into the seat, she handed me the burlap bag that had held Aunt Aida's biodegradable urn.

I pulled back the tissue paper and there, where Aunt Aida's ashes had once been, was the milk mug.

Part Two: Keeping Secrets

As we got close to Charlotte, I thought how Kip and Grandpa Charlie would have liked to look at the evening's sunset, which cast a soft pink light all over. To the west, the colors were bold rosy red to the lightest yellow. I remembered Grandpa Charlie's words, how he had said that the sunset sky will be there for you when you think you have nothing left. I wondered, as we drove, what I had left.

We always parked in the same place at the back of the Warehouse Apartments. It was the spot nearest the lilac caves that I knew Aunt Aida would have liked. The car was full of things that needed to be carried inside; Smiley the parakeet was one of those things. Rosa, Mr. Quinns' daughter, had been outside near the shop as we arrived home. She watched as I lifted Smiley's cage from the back of Mama's car. She took several steps closer, to get a better look at what I held. Maybe she liked birds, too. I already knew that she liked flowers, and I thought that sometimes when people liked flowers, they also liked birds. Mama said hello to Rosa, but Rosa did not acknowledge either of us. I was pretty sure that Rosa only greeted Mama when they were together in the shop when she came in from school. As I closed the car door, Rosa turned and walked back toward the shop.

Rosa came to the shop every afternoon. A bus dropped her off at the entrance to the part where Mama worked. Every day, Rosa opened the door to the warehouse at the back of the shop, slipped inside, and came back out in about three minutes. In that time, she put her backpack away, changed into her overalls and boots, ate an apple and a piece of cheddar cheese from the refrigerator, and put on her garden gloves.

"Hi, Miss Florence," she would say to Mama on her way back from the warehouse. She never looked directly at Mama or me or anyone.

"Good afternoon, Rosa." Mama always smiled as Rosa made her way out to work on weeding the flower patches.

"To the flowers. To the flowers." Rosa always said the same little chant. It seemed she couldn't wait to come to the shop for her work, which mostly involved weeding and sometimes planting. Mama kept a mason jar full of flowers on the counter in the shop. Rosa was responsible for the jar, for making a little arrangement with whatever was in bloom at the time. She loved digging in the flower beds and pulling out the weeds one at a time, and she never said a word to anyone else. I used to wonder if Rosa was lonely, but I was pretty sure she preferred the company of flowers over people.

I never really knew how old Rosa was, but I thought she was younger than Elise and older than me. Rosa's older brother, John-John, was tall and very handsome with black hair that curled like Rosa's. He did some of the garden design stuff at the shop. Sometimes I heard him arguing with Mr. Quinn. Mr. Quinn said John-John never really liked the flowers.

There was still a little bit of the smell of Elise in our apartment. The cat, Myles, was happy to see us. He seemed especially interested in the bird, who watched us all suspiciously from his cage on the kitchen table.

The only place I ever lived was at Warehouse Apartment #4. When Mama and Elise had to leave the yellow cottage, Mr. Quinn said they could live in one of the apartments above the warehouse. I was born when Elise was eight years old, and we shared the same bedroom until the day she left for school. The best thing about our apartment was that there was a ladder built into the closet in the bathroom. If we climbed to the top of the ladder and cranked open the skylight, we could go onto the roof of the Warehouse Apartments, on top of the whole building. Elise and I didn't know if we were supposed to go up there, but we figured there wouldn't be a ladder if you weren't supposed to use it.

The bedroom that I shared with Elise had a skylight, too, but no ladder. The closet was almost as big as the room. It had a little light with a tiny chain, lots of shelves, and a secret door in one corner which I discovered with my friend Gabriella who had come over after school one day. It opened to a small space, just the right size for one of us to fit inside. It smelled musty, like the inside of an old library book. Someone had left an old metal harmonica in there, but besides that, it was empty. I had never told anyone else about the secret door—not even Elise—but she probably knew.

Gabriella had been my first friend. Really, she was my only friend since kindergarten. We always ended up sitting together at school because both of our last names began with "M." She lived on the opposite side of town. Gabriella played with lots of different kids at school, but I mostly just played with her. When the other girls jumped rope at recess, we would join because Gabriella wanted to, but I always just held the end, and that was enough for me.

I heard Mama calling my name from outside. She wanted me to help her finish unloading the car. I wished that Elise and Teddy had been there because they were really good at helping and carrying stuff, and they would have let me be the door-opener. Now, I had to carry things and be my own door-opener. And in a few hours more than one day, I would have to go to junior high.

I really couldn't stop thinking about Kip and how I

had probably ruined the chance of ever hearing from him again. Leaving Heritage could have been so different. I wasn't sure why I had done what I did. Sometimes it seemed like for anyone to understand me or to hear what I had to say, I had to do something big, and even maybe mess up. I knew it wasn't Kip's fault. I knew I had to go home. It had just been so wonderful to be with Kip and Grandpa Charlie and to feel like I really mattered. I wasn't ready to let go. I hoped that he understood and that he could forgive me for the things that I said.

We put all of Aunt Aida's things in the living room, which seemed much bigger than it was because the ceiling was so high. There were two couches and a TV, and three giant windows where we could look out at Charlotte's downtown. Mama said she was going to bed and that I should, too. I held the burlap bag with the milk mug close to me as I carried it to the bedroom.

I thought of so many things as I tried to fall asleep that night. I tried remembering the good things that Kip and I had done together. I hoped that he, too, was thinking of those times and not about how our stay had ended. I thought of Mama, how hard she really had worked the whole week, and about how she had to go back to work right away after all of that. I wondered if Mama looked forward to anything, or to anyone, or if she felt like she had anything left. Then, I thought of Elise, how everyone liked her, and how she never really had bad things happen to her, at least not that I could think of. Then, I remembered that she, too, had lost people that she loved. I wondered if she would call again soon or if she was having too much fun at her school to think of me. After exactly an hour of lying in the dark of that big, lonely bedroom, I slipped out of my bed, into my sister's, and fell asleep right away.

The next morning was rainy. I woke feeling like I had a storm inside of me. I knew I had to get all of my school supplies organized for the next day, and I wasn't in the mood for that. Even after the things that Kip had told me, it still seemed really scary to think about junior high. I had to take the bus, which I had never done before. After that, more scary things would just keep coming. If I went downstairs, I would be away from the supplies and the reminders.

Two girls shared #3, the apartment at the back of the building on our side of the hallway. The girls, Victoria and Robin, were older than Elise, and they had jobs. Victoria, the taller girl, played really loud music and sometimes smoked cigarettes on the back stairs. Once I saw Teddy smoking back there with her, but I never told Elise. I tried to stay close to our side of the hallway when I went down the back stairs because of Apartment #2, which was across the hall from where the girls lived. I never saw anybody come and go from that apartment, but Elise said she heard creepy sounds coming from there, and once Gabriella and I thought we heard some, too.

John-John Quinn lived in Apartment #1, directly across the hallway from ours. He had left Charlotte for a few years to go to landscape design school. John-John rode all around on his black bike. He wore black clothes and black sunglasses, and he smelled like a Christmas tree. He never talked to me, and I sometimes wondered if he even knew about me.

Mama had just opened the shop, which was called *Rosa's Garden Party*, a bit later than most days because it was Sunday. She had worked for Mr. Quinn for a long time, since Elise started school, keeping the store tidy and helping the customers. On that day, a smell of apples and cinnamon filled the shop. Next to the counter where the customers paid was an empty bushel basket. Mama was tying a little sign to the basket. She had written in pretty, gold letters: "Apples, one dollar each."

Mama did so much to make *Rosa's Garden Party* a very special place: the fairy gardens, the little signs, the sparkly lights everywhere, the music that played, and the way she arranged everything to always look so enchanting. I knew little things that Mama did made her feel happy while she was doing them. I wished that there were big things that she could look forward to that would also make her happy. If there were, she hadn't told me about them.

Not long after I got to the shop, Mr. Quinn and Rosa came through the warehouse door. Together, they were carrying a box of tasty-looking apples of different varieties of red, green, and yellow. Mr. Quinn must have known what I was thinking. As soon as he and Rosa set the box down on the floor in the entrance to the shop, he tossed me an apple.

"Goldie! How I have missed you!" he said. "This place just isn't the same without the rest of my girls here!" I remembered how much I liked Mr. Quinn. Sometimes, I secretly wished he were my dad.

Mr. Quinn gave Rosa an apple, too, but he didn't toss it to her. Maybe because he knew she wouldn't be able to catch it, and he didn't want her to feel bad if she dropped it. Then, he put two apples from the box into the empty bushel basket by the counter. He held another apple out to Rosa and gestured for her to put it into the basket. Then, he asked if I might help Rosa with her job. I was grateful to have something to do. I liked how Mr. Quinn gave Rosa things to do to make her feel important, which she was, especially to him.

Rosa and I took turns adding apples to the basket until the bushel was full. Then, Rosa laughed her loud, hearty belly laugh which made me think of the Little Prince and also of Kip.

"Goldie. Bird." I had definitely heard Rosa's voice, but I was startled and confused because nobody besides maybe Grandpa Charlie knew about Kip's name for me. Also, Rosa had never even said my name before.

She said it again. "Goldie. Bird." She smiled and squealed, tapping me hard on the shoulder. Mr. Quinn had a worried look, as he took a step in Rosa's direction. Then, I remembered that Rosa had been outside when I brought Smiley home the night before.

"Oh! Smiley!" I exclaimed. "Yes, Rosa! My...Goldie's bird! That's Smiley. He's upstairs now. I brought him back from my Aunt Aida's place."

Rosa was beaming. I didn't know if she understood anything that I had said, but she knew that I had a bird. She remembered that. Mr. Quinn stepped closer to both of us, but his anxious look had been replaced with a peaceful smile. "Rosa loves birds. I think she likes you, too, Goldie."

"Maybe I can take Rosa upstairs to see Smiley? Maybe once he's settled in his new place?" I asked.

"You know, Goldie, you're a good girl. And your mama here, she's a good lady," said Mr. Quinn. Mama's cheeks turned a little pink when he said that, and she looked down at the counter. Mama was a good lady. She needed to hear that a little more often.

The steady rain kept me from really going anywhere

or even doing anything outside. I thought it might be time to work on getting my school supplies organized. Back at the apartment, though, I remembered my box from Aunt Aida. There wasn't much in there: a few board games, a zipper bag that held Aunt Aida's cross-stitch supplies, a small, framed photograph of Aunt Aida holding me as a baby, and a pink calico drawstring bag.

I put the games and the cross-stitch bag on the bookshelf in the sitting room. My picture with Aunt Aida fit just right next to the lamp on my dresser.

The calico bag was soft and small in my hands. I loosened the strings and poked two of my fingers inside to feel its contents. The bag held Aunt Aida's dollhouse babies, the ones that I had remembered playing with so many times in Aunt Aida's bathroom. I felt a lump rise in my throat; my eyes were hot with new tears. I wasn't sad, though, only full of the best kind of happiness for finding something that I loved, that I was sure had been lost. I thought, then, that my Mama was indeed a good lady.

The next morning, I woke even before Mama. Smiley chirped as I came from my room. I made myself some cinnamon toast while I was in the kitchen. It must have been early, as the sun was still coming up. The morning sky was a rich pink-orange-purple. It made me think of the sunsets that had meant so much to Grandpa Charlie, and I wondered if he felt the same way about sunrises, which were beautiful but in a different way. This morning's sunrise might mean a new beginning for me: one where I would be brave, take the bus, and learn to navigate the halls of Mason Hill Junior High...alone. But I wasn't ready.

My hands shook as I tied the strings to the yellow sundress with the little birds, the one I had worn the day that Kip said I was pretty. I wore my hair up because I remembered wearing it like that on that day, too. Maybe Kip wouldn't think I was pretty anymore after the way I had acted and after the things I had said. I wanted to hope that he still would. I wanted to remember how he had made me feel on that morning in Heritage. Maybe remembering would help me to face this day.

The bus stopped at the corner in the first block of town right next to Piper's Coffee Shop. I could see it coming from the sitting room window in our apartment and also from Mama's shop, but the shop wasn't open that early in the morning, and I wouldn't have made it in time if I waited until I saw it through the upstairs window. I had to walk to the corner to wait with the others. Sometimes, if it were raining or really cold, some of the kids would wait in the coffee shop until the bus came. I wondered if they smelled like coffee for a while once they got to school.

I stumbled a little on the last step before I pushed open

the thick apartment door. The air was fresh from the rain. I took a deep breath, shifted my backpack a little, and started across the street.

"Think about sunsets. Think about pizza. Think about Kip," I told myself, chanting the lines over and over in my head.

A girl that I didn't recognize was the only other person waiting at the bus stop. She was quite a bit taller than me. She smiled when I approached and then she looked away quickly, for which I was grateful because I really didn't like talking to new people anyway.

Once I had made it to an open seat, I remembered that I had never organized my supplies. I had just dumped the whole bag of things that I had bought when I went shopping with Kip and Grandpa Charlie into my backpack, the same one from last year. The ride to the school was only six or seven minutes, which was not enough time to organize supplies. My stomach felt hot and sick. I couldn't cry—not on my way to junior high. I thought of eating the Sugar Babies that had been in the bag since our shopping trip, but after the first couple they didn't taste so good anymore.

"Sunsets…pizza…Kip."

I gripped my backpack tightly as the bus pulled up to Mason Hill Junior High. It looked bigger than it had every other time that I had seen it. The school had been built eight years before, and Elise had been in the first-ever sixth grade class there. I was a tiny girl, holding Elise's hand on the way to the school's fun fair, which hadn't been fun at all. The halls were so crowded. I fell in the middle of some big boys, and one stepped on me but didn't even notice. I was crying, and I couldn't see Elise. I really hoped this day was not going to go like that.

I tried not to make eye contact with anyone in the busy halls, but I didn't know my way around, so I couldn't just look down at the floor. All of the sixth graders had to meet in the gym to get their schedules and locker combinations. I waited just outside the door until most of the crowd had gone. I wasn't sure if it was someone's mom or one of the teachers that was stationed at the "LAST NAMES H-N" table. "Last name, honey?" she asked, as I approached.

"Martell," I managed, "Goldie Martell." I waited anxiously, wondering if others were behind me while the lady filed through the papers in front of her with a #2 pencil.

"Here we go...'Martell'...oh, wait, you didn't say 'Jane Martell'...What was it again, honey?" The lady put the #2 pencil behind her ear and looked up at me.

"'Goldie.' I said 'Goldie,' but Jane is me." The lady looked a little confused, so I kind of told her a half truth, that everyone called me by my middle name. I didn't bother about the 'Goldie/Golden' explanation because I figured she didn't care. Also, a line was building behind me, and I was feeling shaky and still a little sick.

The lady pulled the pencil from behind her ear and handed me my schedule. "There you go, Jane," she said cheerfully. "That's a beautiful name, honey."

The hallway leading to my homeroom class was lined with lockers on both sides. A few other students were also still making their way to their first period classes; I had to find my homeroom before the bell rang. One boy that passed from the opposite direction made me think of Kip.

"Sunsets...pizza...Kip."

The bell sounded just as I walked into A107, my homeroom section. The teacher looked barely as old as Elise. He was dressed in a suit, and he smelled a bit like John-John Quinn. He was calling names from a list using an unreasonably loud voice. I slid into the first chair inside the door. As the teacher bellowed out "Jane Martell," I hesitantly raised my hand in the air. I wasn't sure I wanted to be known as 'Jane Martell,' but I wasn't sure I had the courage to speak up.

"Goldie!" I heard someone call my name from the other side of the room. Gabriella left her seat and hurried to sit just behind me. Some of the other students giggled, but the teacher kept on calling names, and "Gabriella Martin" was right after mine. She raised her hand, but then spoke.

"Jane Martell, right here," she gestured toward me, "likes to be called 'Goldie.'"

"Alright, Miss Martin. Thank you. I will remember that." The teacher carried on calling names. I thought, then, that Kip was right, that there might be some good things about junior high, like having Gabriella in my homeroom.

It turned out that Gabriella and I had half of our classes together and also lunch. That was a relief; I didn't have to sit at a lunch table all alone. Throughout that first day, and the days following, Gabriella reminded everyone that I preferred to be called, "Goldie." By Friday of the first week of school, nobody called me "Jane Martell" anymore.

The hardest part of junior high was switching classes. There were students everywhere, and it was so hard to find my way around. Gabriella didn't care at all about crowds, or noise, or anything like that. I guess we made a good combination because I didn't feel so alone or afraid in the halls when she walked with me, and I helped her with some of the confusing stuff from our classes when we had extra time. She didn't like balancing on the backs of the benches, though, and there were lots of benches outside Mason Hill. I didn't mind doing that alone.

Sometimes I wondered if I needed Gabriella more than she needed me. There were more girls like her, that didn't mind being around lots of people or doing loud things. I didn't really notice anyone else balancing on benches or hoping the day would go faster. I wondered if anyone else said little chants over and over to feel better, like I did. Sometimes I wondered, too, if I was supposed to be more like Gabriella and the other girls.

I thought every day about writing to Kip. I remembered that he said he would write first, but I worried that he wouldn't write to me at all, especially if he was mad at me for hiding in the secret cave.

In the afternoons when the bus dropped me off at the corner by Piper's Coffee Shop, I would push open the heavy old glass door that led to the apartments above the warehouse. Before going up the stairs, I would check mailbox #4, twisting the little old-fashioned knob. Each time, I hoped for a letter from Kip. There was never much mail at all, not for Elise or Mama, nor for me. I still looked, every day.

Elise wasn't much for writing letters. The evening after my first day at school, Elise called Mama's phone and asked to talk to me. She remembered that I had started at Mason Hill, and she wondered how my day had gone. I told her about the bus and the halls and how Gabriella had helped me.

The whole time we were talking, I thought about telling her about Kip. Just as she was getting ready to hang up, I told her that I had met a boy in Heritage and that he was really different from anyone that I had met before. Elise was probably smiling because that's how her voice sounded. "Aw, Goldie! That's so sweet!" she said when I told her about reading *The Little Prince* together, about the lemonade sale, and even about birch-bending. I never told her about the morning when I hid in the secret cave, though. I didn't tell her about the secret cave at all.

On a Monday, two weeks after the start of school, I turned the key to mailbox #4 to find a small white envelope addressed to "Goldie Bird Martell." I knew it could only have been from one person.

I could tell that the envelope had something inside, something besides just a note. My heart skipped as I made my way up the long flight of creaky stairs. My cheeks flushed hot like fire. Kip had not forgotten me!

My hands were shaking as I tried opening the envelope without tearing it at all. Inside was a folded piece of loose-leaf paper—college-ruled—from the pack that Grandpa Charlie had bought for him when we went shopping in Heritage. Also contained in the envelope was something tiny, wrapped in brown paper and fastened securely with masking tape. I took a deep breath and decided to open the little package first.

It took a while to get through the tape and the layers of paper. I recognized the stone right away; it was the one that I had spotted the day Kip and I walked home from town. Kip had put it in his pocket to give to Grandpa Charlie for his shop. I just didn't think of it again. This little stone that we had found together was a million times more beautiful than I had remembered.

A tear rolled down my cheek and landed on the kitchen table. This caused Smiley to cock his head as he stared. He didn't make any noise, but I kept wondering if he knew more than just bird things. Slowly, holding the sparkly stone tightly in one hand, I unfolded the paper which would have fit just fine in the envelope if it had been folded a few less times. I liked how it was, though, because it stretched out the good feeling of opening Kip's letter.

Kip's handwriting was much neater than mine. I took a deep breath and read what he had written.

Dear Goldie Bird,

I wanted to wait to write to you until I started school, so I would actually have something to write about. It has been boring around here without you. I guess it's okay that school started. Seventh grade seems alright so far. At least I have something to fill up my days again. My Little Prince test went really well, so thanks for helping me with that when I really didn't want to read the book.

Do you think I should go out for the soccer team? Then I would have something else to do besides nothing. Oh, and Grandpa Charlie said to tell you that if your mom ever changes her mind about letting you stay in Heritage, he will come and get you.

I almost forgot about the stone until I had to wash my pants. Do you remember when we found it? I thought you should have it.

Goldie Bird, I'm really sorry that I had to tell your mom where you were when it was time for you to go back to Charlotte. I wanted you to stay, but I knew you had to go. I was trying to do the right thing. I hope you're not mad.

Please write back to me when you have time. And don't ever forget about birch bending.

Love, Kip

I looked at the letter for a little while longer and then I read it again a few times before folding it up and tucking it back into the envelope.

All that time I had worried that he wouldn't want to talk to me again because of how I had acted, but he had been wondering if I was mad at him. How could I ever have been mad at Kip?

I decided to hide the letter inside the secret door in the closet. The stone, though, I would keep that with me. As I held it in my open palm, it caught the light from the afternoon sun, casting little rays of color that danced and jumped around the room like happy little bits of fairy dust and magic, which I could feel inside my soul.

Maybe I would show the stone to Gabriella, and I would

even tell her about Kip. She did talk a lot about boys now that we were at Mason Hill. She would tell me when she thought someone was cute, but I acted like I didn't care. Really, I didn't care about any of the boys at Mason Hill. I did care a lot about Kip, though. Sometimes I wondered if I was in love with Kip. I thought that Elise would know. I figured I could ask her what she thought the next time we talked. Mama wouldn't want me to have a boyfriend in sixth grade, but I thought I could still love Kip and he wouldn't really be my boyfriend. After all, he had written "Love, Kip" at the end of his letter. And I hoped he wasn't joking about Grandpa Charlie coming to get me.

Somehow, having the stone with me made me feel better when I was at school. I felt less alone. If I was one of the six hundred kids at Mason Hill, at least I was important to someone. When I was nervous about something, I would reach for the stone, just to hold it in my hand, and I would always feel a little bit better. Gabriella always made me feel safer and less alone when she walked with me in the halls, but she wasn't always with me. The stone was, as long as I remembered to put it in my pocket or to stick it inside my sock.

Gabriella had grown taller over the summer. She had always worn her dark hair braided close to her head, but since starting at Mason Hill, she had smaller braids that she could wear lots of different ways. As she approached our homeroom one morning, I heard two boys whistle at

Gabriella from just down the hall. "Hey, Gabriella," said one of the boys. She turned and waved to him. Sometimes I wished that I were Gabriella, or at least that I was more like her because things that were hard for me seemed to come easily to her. I wondered if Kip would have liked Gabriella if she had gone to Heritage or if he would still have sent me the stone if Gabriella had been there, too.

About a week passed before I gathered my courage to write to Kip:

Dear Kip,

You were right about junior high. It's not as bad as I thought it would be...

I told him that I would still rather be in Heritage because it was more fun than Charlotte. I wrote that I loved that he had sent the sparkly stone, that I kept it with me always, and that it reminded me of the sunsets that I had seen with him and with Grandpa Charlie. I told him that I had told Elise about him, about the things we had done in Heritage, and how I missed her, too. I asked if he missed his mom, dad, and sisters, but I couldn't really think of anything else to say, except that I thought he would be really good at playing soccer.

Please write back again.
Love, Goldie

Maybe I shouldn't have written the part about the sunsets. Maybe that was dumb. Maybe I shouldn't have written "Love, Goldie," but I did. Kip had signed his letter the same way, and I wondered if he had really meant that he loved me or if that's just what most people write at the end of letters. I guess I would have to talk to Elise about that, too. Still, I sent the letter.

Toward the end of September, there was a dance after school in the gym. The people in charge had decorated the gym with balloons, streamers, and flashing lights. There would be free snacks and a DJ. Gabriella wanted me to go with her. She told me that she was going with one of those boys that had whistled at her in the hall at the beginning of the year and that his friend would be going, too, so I could dance with him. I knew, though, that he probably wouldn't want to dance with me, and I knew that I definitely would not have wanted to dance with him. Besides, I was pretty sure that Mama wouldn't have wanted me to go anyway, so that's just what I told Gabriella. She kind of rolled her eyes at me and walked off without saying anything. I took the bus home that day, and Gabriella went to the dance.

After that, I wondered if we were going to be the same kind of friends that we had always been, and it was mostly because of boys.

Most days on the bus, I sat next to Kate, the tall girl that I had noticed outside of Piper's Coffee Shop on the first day of school. My spot was by the window, and she sat on the outside. She didn't say much, but neither did I. Often, Kate read a book on the short ride to Mason Hill. I usually looked out the window. Sometimes, she brought her breakfast, usually a chocolate chip cookie, to eat on the ride to school. She always asked me if I wanted part of her cookie. I never took a bite, but still she always asked. I liked Kate. In some sort of way, she reminded me of Elise, even though she was about a year older than me, because she made me feel okay while I was sitting on the inside of that bus seat.

Sometimes, Kate would put her book down, and we would have a little conversation. She once told me that she didn't live with her mom or dad. She had come to Mason Hill the year before, at the beginning of her sixth-grade year, to live with a lady that was taking care of her. This lady, who was her foster mom, had a lot of other children that she was taking care of that also did not live with their parents. Some of the other kids were little, even too young for school, and two were older than Kate, in high school. I wondered why none of those kids lived with their families, but I didn't ask Kate. Maybe they were like Kip, and their parents had to work on some things. I thought that maybe someday I could tell Kate about Kip. Maybe she was a little like him.

In the mornings, Kate came to the bus stop from the other side of downtown. I didn't know where she lived but she couldn't have lived too far from the warehouse and the shop because we shared the same bus stop. One day, after we were dropped off by the coffee shop, I stayed at the bench to tie my shoe. Kate carried her purple backpack over one shoulder. Her hands were in her pockets. She was wearing the same long brown sweater that she wore every day, even when it wasn't the slightest bit cold outside. Her brown hair was shiny and pretty, falling just to her shoulders. Kate did not seem to be in a hurry to get home, or to the house where she was staying. She stopped to pick up a leaf from the sidewalk along Follaton Road. The first of the autumn leaves had begun to drop from the trees. I looked away for a second. I did not want her to know that I had been watching her. I moved to the top of the bench, balancing on the back. Kate tossed the leaf and kept walking as it spun to the ground beside her. She did not really seem happy or sad. She was just Kate, the girl from the bus stop. My friend from the bus stop.

I watched from the bench until she turned down one of the side streets and I could no longer see her. As I made my way to the apartment, I wondered if Kate would like birch-bending.

Elise called Mama's phone every few days. Sometimes she asked to talk to me. I would tell her about what was new at Mason Hill, and she would tell me about her classes or the dining hall or the parties that she would go to on the weekends, which sounded a little like the school dance that I hadn't wanted to attend. Elise, though, seemed to like these parties. She asked about Gabriella, and she assured me that we could still be friends even if we didn't always like doing the same things. I told her about my new friend, Kate, and about little things that I remembered from my time with Kip in Heritage. It definitely wasn't the same as having her home, but I knew she still thought of me even though she was away at the university. On those nights, after our phone calls, I always slept in Elise's bed, just to get a little bit more of her.

Another letter came from Kip. This time, it was just a regular letter.

Dear Goldie,

I made the school soccer team! Grandpa Charlie is going to come to watch my games when he can. We'll both have something else to do besides just hanging around his shop.

Nina brought brownies — the amazing ones with

the frosting and sprinkles — and two jars of honey for me and Grandpa Charlie. She said she wished you and your mom were still here.

It's pretty good being here with Grandpa Charlie, but I miss my mom and my sisters, and I miss my dad, too, even though Grandpa Charlie doesn't like the way he treats my mom.

Goldie Bird, are you going to dress up for Halloween? Does your school have a soccer team? Are there any good ice cream places in Charlotte? I have been wondering about all of those things.

Write back soon.
Love, Kip

The "Love, Kip" part made my heart skip a few beats, even the second time around.

I thought Kate would understand about Kip in a lot of ways. She probably knew just what it was like to care about someone that you didn't get to see very often and to wonder if you actually ever would see that person again. I decided that the next time Kate put her book down on the bus, I would tell her about Kip, and that's just what I did. I told her everything about him, everything except the birch-bending and about hiding in the secret cave on the day that we had to leave, even though she would have understood perfectly well why I had done what I did. It turned out that Kate had read *The Little Prince*, too.

It was homecoming weekend in Charlotte. Mama would usually take me to the parade, which was always a little too loud. I liked going, though, because the football players always threw out candy, the good kind, like chocolate kisses and peanut butter cups. Last year, it was so hot that the candy was a melty pile of chocolate and foil wrappings by the time we got back home.

I didn't mind missing homecoming that year because Teddy was taking me to visit Elise. It had been over a month since I had seen my big sister, forty-one days, to be exact. I was going to get to share her bed in her dorm room, and Teddy was going to stay with one of his buddies from his old baseball team who went to Elise's school.

Mama and I baked oatmeal chocolate chip cookies for Elise. We also packed a loaf of cheese bread, Elise's favorite, from Piper's Coffee Shop. Mama gave me money to buy pizza for Teddy and Elise from one of the college places. Elise loved pizza, too, but just not the kind from Gas Mart.

Clover the fox was packed in my backpack. I also brought the quilt from Aunt Aida, the one that I had taken to the secret cave, because Mama wanted Elise to have it. Mama had to wash it because it had some dirt and grass marks on it from being dragged around outside. I wished that Mama wanted me to have the quilt, but I knew it would look nice on Elise's bed in her college room.

Teddy came to pick me up after I got home from school. I was at the shop helping Mama arrange one of the outside flower boxes with tiny pumpkins, kale, and yellow and purple pansies when he pulled up in his little red car, which always made lots of noise. Teddy hadn't come around since Elise had gone away to school. I thought Mama liked Teddy, but I couldn't always tell. Maybe he took Elise away from her when she hoped they could spend time together. It didn't matter much once Elise went to college because nobody really got to see her, unless someone made a special trip. And I thought Mama must have been grateful to Teddy that Elise wouldn't have to always be alone.

The drive down state seemed much shorter than last time, when I was dreading leaving Elise at the new place where she was going to live. Teddy played loud music in the car, and I could feel it inside my bones. I liked it. We didn't talk much. We were probably both thinking of Elise. The leaves on the trees along the stretches of highway had turned from green to red, orange, and gold.

It was dark when we got to the campus. Teddy had to park his car in the visitor's lot, which was a long walk to

Elise's dorm. I could feel a little chill in the air, not like the last year when the chocolates had melted. I zipped my sweatshirt and walked quickly to keep up with Teddy. Once we were finally inside the building where Elise lived, we walked past a giant desk that had rows and rows of little mailboxes, each with a tiny keyhole, like at the Warehouse Apartments. I knew that one of them belonged to Elise.

Teddy knew the number for Elise's room. He had to enter a code on a special phone and then we waited for Elise to come down in the elevator. It had been so crowded in the elevator on the day that we dropped Elise off. This time, we were the only ones in the lobby. It seemed much better without so many people. Most things did.

The elevator made a clunking noise, and a light went on as the door opened. There was my beautiful sister, looking out at us with her violet eyes. Her hair was swept onto one shoulder, and it looked much longer than I had remembered. She just stood there for a little second, and I could smell her familiar scent as the elevator doors closed behind her. Teddy moved to her and hugged her tightly for a long time. I felt just a little bit jealous. I turned to look in the other direction, to wait for my turn with Elise, but she surprised me from behind and lifted me off the ground and swung me in a circle, just as she had done so many times before.

"Goldie! You look more grown up! Is it junior high or the boy?" I didn't think she expected an answer, and I didn't say anything.

We went back to the elevator so Elise could show us her room. I expected to see her roommate, but she wasn't there. "Where's Meredith?" Teddy asked, even before I could.

"Oh, Meredith left for the weekend. Her family was going somewhere, and I guess she decided to go along. Goldie, she said you could sleep in her bed," Elise said with a lilt to her voice, expecting that I would be happy to have a whole bed to sleep in. Truthfully, I had been looking forward to sleeping back-to-back with Elise again.

Teddy sat really close to Elise on her bed, and I stretched out on Meredith's bed with Clover and listened to Elise and Teddy exchange stories about how their days had gone.

Elise wanted to take us to State Street Pizza, which was just a short walk from the dorm. I walked behind Teddy and Elise. Teddy had his arm around Elise, just the same way that Kip had his arm around me that last night after the marshmallows when he had walked me back to Aunt Aida's apartment. I wondered if someday Kip and I could be like Teddy and Elise. I hoped so, anyway.

The last time I had remembered being at a pizza restaurant was that awful day with Mama and Nina, when we finished Aunt Aida's "arrangements." This time, we had a booth with a soft red lantern that cast just enough light to read the menus. I sat across from Teddy and Elise, but we could easily have fit all on one side because they were sitting so close together. Elise was right: the pizza was amazing. We even got free garlic bread and free ice cream after we had finished eating. I paid with the money that Mama had given us, and Elise got to keep the change, which she said she would use for coffee the next week.

I was so sleepy on the walk back to Elise's room. Elise must have known because she turned to ask if I wanted a piggy-back ride. Before I could answer, Teddy stopped in front of me. He carried me on his back as I nearly fell asleep with my head on his shoulder. Every so often, Elise looked up at Teddy. Her eyes were bright and happy, which made me feel the same.

Teddy was talking to Elise about there being nobody at the desk when we had come in earlier, and still nobody was there. I wasn't sure why that mattered. I was sleepy enough, though, that I couldn't pay attention to much conversation. I could tell that we were moving up the elevator, but I didn't remember anything else until I woke to Elise's voice. She was whispering. It took me a few seconds to realize that I was in Meredith's bed, and Clover was with me underneath the covers. Teddy must have carried me all the way to the bed, and Elise had probably tucked me and Clover in.

I tried hard not to move. I thought I heard Teddy saying something, too, which didn't seem right, because he had planned to stay with his friends. I didn't know what time it was, and I was a little bit scared. Ever so slowly, as if I wasn't moving at all, I turned my head in the direction of Elise's bed. Even in the dark I could tell that Teddy was there, on the side closest to Meredith's bed. He was kissing Elise, probably because they thought I was asleep. As quietly as before, I turned my back to Elise's bed and tried hard to fall back to sleep.

A few times during the night, I woke to see that Teddy was still in Elise's bed, and they were both sleeping, as far as I could tell. When a creaking sound stirred me from a deep sleep, the sun was already shining through the window into Elise's room and right onto Meredith's bed where I was. This time, when I looked to the other side of the room, Teddy was gone. Elise was sleeping soundly. I had to go to the bathroom, so I crept out of Meredith's bed. I didn't have much to do except stare out the window while I waited for my sister to wake up.

After what seemed like hours, Elise's buzzer rang. She opened her eyes wide, smiling when she saw me. She spoke in a raspy voice and asked me to go down in the elevator and let Teddy in while she got dressed. When the elevator opened, there was Teddy with a little box of donuts and three cups of coffee, which made me know that I couldn't be mad at him for taking up some of my time with Elise. Nobody had ever brought me coffee before.

Elise took us around campus and to a football game on Saturday. Teddy stayed with his friend the next night. On

Sunday, we went to a theater and saw a movie that didn't make any sense, at least not to me. I liked it, though, because I had a whole box of popcorn to myself.

Elise walked with us to Teddy's car when it was time for us to return to Charlotte. She told Teddy that she loved him a bunch of times, and they hugged again for a really long time, long enough for me to buckle myself into Teddy's car and get all settled in for the ride home. We didn't say much during the drive, but I knew we were both thinking lots of things, mostly about my sister, while the loud music muffled the sounds of the highway.

The first quarter of sixth grade was nearly finished. I looked forward to my bus rides to and from school with Kate. Each day I checked the mailbox at the Warehouse Apartments just in case I had a letter from Kip. I had begun writing to tell him some of the things about visiting Elise with Teddy, like the football game and walking around the campus. I didn't tell him everything, but I did tell him that I wasn't sure if I had had a good time or not. I waited for a few days; I couldn't think of a whole lot more that I thought Kip would want to know. When I dropped the letter in the mailbox at the corner by the ice cream store (which I told him about), I wondered if I would ever hear back from him again.

It turned out that I didn't really mind Mason Hill Junior High. Reading and Art were my favorite classes, and the others were okay. I was managing without feeling like I had to rely on Gabriella. She was friendly toward me as I was to her, but it was becoming clearer that we liked to do different things. We shared the same lunch table and sometimes walked to our classes together, but Gabriella was spending time with a group of her new friends which included the whistling boys from the hallway and a few other girls who also seemed interested in boys. A few times, Gabriella gave a certain look to the other girls when she was with me, like she was bothered to be with me. It wasn't really that Gabriella made me feel left out, but like when I would hold the jump rope at grade school recess, I knew I didn't exactly fit in. I thought Kate would understand, since she seemed very much the same way.

The school band was having an organizational meeting during lunch and recess one day, and Kate asked me if I would go with her. She had always wanted to play music, she said, and this could be her chance. I thought of my harmonica, the one that Gabriella and I had discovered inside the secret door in my bedroom closet, and wondered if there would be any harmonica players in the band. The band director, Mr. Shankman, ordered sub sandwiches and cookies, and everyone that came to the meeting got to have some. I thought I was going to like the band, though I had no idea what instrument I would be able to play.

Kate was a little worried about paying the fee for the band. She said that she was going to wait until the weekend to ask her mom if she could give her money. She knew she couldn't ask her foster mom, Miss Marie, because she knew Miss Marie didn't have extra money to give away to all of the kids for lessons or that sort of thing, even though she would have given it to her if she knew she wanted it.

I wondered even harder why Kate didn't live with her mom. She was going to ask her for money, so it couldn't be that she didn't have enough money to take care of Kate. I wanted to ask more about her family, but something inside of me was afraid. Kate, though, asked me about mine on the ride to school on Friday morning, the same week as the band meeting.

"So, Goldie, who lives with you above the warehouse?" I wondered if I should tell her about Myles and Smiley, and if Elise counted as actually living with me.

"It's just me and my mom. My sister is away at school," I said, deciding only to mention the people.

"So, your dad doesn't live with you?" asked Kate.

"I don't have a dad," I said, as I turned to look out the window, not really at the downtown shops or trees or anything, but just to make talking about the hard stuff a little easier. "Well, I mean, I have a dad, but...I never knew him." I was worried that I had said too much, even though it hadn't been a lot of words.

I felt her hand on my knee, which startled me just a bit. "Goldie," Kate whispered, "It's okay. You can tell me stuff. I think we are the same in some ways. I don't ever see my dad, either. I haven't for a really long time, since I was like two years old."

I turned then to look at her, and I felt that I had known Kate for much longer than just a few months. My eyes were misty, and I think hers were, too. She continued to tell me her story. "When I was two, that's when my dad left me and my mom. That was the last time I saw him. He hurt my mom badly enough that she had to be in the hospital for a while. That's when I went to a foster family for the first time, but not with Miss Marie. All this time, it was just me and my mom, and it was pretty okay, until she got in some trouble last year. If she keeps doing what she is supposed to do, I'm going to get to go home pretty soon. At least I hope so."

I hoped so, too, for Kate, but I worried that I might not see her anymore if she left her foster family.

The bus had pulled up at school.

"Thanks, Goldie. Thanks for listening and for being my friend," said Kate, as she stood up in her seat. I stood, too, and hugged her, which wasn't something that I could remember ever having done before—hugging someone first—without it having been their idea.

The following Monday afternoon when the bus dropped me in the usual spot in front of Piper's Coffee Shop, I didn't want to go to the apartment. I missed Elise too much. And Kip. I also missed Kip. Kate hadn't been on the bus that day, so I was even missing her. I didn't want to be alone, so I went to Mama's work after school because at least there would be other people there.

Mama was surprised to see me. She smiled, though, and came up to me as I entered the shop. She had been stringing ruby glass stars onto long pieces of twine. Her hair was mostly light brown with a few silver-gray strands here and there. On that day, she had worn it high up on her head as she often did when she was at work. Mama's cheeks were as rosy as the stars. When Mama had a lot on her mind her cheeks would get red from so much thinking. I wished that I knew what she was thinking about as she chose the stars, one at a time.

Just then, Rosa came through the front door of the shop. She greeted Mama without really looking at her and disappeared into the warehouse, just as she always did. A short time later, Rosa emerged, clad in her overalls and clutching her garden gloves. She grabbed her tools and headed out to the flower beds where there were no more weeds growing since it was nearly winter, and the days had turned chilly.

I wondered what sort of things Rosa worried about. She was definitely not a grown up, so she didn't have to worry about adult things like paying bills or making the shopping list. I was pretty sure she didn't worry about boys, and she already had a job, so she didn't have to think about love or money or anything. Maybe she worried about the flowers, or maybe she just thought about them. She probably missed them during the winter. I wondered if Rosa would like to climb trees, or if birch bending would make her laugh as hard as Kip and I had.

Still, Rosa grabbed her trowel and weeding fork, and the little pad that she always sat on, and headed to the gardens. She also carried a bushel basket full of something like onions separated into tiny mesh bags. I wondered what she was going to do with those onions.

I watched her from the shop window. Her mouth was moving as if she was talking to someone, but I saw nobody near to her. I thought about the time when we were filling the bushel baskets with apples and just how excited I was when we seemed to connect in that moment of time. She seemed far away again. Rosa settled in a spot close to the weathered picket fence that separated the garden grounds from the parking lot. She started digging little holes at even distances apart in the earth. I heard Rosa laugh: first, an explosion of giggles that made me think of bubbles dancing high into the November sky, then a deep belly laugh, much like how I imagined the laughter of the Little Prince, a sound which caused John-John Quinn to come out from inside the landscape barn where his office was.

"Rosa! Enough!" John-John looked very stern as he put one finger to his mouth in a gesture of silence. I wondered what was wrong with laughing. I wondered if he even knew why Rosa was laughing. I wondered if Rosa even knew why she was laughing.

"Mama, what's Rosa doing?" I asked, curious about what made Rosa do the things that she did. The things that made her happy were pretty simple things. I thought Rosa had a higher kind of happiness than most people. Sometimes I wanted to trade places with her.

"She's planting bulbs. In the springtime, they will come up as flowers. Why don't you go out and see?"

I got myself a cup of tea—Earl Grey with just a bit of milk—from the little shelf by the door and went outside to the bench in front of the shop. There was just enough room on the bench to put my cup and saucer next to me. Steam rose from my tea and lingered in the cold air, adding a tiny bit more mystery to Rosa and to what she was doing. She laughed again, this time with just a few giggles and then that deep burst of laughter which again made John-John Quinn angry. This time, though, he gathered Rosa's tools, put them on top of the bulbs that were left in the bushel basket, and pulled Rosa up by the arm, more sternly than I thought he should have. Rosa let out a scream that was more disturbing than any of the laughter ever could have been to anyone. She dropped to the floor and stayed there, knees pulled to her chest and face in the dirt. She made a rhythmic sound—a whine and cry—over and over. John-John said something that I couldn't understand and turned to walk back to where he had come from. He noticed me on the bench, but I looked away, and he kept on going.

Rosa's sound grew quieter until she stopped making any noise at all. She rocked back and forth from that same position on the floor for a few minutes before lifting her head and pushing herself to a seated position. After pulling the bushel basket a little closer to where she was, Rosa laid out her tools, lined up the little bulbs next to the basket, and went back to digging. At once, I felt sad for her but also a bit envious that she could just go right on back to what she had been doing as if nothing had happened. Maybe to Rosa that really wasn't a big deal.

As I set my teacup down on the saucer, my hand slipped just enough to make a loud clanking noise. Rosa looked over to where I was sitting. I didn't think she knew that I had been there. She went back to planting her bulbs.

"Hey, Rosa," I said. Rosa did not acknowledge that I had spoken to her. I stayed on the bench for a few more minutes, but then I decided to move a little closer.

"Do you mind if I watch you plant those things... those bulbs?" I asked. Still, Rosa did not look up. I sat at the edge of the sidewalk, near to where she was working. She had taken off her gloves. As she placed each flower bulb, she sifted the dark brown earth through her fingers to make a gentle covering. Once the bulb was no longer visible through the layer of soil, she used her hand to pat the dirt before scraping with her shovel to fill the hole to ground level. I wondered how she knew where she had already worked and where she still needed to plant the bulbs because she didn't seem to be going in any pattern or marking the dirt in any way. Rosa knew a whole lot. There were plenty of things that she seemed to struggle with, like talking to people, but there were also things that she was much smarter about than almost everyone else. If Rosa had gone birch-bending with me and Kip, I had a feeling that we would still be able to hear her laughter.

I stayed out there for a very long time until the sun was nearly all the way gone. Mama turned off the porch light to the shop. It must have been close to five o'clock. I stood up, and right then, Rosa looked at me.

"Goldie. Bird." She had remembered. Rosa repeated what she had said, this time pointing over to the shop, above the warehouse, at the apartment that I shared with Mama.

"Yes!" I said. "Goldie's Bird. He's up there. His name is Smiley." Rosa's face lit up, as though she knew she had been understood. She laughed the longest, loudest, best laugh of all.

Mr. Quinn emerged from the shop. "It's getting late, girls," he said. I wasn't sure if he, too, was trying to redirect Rosa, or if he had just come to take her home. He was mostly always happy, and he was extra nice to Rosa and to me. John-John didn't seem very much like Mr. Quinn.

Rosa pointed to the apartment again. "Goldie. Bird. Smiley."

"She remembered about the bird that we brought from my great aunt Aida's place," I said. "Do you think I could take her upstairs to see Smiley sometime, Mr. Quinn?"

"I think that would be just fine," he said, and I thought that Mr. Quinn's face had lit up a bit, too. Maybe because he knew Rosa might be a little less lonely if she was my friend.

"Well, good night, Mr. Quinn," I said, "and good night, Rosa."

Rosa didn't say anything this time, but she did laugh just a little bit as she gathered her gloves, tools, and bushel basket, along with the rest of the bulbs that had yet to be planted.

"Good night, Goldie dear," said Mr. Quinn, as he waited for Rosa to finish collecting her things. They walked alongside one another up the path, lit now by the moon, toward their home.

Mama was happy to give me thirty-five dollars for the fees to join the band.

"Goldie, I think it's a great idea. You will have something else to do to keep busy," said Mama. She didn't ask me any questions. She just said that she thought I would be good at playing an instrument. Mama must have been in a good mood that day.

When I got to the bus stop on Wednesday, which was the last day to turn in the money for the band, I didn't see Kate. This was the third day in a row that she had missed school and the only three days this year that she had been absent. I knew, because I had been at school every day, and I remembered when I saw Kate outside of Piper's Coffee Shop on that first day, and each day following, until those days.

I hoped Kate wasn't sick, or in trouble with her foster mom, or that something bad hadn't happened to her. Trying to stop the thoughts in my brain was hard. I just missed my friend, which made me miss my sister and Kip even more than I already did.

On that day at recess, I knew I had to give Mama's money to Mr. Shankman. Without Kate, I felt lonely and sad. I was even a little bit mad at Kate. This was all her idea, and now she wasn't here to go through with it with me. It wasn't fair, really, to be mad at Kate if she was sick or something, but I wasn't sure I could do this alone, or if I even wanted to be in the band if Kate wasn't there with me. Still, I found Mr. Shankman.

I handed him the envelope. He was younger than most of the other teachers at Mason Hill, and about the same age as my homeroom teacher. He always wore a tie. The one he wore on that day had little music notes all over it.

"Name?" Mr. Shankman smiled at me as he adjusted his tie.

Just then, I had a thought. What if Kate hadn't been able to get the money from her mom and that was why she wasn't at school? She really wanted to be in the band. Maybe she was just upset, too upset to come to school because she couldn't pay.

"Kate. It's for Kate, in seventh grade. My name is Goldie Martell, but I'm paying for Kate." I pushed the envelope closer to him. I could feel my heart beating faster.

"Oh, sure, Kate. I know you girls were together here at the first meeting. So, you're paying for her?" he asked.

I nodded. "I decided not to join," I told him, which was the truth, because I had just decided right then that it would be better for Kate to be able to do what she had always wanted to do.

"Very good, and that's too bad, that you won't be taking part. I think you would have done well. Thank you for letting me know. I have Kate marked as "paid," so she is all set. First practice will be this Friday after school, if you could pass that along to your friend, please."

"Thank you, Mr. Shankman," I managed to turn away before the tears began falling. Thankfully, I had a few more minutes before the bell would ring for my next class. I tried thinking about the cheerful little music notes on Mr. Shankman's tie, hoping to make myself feel better. I wondered what I had just done and whether I would even see my friend again, and whether she would be able to be in the band at all.

I ran from the bus stop all the way to the apartment, directly to the mailboxes with the hope of finding something to make me feel better, but there was no letter from Kip.

Maybe Kip had made new friends at the school in Heritage. Maybe there was even a special girl, one that had made him forget me. I thought of the secret cave, and if Kip might have taken someone else there, to show her his secret place, and even to take her on a birch-bending adventure.

Smiley was making some bird noises when I got back to the apartment. For a little while, I wished that I was Smiley, only I would be called Goldie Bird. I would stay in that cage and not care if anyone paid attention to me or if I had any friends at all. I could stand on the highest perches, and I could sing, and no one would care. And I would never be lonely because I wouldn't need anyone else.

I went to my room and lay down on Elise's bed and cried.

The sky looked dusky through the big window in my bedroom when I was awakened by a knock at our apartment door.

"Goldie!" I heard a familiar voice. It was Mr. Quinn.

When I slid the chain from the door and pulled it open, the first person I saw was Rosa. I didn't remember ever having seen Rosa above the warehouse before. Mr. Quinn had been to our apartment many, many times because he owned the whole warehouse, the shop, and everything.

"Goldie. Bird. Goldie. Bird. Smiley!" Rosa beamed.

"Florence said it would be a good time to visit. Rosa has not stopped asking about the bird!" Mr. Quinn was smiling, as usual, as he led Rosa through the living room. I thought of the way John-John talked to and treated Rosa when she was planting the bulbs. Once I asked Mama if Rosa had a mom. She told me that Mrs. Quinn had gone away from the family when Rosa was a little girl. John-John and Rosa stayed with Mr. Quinn. I wondered why she had left. I wondered if she was mean to Rosa like John-John had been.

Smiley's cage was still on the kitchen table. Myles was

happy about this. Since Elise was gone, there was plenty of room for the bird and the cat, with two spots to spare for me and Mama.

"Goldie. Bird. Smiley." Rosa repeated her chant over and over. She stood with her face close to the cage, watching the bird for a very long time and exploding with a burst of laughter every once in a while.

Mr. Quinns' phone rang. He stepped outside the apartment. I could still hear his voice from the hallway.

Rosa moved back from the birdcage. She stood very still for a minute, listening to her dad's voice. She looked all around the room before moving toward the bookshelf. She laughed. After staring at the books for as long as she had stared at Smiley, Rosa spoke in a loud voice that startled me just a bit.

"Goldie, read!" exclaimed Rosa, who was still looking at the bookshelf.

She insisted again. She must have been waiting for me to choose a book. Rosa stood still as I moved toward her. I wondered what sort of book Rosa would like. I pulled *The Little Prince* from the shelf in our living room. Rosa had said my name again, and this time it wasn't about the bird. Maybe she knew that I was her friend. We could tame each other in the same way that the Little Prince had tamed his fox.

She moved to sit on the couch. "Goldie, read," said Rosa.

I opened the book to the beginning of the story.

"Goldie, read," Rosa repeated. Her laughter filled the room.

I wasn't sure how long Mr. Quinn had been watching us. Rosa was listening intently to the pilot's story of meeting the Little Prince and trying to please him with his drawings.

"Rosa loves when others read to her. She remembers every word! You are a wonderful friend to read to her. You know, you're a lot like your mama," said Mr. Quinn. I smiled at him before returning to the book.

Before long, Mama came through the door. It must have been late enough that she had already closed the store. "Calvin!" she exclaimed. "I wondered where you were. It was so quiet in the shop today." Mama laughed a little after she said that, and Mr. Quinn laughed, too.

Mr. Quinn told Mama that I had been reading with Rosa and that they had come to see the bird. He also told her that she should be proud of having such a kind daughter.

"Yes," said Mama, "my Goldie has a good heart."

Elise called a bit later, just as I was getting ready for bed. If she had called earlier in the day, I would have told her that I was having a terrible day. After the visit with Rosa and Mr. Quinn, though, I felt much better. She told me that she missed me and that she would be coming home for her school's winter break in just over a month. As I tucked myself into Elise's bed, I thought about Kip and whether he would write again. I wondered, just for a little while, why so many of the people that I cared for went away. Elise, though, was coming home soon, and now I had Rosa to keep me company, so there were lots of reasons that I might not be lonely, even if Kate was gone for good.

That next morning, Kate was already waiting when I reached the bus stop outside of the coffee shop. I nearly knocked her over when I ran to her and hugged her. "Kate! I missed you! Where have you been? Were you sick?" She looked a little overwhelmed.

"I missed you too, Goldie. I was gone for a good reason, though. At least, I think. I was with my mom. I might be going home soon," said Kate, with a lilt to her voice. "I didn't even know I was going to get to stay with Mom until Sarah picked me up." Sarah was her caseworker. She continued, "Mom's been doing the stuff that she is supposed to do for me to be able to come home. That means we'll get to have more visits, and longer ones. If she keeps doing well, I can live with her again."

The bus pulled up, and we went to our usual seat with me by the window and Kate right next to me. "It's not near here, where your mom lives, is it?" I asked. I could feel the lump building in my throat, but I didn't want to spoil Kate's happiness. Maybe if I told her that she was all signed up for the band, she wouldn't want to go home. I felt bad for wanting her to stay.

"It's a couple hours away," Kate began. "I would go back to the junior high where I started sixth grade, before the stuff happened with Mom. It's okay there. And they have a band, too."

I turned my head harder to the window so Kate wouldn't know I was upset. She knew, though, because she reached for my hand.

"I know, Goldie. I'm not going to forget about you, ever. Besides, it's not going to be for a while, if it even happens. She's my mom, though, and I love her."

I guessed it was okay for Kate to see me cry because she would know just how much she meant to me. All day I thought about whether I should tell her about the money that I had given Mr. Shankman. The next day was going to be Friday. I decided that I should at least tell her about it to be fair. She said she "might" be going home, so maybe she wouldn't even leave at all. I secretly hoped she wouldn't, and I knew that was a terrible thing to hope for. It was a bit like when the Little Prince knew he had to return to his planet: he was sad to leave, but he knew he had to go back to his rose, even if it meant leaving people that meant a lot to him.

Kate was quiet on the bus ride home. Just before we arrived at our stop, I asked if she had talked to her mom about joining the band.

"She was so excited about having me stay for the extra days, Goldie. There's not a lot that has made Mom happy during the past couple of years. I knew that if I told her about wanting to sign up for the band, she might feel like I didn't want to come home to her. And I knew she wouldn't have the money. It seemed like a good idea at first, but I just couldn't do it. I hope you understand, Goldie."

I tried to think of what to say next, but I wasn't sure how to tell her.

"Oh, no! You signed up, didn't you? And we were going to do it together! Goldie! I'm so sorry!" I could tell Kate really felt bad. She stopped on the sidewalk instead of going her usual route down the block.

"No, Kate, really, it's okay! I had no idea what instrument I would play, or even if I would want to play one at all. But, you would still want to do it, I mean if you could, if you didn't even have to pay, right?" I hopped up on the back of the bench outside of Piper's. Somehow, I always felt braver and stronger when I was off the ground.

"How do you even do that?" asked Kate. "I would fall right down. You're like a little bird up there. Like a little goldfinch or something." She smiled, and I returned her smile, for more than one reason, before sharing what I had wanted to tell her all day.

I told Kate about the money from Mama and how I had given it to Mr. Shankman for her because I was worried that she wouldn't be back in time to pay her fee and that she wouldn't be able to do what she had wanted to do for so long.

Kate jumped onto the bench seat, but not onto the top. Her hair lifted a little bit in the cold breeze, and she shivered beneath her brown sweater. Her face flushed.

"Goldie, you did that for me? I can't believe you did that for me. You're the best friend I have ever had," said Kate.

"Your first rehearsal is tomorrow. Mr. Shankman said to let you know," I said, as I jumped from my spot and landed on the ground. I was happy for Kate, but I was a little sad for me. Kate hugged me and headed down the block as I crossed the street toward the shop.

"Goldie," called Kate, just as I had reached the gate to the worn white picket fence that led to the shop, "thank you!" I knew I could never tell Mama about this. I hoped that she would never ask how my music lessons were going or what instrument I was playing. I hoped even harder that she would never show up at Mason Hill for a band concert. I hoped, hardest of all, that Kate would love being in the band for as much time as she had left here in Charlotte.

The moon was bright in the window when I woke in the middle of the night to some sort of noise coming from the kitchen. The big moon made me think of the Little Prince, the stars, and Kip. He was out there somewhere. I just needed to know that he still remembered me.

A little more noise came from the kitchen—water running, this time—and then the bird made a peep. So slowly, I pushed open the bedroom door. I could tell Mama was in the kitchen.

"Goldie. You can't sleep, either?" asked Mama.

I went to her, standing close enough to feel the steam rising from the tea in her mug.

"Want some tea?" she asked.

"No, thanks, Mama." I stayed next to her, breathing her air, until she had finished the tea. After a couple minutes, Mama stood, leaving her tea on the table. I followed her to her bedroom. Mama pulled the covers up to her shoulders. I hopped in the bed beside her and curled up with my back pressed against hers. We both fell asleep until morning.

"Goldie! I have been looking for you! You're not going to believe this!" It was just nearing the end of recess when Kate found me outside on the swings. She told me that Mr. Shankman asked her if she thought I really wanted to be in the band with her. When she told him that she thought I did, he said he would take care of my fee.

"He told me to tell you that he would love to have you! He hopes to see you after school for the first rehearsal!" Kate said excitedly.

I thought for sure that I would sail over the trees if I let go of my swing right then. He would love to have me! I was going to be in the band after all.

Kate waited for me at the entrance to the cafeteria after school. There were already a lot of students with instruments. Others were looking at all sorts of shiny brass horns, bells, and drums that had been laid out on two of the long tables. The afternoon sun shone brightly through the high cafeteria windows, making little rainbows that danced off some of the instruments.

Mr. Shankman waved from across the room. He told me he was glad I had decided to come. He also said he thought I would be perfect as a flute player, and there were only two other flute players in that year's band. Kate had also chosen to play the flute, which seemed like the best idea because we would be able to practice our music together. I thanked him for letting me come without having to pay, and I watched a little rainbow dance behind his head as he assured me that indeed I had paid already with my kindness. As I waited for the late bus with Kate, I held tightly to the little black case which held my flute.

There was a break from school during the week of Thanksgiving. Every year for as long as I could remember, we had eaten Thanksgiving dinner at the little church outside of Charlotte, where they hosted a turkey feast with stuffing, cranberries, green beans, lots of pies, and so much more food. The church served the meal free to anyone that wanted to eat there. Mama, Elise, and I would go early to help out in the kitchen, usually peeling what seemed like a hundred potatoes. Then we stayed to eat as much as we wanted. I didn't mind going, mostly because of the pie. I told Kate about it. She said she would have loved to go but she would be gone for a visit with her mom.

Mama said she could really use my help getting the shop ready for Christmas. That year, she put me in charge of the fairy window box gardens, which were my favorite things in all of Rosa's Garden Party. One morning before the shop opened, Mama took me into the warehouse to look through the storage for things I might use. The warehouse was as big as my school's gym. There were tables and shelves everywhere, and so many little hiding spaces. I loved how it smelled in there; it was a mix of flowers, spices like ginger and cloves, and the old musty smell that was always inside library books, a little like the secret closet. Mama said it would be okay if I looked through the fairy garden boxes while she set things up in the shop. I hadn't been in the warehouse alone before. Silver bells, little glass balls of red and green, old Christmas ornaments, fresh pine boughs, little ceramic animals, and golden stars, all glittery and sparkling— there was so much to pick from! I gathered what I thought

I would need for the window boxes and put it all into one of the empty cardboard boxes behind the storage shelves. When I turned to leave, I heard Rosa.

"Goldie! Bird!" She moved toward me. I noticed that she was wearing her garden overalls, but she did not have her tools with her.

"Hello, Rosa!" I said. "I'm helping in the shop today. Smiley is upstairs at my house." Rosa looked a little disappointed, but it seemed she was happy to have been understood, even if she couldn't see the bird right then.

Mr. Quinn came through the warehouse. "Oh, good morning, Goldie! Rosa's a little lost today without her usual school routine and without really being able to work outside in the cold and snow."

I asked Mr. Quinn if she could stay with me for a while to help with the window boxes. Rosa helped me carry the box of treasures that I had gathered from the warehouse. I wasn't sure if Rosa understood the point of what we were doing, but she was really good at arranging the little pine boughs just where they looked their very best, and that's what seemed to matter. We were nearly finished with our work when it was time for the shop to open for the day.

"Oh my, girls! Your art direction is so lovely!" exclaimed an older lady with a white fur-lined hat as she approached the door to the shop. "That's great marketing right there. You can help me make some decisions after I look around."

Rosa laughed, and I knew then that she understood that we had done good work.

Mama came out to see what we had done. She said the lady with the hat was raving about the fairy garden window boxes, and she wanted to have a look at them. Rosa kept saying "Goldie!" and laughing, which made Mama smile. The lady with the hat ended up buying a lot of little treasures to make her own fairy window box, and she even let Rosa and me choose some of the things. We stayed for the whole day to help Mama in the shop. Mr. Quinn brought sandwiches and lemon shortbread from Piper's Coffee Shop for all of us to eat for lunch. Rosa didn't even seem to miss her flowers on that day.

I thought a lot about Elise and how I missed having her home. Just three weeks later, though, she would be coming home for a whole month. Teddy had asked Mama if he could take me to get a Christmas tree sometime before Elise came home. Elise usually helped Mama with the tree and with all the decorations on the Sunday after Thanksgiving. Teddy must have remembered this.

It was a little hard passing the time without much to do. I tried practicing my flute. It was a lot different than the harmonica. Somehow, though, Monday turned to Thursday, the day of the feast. The shop was closed, and Mama and I both slept later than we had for a long time. Mama was making coffee, and I was getting dressed in my room when we heard our buzzer. Someone was ringing from downstairs.

"Goldie, are you expecting anyone? Will you run down and see who it is?" I still had on my clothes from the day before. I hadn't managed to comb my hair or anything, but I shuffled into the hallway. Once I reached the top of the stairs, I stopped for a second as I recognized the shoes and the bottom of the brown sweater. Kate! I thought she was with her mom. I raced down the stairs. The loose, cracked, hundred-year-old tile made clicking sounds under my bare feet.

Kate had been crying. She looked up at me with her dark brown eyes, and the tears that fell down her cheeks made me think that her sadness had been waiting to come out for a long time.

"Hey," she asked, "would I still be able to go with you to that church today?" Kate asked.

"I'd love that," I told her. "Want to come up and meet my mom?" Kate sat on the stairs and put her head in her hands. I knew I wasn't good at saying the right thing, so I just sat next to her. After a little while, she lifted her head.

"I'm not going with Mom," she said, her voice breaking a bit. "She wasn't at her place last night when the caseworker showed up. She hasn't answered any of the messages, so the visit is canceled for the weekend. I was supposed to be with my mom for four nights, but now I don't even know where she is. I'm so worried about her. She wouldn't just not show up for me on purpose." She put her head down again, and this time I sat a little closer to her and put my arm around her shoulders, kind of like Kip did for me when I was sad about the same sort of thing.

After a little time, she told me that she was ready to meet Mama, who welcomed her in and gave both of us coffee with milk. She offered to make eggs for all of us, which seemed to make Kate feel a little better, at least for a time. Kate said that her foster mother, Miss Marie, was fine with her coming to our place, and even with her going to the feast later in the day. She just wanted to talk to Mama first.

Kate was waiting by the door when we stopped at Miss Marie's house on the way to the church. Mama chatted with Miss Marie, who was holding a little pink baby over her shoulder. Kate introduced me to her two toddler foster brothers who sounded and acted like an entire circus.

A small crowd was already gathered in the banquet room at the church when we arrived. Kate and I got busy in the kitchen, peeling sacks, and sacks of potatoes, which did not seem like work at all, because we filled the time by telling stories, laughing until our bellies hurt. I hadn't laughed that hard since Kip and I fell into the lagoon during our birch-bending adventure. I decided to tell Kate about that, too.

When we had peeled all of the potatoes, we waited for

Mama to finish cutting a pumpkin pie and then it was our turn to eat. We went through the line three times, piling our plates with ridiculous amounts of food and finishing an entire pumpkin pie between the three of us. I thought on our way home that I really hadn't even missed Elise, but I would never have told her that.

The shop was crowded when it opened the next day. Mr. Quinn brought Rosa to help pass out cookies and cider. Rosa didn't like looking at all the people, but she loved pouring the hot cider, probably because of how the steam looked. She was very careful.

At one point, John-John came into the shop looking for Mr. Quinn. On his way back to the warehouse, he asked Mama if she thought it was a good idea for Rosa to be handing cider to the customers. Mama assured her that Rosa was doing a good job, and John-John rolled his eyes to the tin ceiling.

"Hey, Goldie," John-John addressed me, which made me nervous because I wasn't even sure most days if he even knew I existed, "when is your big sister coming home?"

"Pretty soon, I think…in like three weeks," I told him.

"Good," he said, "because my dad said she would be able to help me with some of these design orders. I sure hope so." As he left the shop, I thought that it didn't really seem like John-John liked his job, or even being around his dad and his sister.

Shortly after returning to the shop from making a sandwich in the apartment, I saw Kate, Miss Marie, and the two little circus boys coming through the gate. Miss Marie was wearing a baby sling. The baby that she had been holding the day before was tucked inside. Rosa handed the bigger of the toddlers a cup of cider, nearly filled to the top, which he promptly dumped on the pine floorboards. Rosa laughed and jumped up and down. Mama looked overwhelmed. Miss Marie barely noticed the sticky spill that the boy had made.

"Goldie! Grab the mop bucket from the sink just inside the warehouse, would you?" asked Mama. I was quick to clean up the mess. The circus boys had moved on to the fairy garden area, but not before grabbing one gingerbread man for each of their hands. Miss Marie was looking around the shop, juggling the baby and trying to catch up with the two toddlers. Kate followed me inside the warehouse while I dumped the mop bucket.

"Ugh, I miss school. It's hard when everyone's home. The babies won't leave me alone," said Kate. I had always thought I would like to have younger siblings, but I doubted it would be much fun to live in Miss Marie's house.

Then, I had an idea. "Kate, do you think Miss Marie

would let you stay at our apartment? For a sleepover? I mean, you weren't going to be home anyway, right?" I felt a little bad for saying that last part. Kate didn't need to be reminded that her mom didn't show up for her.

"Really?" Kate's enthusiasm took me by surprise. "Goldie, can I? I'll ask Miss Marie," said Kate. She made her way across the floor, carefully stepping to avoid the partially eaten gingerbread boy limbs, fairy garden accessories, a discarded cider cup, and her two gooey little foster brothers.

"I'm sorry, Goldie," said Miss Marie, as she tried to bend to the floor, with the pink baby still strapped to her. I promised I could take care of the mess, mostly because I was hoping that she would let Kate stay with us, but also since I knew Mama would be happy when the little boys left the shop.

Kate came later that evening after Mama had closed the shop. She carried her school backpack, a pillow with Snow White and a little squirrel stitched on one side of the pillowcase, and a grocery bag which she handed to me as soon as I met her at the bottom of the stairs. "I brought these for you. We can decorate your room or something." I looked in the bag to find three boxes of multicolored string lights.

"I had planned to bring them to decorate my mom's place for Christmas," Kate said. "Since I don't know when I will be seeing her," she continued, "I want you to have them."

I wasn't sure what to say. And then I remembered.

"You remembered about the lights!" I wanted to hug Kate, but I didn't. On one of our bus rides, I told Kate that I had always loved little lights and stars and sparkly things, but ever since sitting with Kip on the hill in Heritage, looking out at the lights, I loved stars...and lights...even more.

Kate said she knew I would appreciate them more than her mom would, anyway. This made me happy and sad at the same time, like a lot of things with Kate. We got straight to work hanging the lights with some little push pins that were in Mama's junk drawer. One box of lights was all that we needed for my and Elise's room. We left the bedroom but kept the string lights lit so we would be able to see them right away when we opened the door.

Mama wasn't back yet from whatever she had been doing after closing the shop. Kate and I decided to hang the other two boxes of lights in the living room. We had to move the tall stools from the kitchen to reach the highest places. It was dark by the time we heard Mama fumbling to open the apartment door. The only light in the big room came from the Christmas lights that we had worked so hard to hang. When she opened the door, she nearly dropped the pizza that she was carrying. She smiled as she looked around the room. "How festive!" exclaimed Mama, as she set the pizza on the table next to Smiley's cage. I noticed the "Gas Mart" stamp on the pizza box. It had been a great day, and it wasn't even over.

Kate and I were watching our second movie of the night when Mama's phone rang. Mama had been sitting with us, waiting for her nail polish to dry before going for a second round of pizza. That's when Elise called. I knew something wasn't quite right because I could tell that sort of thing about my sister, and because Mama left the room while she talked. After a short time, Mama came back to let us know that she was going to bed. She didn't say why Elise called. I didn't ask, but I wondered if she was okay.

After eating the last pieces of the Gas Mart pizza and watching *The Elephant Man*, our third movie of the night, Kate and I settled into bed under the sparkling lights. Kate fell asleep right away in my bed, but I lay awake under Elise's blanket where there was still a little bit of the scent that my sister had left behind, wishing that nothing would be wrong. Every so often, I peeked from under the blanket to look at the lights. I knew, even though there was hard stuff, that there was a lot of good.

Teddy came, as promised, on that Sunday afternoon. I hadn't seen him since we visited Elise at the university in October. We were going to get a Christmas tree. I wondered if we were going to the home store just outside of Charlotte, as we had every year before. There were always lines and lines of trees, chopped and ready to go, just outside the store's entrance. Sometimes people spent crazy amounts of time walking up and down the lines, looking at every single tree, and then starting again. This was hard to understand because most of the trees looked the same to me.

Teddy drove right past the home store, through the neighboring town, and through the town next to that one. After what seemed like about an hour, he turned the car down a gravel road. I watched through the window, looking back from where we had come a time or two just to make sure I would know which way to go in case something went wrong. The music was loud, and Teddy wouldn't have heard me if I had anything to say, so I just kept quiet. He stopped the car about a mile or so down that gravel road. The little road was now framed on both sides by pine and fir trees of every shape and size. The people walking the lines at the home store would never have been able to choose.

Teddy opened the hatch to the back of his car and pulled out a saw. It looked brand new. I wondered if he had bought it specifically for what we were about to do.

"Where should we start, Goldie?" asked Teddy, who looked all ready to chop down a tree. I could see why my sister loved him. He was a good person, at least to me, and definitely to Elise.

"Which one looks good? You get to pick, Goldie. That way, if Florence or Elise thinks it's a bad tree, it won't be on me," Teddy laughed.

The ceilings at the apartment were so high that I could have chosen any tree in that part of the forest. We settled on one that was about two feet taller than Teddy's head. He got down on his knees and began sawing the tree as close to the ground as he could while I held tightly to the trunk. I could feel the spiky little pine needles poking at my hands through the wool of my mittens. When he had nearly cut through the trunk's thickness, he told me to let the tree fall. As I let go, I breathed in the deep, rich winter air around me. I helped Teddy drag the tree to his car. He said he was glad it wasn't too cold in case I needed to hold onto the tree while we drove. I didn't, though, because he had done a good job tying it to the top of the car.

"Thanks for your help, Goldie," said Teddy, reaching across the car to give me a high-five. "I think you picked a great one!"

"I hope so," I said. "Thanks for taking me."

"Teddy, can I ask you a question?" I felt a little butterfly in my stomach. I didn't wait for his answer. "I'm a little worried about Elise. I think she was crying when she talked to Mama last night. Do you think something happened at school or something?"

Teddy looked out the driver's side window. "She's okay, Goldie. It's hard for Elise to be away. She misses all of us. It's sweet that you're worried about her."

"Do you promise that she's okay? Or, well, if she's not, do you promise to take care of her?" I asked.

"I promise, Goldie. I promise," said Teddy, as he drove on.

Kate and I had a lot more to talk about than usual when we returned to school on Monday. Kate said that she still hadn't heard from her mom, so she was trying not to think about her for a while. I knew what that was like, to try not to think of someone. I knew it wasn't easy.

"Goldie, can I ask you something?" said Kate.

"Sure, what do you want to know?" I asked.

"Do you..." she hesitated, "Goldie, don't you wonder about your dad? I mean, your mom has to know who he is, right? Did you ever just ask her?"

Her question caught me with such surprise that I turned my head toward the window.

"I'm sorry. I don't want to make you sad, but don't you wonder? I mean, shouldn't you be able to know...if you want to?" Kate asked.

"Really...I think Mama would tell me if she wanted me to know. I mean, don't you think she would?" It's just not something that I thought I was allowed to know, but Kate was right.

We were both quiet for a while. I mostly just looked out the window. I wondered why Kate had mentioned the idea of my dad. She did, though, know what it was like to wonder and to try to understand why parents do the things that they do. Maybe she was thinking about her dad. Maybe our questions and sadness were all mixing together.

Once we got off the bus, Kate put her hand on my shoulder. "We're going to be okay, you know," she said, "I promise."

Kate decided to walk to the apartment with me after the bus stopped at the corner that afternoon. Mr. Shankman had given us the music for our holiday concert. We were going to play our songs at the retirement home just outside of Charlotte. We checked the mailbox on the way upstairs. Finally, there was a letter from Kip. He hadn't forgotten about me! I couldn't tell who was most excited about the little white envelope: me or Kate.

We sat at the top of the stairs in the hallway.

"Open it, Goldie!" Kate said, as she elbowed me hard in the side. I opened the envelope and read the letter to myself, just in case, before I shared it with Kate.

Dear Goldie Bird,

Can you believe it's almost Christmas already? I bet it's cold up there! I drove with Grandpa Charlie to Penny, where my family lives in Ohio, for the Thanksgiving holiday. I think things are better with my parents. That made me and also Grandpa Charlie really happy. Mom and Dad want us to come back at the end of the school year, and they want Grandpa Charlie to stay for good.

Mom worries a lot about Grandpa Charlie being alone in Heritage now that Grandma Ellen is gone. Grandpa Charlie said he is going to think it over.

I really do like being in Heritage. Soccer was a great time, and I might run track in the spring before baseball. Playing sports keeps me busy, and it takes my mind away from what I worry about, mostly my family. I wonder what would happen if my parents kept fighting, and if they had to split up. I guess I'm not as worried about that anymore. If we were all back in Ohio, even Grandpa Charlie, that might be really good. Then you would have to visit me in Ohio instead!

How is your family, Goldie? How is your sister doing in college?

Also, what do you want for Christmas? I hope you get it. Write to me soon.

Love, Kip

Kate read the letter aloud after I handed it to her. She said she thought it was funny and surprising that he called me "Goldie Bird" when she, too, thought I was a little like a goldfinch when I balanced on the backs of the benches. "Kip seems so nice, Goldie. I don't blame you for having a crush on him," she said.

I shouldn't have been surprised; Kate already knew me pretty well.

"You like him a lot, don't you?" she asked.

My cheeks were hot. "Come on," I said, as I stood up from our spot at the top of the stairs. "We better go and practice." I reached for Kate's hand and wished it were Kip's. I didn't tell her, though I was sure she would have understood.

That afternoon, we took turns playing our flutes and talking about so many things, good things and hard things, too. It felt so good to have someone to listen to me and to have someone that really seemed to care about the things that mattered to me.

"Hey, Goldie, you should get something for Kip for Christmas, don't you think?" Kate asked.

"I don't know. What would I get him?" I asked. "I don't have any money, anyway."

Kate said that she didn't have any money, either. "Why don't you make something for him? You're pretty good at art, aren't you?" she asked.

"My sister is! She's great at painting. I will ask her to

help me when she gets home. That's just two weeks from now." I loved Kate's idea. I already had a few thoughts about what I wanted to ask Elise to do.

Kate left just before Mama closed the shop. I hadn't thought anymore about the question Kate had asked me that morning until I saw Mama come through the door to the apartment. She had her hair up high on her head and a pencil tucked behind her ear. She looked a lot like Elise. Mama was wearing a long skirt that actually belonged to Elise. They were so much the same that sometimes I wasn't sure where I fit in. Kate was right. Maybe I could work up the courage to talk to Mama about my dad, someday.

I went with Teddy to pick up Elise from the bus stop. She took a student route from the university that stopped at lots of places, including the home store. She was waiting on a bench next to the outdoor fire pits and cooking grills, in front of the store. She was all alone. Her face was pale. I thought for sure it must have been from the long bus ride. She ran to Teddy and buried her head in his coat as he tried to get out of the car.

"Goldie..." Elise let go of her hold on Teddy and hugged me tightly. She said she couldn't wait to get home and that she was going to get right in bed and sleep for days. Elise looked worn out alright; she didn't feel good.

She said she threw up on the bus. She said she was tired of feeling sick, she was tired of being tired, and she was just happy to have some time away from school to rest.

As I climbed into the back seat of Teddy's car, Elise noticed the little bulge from the stone in my pocket. When I showed it to her, she said it was the prettiest, most sparkly stone that she had ever seen.

Elise's eyes brightened when she saw the Christmas tree, now sparkling with lights and ornaments, that Teddy and I had secretly cut down from the forest. Then she did what she said she would do. She crawled right into her bed and slept all the way to the next day. I went to bed early, just so I could be near to her.

The next morning, I asked Elise if she would help me make a little painting for Kip. My idea was to try to paint a goldfinch bird sitting in a birch tree or balancing on the back of a park bench. I didn't know where to start, like what supplies to use or even how it should look.

I was having my cinnamon toast when Elise came from the bathroom. "You like Aunt Aida's bird, Goldie?" she asked.

"I don't know. He's okay, I guess. He probably misses his old life in Heritage. Rosa, though, she really likes him," I told Elise.

"I'm with Rosa," said Elise. "I like birds. I guess I like them better when they're outside."

"Are you feeling better this morning?" I asked.

"I'm not sure, but I'll be fine," she answered. Then, she brought a small piece of heavy painting paper to the table along with a mason jar which she had filled with water, a couple of paintbrushes, and her palette of watercolors that she had bought for one of her painting classes at the university.

"You're going to let me use that?" I asked, worried that I might mess up the colors.

"Of course! Anything for Kip," said Elise, as her face lit up with the sweet smile that I had been missing.

Elise helped me sketch, with the pencil that she pulled from behind her ear, a simple drawing of a little goldfinch perched on the back of a bench, with a birch tree in the background. Then we used her college watercolors to make it come to life. It was small and simple, but I thought it turned out okay. We left it in the middle of the table to dry, where Smiley could admire it for the day.

Dear Kip,

Elise is finally home! I bet your sisters will be happy when they get to see you again...

I thought I should write a little note to Kip to go along with his painting. I wrote that I had a new friend named Kate and that we had joined the band together and both of us were playing the flute. I told him about Rosa and how much she liked Aunt Aida's bird. Elise, I told him, had helped me with his Christmas present.

I hope you like the painting. Merry Christmas to you and Grandpa Charlie.

Love, Goldie (Bird)

Elise was asleep on the couch when Kate and I got back from school that next afternoon.

"Oh! She is pretty," whispered Kate. Elise's arms were stretched above her head, and her hair spilled over the arm of the couch and across her face. She looked peaceful, like she could sleep forever.

"She smells good, Goldie!" said Kate.

"Let's go practice our music," I suggested. "I'm sure she'll be awake soon."

"I'm sure," Kate laughed, as she followed me to the bedroom. We closed the door, but our flute version of "Jingle Bells" woke Elise.

"Ugh! Goldie!" Elise groaned, as her words shot through the bedroom door. "Didn't you see I was trying to sleep?"

I could feel my cheeks flush. I looked at Kate and then stood up to open the bedroom door. I wasn't used to Elise talking to me that way.

Elise was sitting up on the couch by the time I opened the door. "Aw, I'm so sorry, Goldie! This must be your friend Kate," she said, with her usual sweetness. "I just laid down to rest for a bit. I didn't expect to fall asleep. John-John wore me out, I guess, trying to get me to help him with a bunch of stuff." She stood, took a second to regain her balance, pulled on her skirt to straighten it a bit, and extended her hand to Kate. Kate was about the same size as Elise.

"Goldie has told me so much about you. I can't wait to hear your music!" said Elise.

"Well, you already kind of did," laughed Kate. "I've heard lots and lots about you, too, Elise. Goldie sure is lucky to have you as a big sister."

"I'm lucky to have her, really," Elise said, as she pulled me close to her. "Now, let me hear you play your song. I promise I won't interrupt this time."

Kate and I played "Jingle Bells" two times. Kate told Elise that we would be playing a holiday concert at the retirement home on Friday during school if she wanted to come. People in the band got to skip two periods of school and take a bus with Mr. Shankman. Elise promised to try her best to be there. I hadn't mentioned it because I knew Mama would have to mind the shop. I didn't want to make her feel bad. And I didn't think Elise would really have wanted to go.

"Let's go to Piper's for a little treat," said Elise. "I could really go for some cheese bread, and I think I need some coffee to wake me up!"

We sat at Piper's for hours, nearly finishing a whole loaf of cheese bread along with our lattes.

Kate looked at the clock. "I should go," she said. "I told Miss Marie that I could help her with the babies tonight while she went to the grocery store." She rolled her eyes, but she still smiled as she stood, shook Elise's hand, and thanked her for the coffee date.

"Goldie was right about you, Kate," said Elise, as Kate turned to leave.

I was watching Kate through the glass window as she walked around the corner and down the street toward Miss Marie's. Elise pushed her chair back quickly and put her hand to her mouth. "I shouldn't have eaten so much cheese bread," she said, as she headed to the bathroom at the back of the store as quickly as she could through the maze of tables and toddlers. I was getting worried about Elise. I hoped there was nothing wrong with the cheese bread because I didn't want to be sick for the last few days before winter break.

Elise came out from the bathroom with teary eyes and her face a pale whitish-yellow color. "I have to go home and lay down," she said, but I already knew that. I put my arm around Elise's back, in case she needed me.

My stomach was in knots about the concert at the retirement home. I wondered if I was the only band member that was nervous. Kate was so happy she skipped all the way to the bus. She pulled my arm to try to get me to skip alongside her, but I had all I could do to manage my flute case, my music folder, and my coat.

"I'm going to see Mom tonight, Goldie, right after school!" Kate was so excited. "The office sent a note to Mr. Shankman that my caseworker is going to meet me when we get back from the concert." No wonder she was skipping. It had been more than a month since Kate had seen her mom. I wondered if I would get that excited about Mama if I had to go for a while without seeing her.

Kate kept on talking.

"Mom called Sarah and told her that something had come up last time," said Kate, "which happens often. I'm just so excited to get to see her again!"

Knowing Kate was happy made me feel like skipping, too. Gabriella and I had first become friends because our last names began with the same letter, and we always ended up sitting next to one another. Kate and I had a different kind of friendship. We were best friends because we had both been through stuff that made our hearts hurt in the same place.

We lined up with our instruments and music stands behind the ruby red curtain on the stage in the auditorium at the retirement home. Mr. Shankman peeked out to the audience, then back at us—his musicians—before pulling a long, golden rope to open the show.

About twenty rows of fancy velvet theater chairs, separated by a center aisle, made up the audience seating area. Most chairs were filled with residents that had varying levels of awareness. In the very last row, in the two seats closest to the center aisle on my right-hand side were Teddy and Elise! Elise had promised to try to come. She was good at keeping promises.

I played all the notes for "Jingle Bells," squeaking only a few times. Kate, of course, did not squeak at all. Marcy Clown, the other flute player in the band, also played perfectly even though one of her eyes seemed to be twitching every time I looked at her. When we had finished our song, I tapped Kate's knee and tried to draw attention to Teddy and Elise, but it was after the show when she realized that they had come to see us.

"Goldie, you have the best family!" Kate said, and I know she really meant it. I thought then that I did have a great family. I wondered if I really did want to try to mix things up by asking Mama about my dad.

When the curtain closed, we were allowed five minutes to visit with the audience before boarding the bus. Kate and I walked down the stairs together, outside the curtain. There was Elise, waiting for us with two bouquets of the most beautiful pink roses I had ever seen. Actually, they were the kind of pink roses that I was used to seeing, but they were especially beautiful because they were from Elise.

Elise took me shopping later that evening. We walked around the outdoor mall, which was on the other side of the highway from the home store. It was a cold, crisp night. The glow of the moon turned the snow around the shops to sparkling silver, and it seemed like we were in a fairy tale.

It was hard to decide what to get for Mama for Christmas. She worked hard, and she didn't really ask for anything. We decided to get her some flannel pajamas, some new slippers, and a gift certificate for the massage therapy studio at the mall, all with Elise's money because I didn't have any. On the way back to Mama's car, we passed Santa's Workshop, a temporary photography studio which had been set up in one of the mall storefronts. Elise and I looked at each other. The jingle bell tied to the door made a festive noise as I pulled it open. We left Santa's Workshop laughing until our bellies were sore with the last photo of me and Elise ever to be taken on Santa's lap.

For as long as I could remember, Mama, Elise, and I had baked cookies on the morning and afternoon of Christmas Eve. Mr. Quinn always gave Mama the day off. The shop was closed for Christmas Day, so it was like a little vacation for her. We made gingerbread men, chocolate star cookies, frosted sugar cookies, and little green rice cereal wreaths. Elise had a special candy cane cookie that she made, too, but Mama and I could never get the twisting right, so we always left that one to Elise. We had to move Smiley into the living room, by the window, because we needed the whole kitchen table for our baking day. Mama remembered that she had brought back some old aprons, stitched by hand in some places, all festive and flowery, from Aunt Aida's place. There was one for each of us. Mine had red roses and a yellow blanket stitch at the edges. I thought it looked prettier than Mama's or Elise's, and I knew Grandpa Charlie would have loved the aprons. In a way, it seemed like Aunt Aida was with us this year. I was sure she would have been good at rolling out Elise's candy canes.

Elise played Christmas music from the kitchen radio. We didn't stop for lunch; our bellies were plenty full of frosting and dough. By early afternoon, we had made enough plates of soldiers, stars, and bells to share cookies with the whole town of Charlotte. We would share with the Quinns and with Teddy's family, as usual. This year, Mama said we could give some to Kate and Miss Marie, too.

Kate rang the bell as we were beginning to clean up our cookie baking mess. She jumped right in to help. She seemed as happy as she had been at the concert just before she visited her mom. She was wearing a necklace that I hadn't seen before.

"Mom gave it to me," Kate beamed. It was a gold heart with a lace pattern around the edges. She pulled one side of the heart, and it opened to reveal two tiny photos, one on each side. "This is my mom, and this is me as a baby," she said, "to remind me that we will always be together, even when we are apart."

"That's so sweet, Kate! How was your time with your mom?"

"It was so great," said Kate. "We went for dinner at a restaurant right near her apartment, one where we used to go all the time. The people have known us forever. It was so good to be back. I know it was just for a couple of hours, but Mom promised that she wasn't going to let me down again."

I smiled, and she continued while Mama and Elise worked in the kitchen. "Mom said she is thinking about looking for a place around here once she is settled in her new job. Or, well, I guess once she has saved a little money.

That's probably what she meant because I think she would have to quit that job if we moved. I told her about you and about how much I like school and playing in the band. I'll get to see her again next weekend and then again one more time before we go back to school." Kate had been holding the locket between her fingers the whole time she talked, moving it up and down the chain.

She pulled a little box out of the pocket of her brown sweater. "Here, Goldie. Merry Christmas," Kate said, as she handed me the little box, which was tied with red and green embroidery thread. I pulled the lid from the box. "It's a friendship bracelet. I made it for you," she said. I held it up to admire the rainbow of colors and the intricate woven design.

"I love it, Kate. Thank you so much!" Kate tied and knotted the bracelet around my wrist. It fit perfectly. I told her that I wished I had something for her. She told me then that I had already given her the best gift she could ever have. Kate helped with cleaning the rest of the kitchen before taking a plate of cookies back to Miss Marie and the rest of the family.

Elise was going with Teddy to have Christmas Eve dinner with his family. All three of Teddy's older brothers were in town for the holiday, and they were all staying with the Meyers. One of the brothers had just gotten engaged, which made Teddy's mom very happy.

Teddy's mom, Mrs. Meyer, taught special education at the high school. Rosa Quinn was in her class. I secretly wished that I were in Mrs. Meyer's class because her students got to go to the shops downtown, out for pizza, and to the pool during the school day. Teddy's dad came to every one of Teddy's baseball games, usually dressed in his work outfit.

Sometimes Elise took me to watch Teddy's games. I always brought the mitt that he had given me for my tenth birthday. College scouts came to see him play. One offered him a scholarship at a school outside of the state, but he didn't go.

Elise and I would sit on the highest row of the bleachers at the high school field. Sometimes, when she got up to talk to Teddy or some other high school people, I would climb all the way up to balance on the bar at the top of the stands. I felt like I was flying. Birch-bending was like that.

One day, after Teddy's team won a game, the Meyers took me, Elise, and Teddy out for ice cream. Everyone talked a lot, except me because I was trying to keep my Rocky Road from dripping down my arm. We sat outside on two different benches. Elise sat with Teddy and me, and Teddy's parents had a bench just across from us. Mr. Meyer had his hand on Mrs. Meyer's knee, and he looked at her in a really soft way when he talked. I could tell that he loved her by some little things he did, though I never even heard him say it out loud. I bet that's how Davy, Elise's daddy, had loved Mama. I watched the Meyers eat. Mr. Meyer had a strawberry cone, and Mrs. Meyer's was plain vanilla. I never saw the point in getting plain vanilla, but Mrs. Meyer seemed to like hers a lot.

I remember looking up at Elise. I could feel her leg against mine, and I wanted everything to be just like that forever, with me and my sister in the same place. I noticed that Teddy's hand was on Elise's knee, just like his dad's hand was on his mom's knee. I thought then that Teddy must love Elise. The Meyers loved Elise, too, or liked her, at least. People always liked Elise.

On that Christmas Eve, Elise looked beautiful as ever with her hair tied up on top of her head and a few curls spilling across her face. She said she thought she was finally feeling better.

"So tonight, Elise? We'll go and see the lights before church?" asked Mama.

"Yes, for sure. See you a bit later. Bye, Goldie Girl!" Elise hugged Mama, took the plate of cookies for Teddy's family, and closed the apartment door behind her, leaving a little trail of her good smell behind. I couldn't wait for her to get back from dinner.

Mama and I watched a movie, an old-fashioned one about Christmas that made Mama cry a few times. We had sandwiches and cookies for dinner and some of the cider that they served at the store. It was getting late. Mama sent me down to deliver cookies to the Quinns at their house, which was across the road that ran behind the warehouse, alongside the alley. As I opened the door to the back stairway, I stopped to admire the sunset. I hadn't seen one quite so beautiful since our time in Heritage. If only Kip had been there, then Christmas Eve would have been pretty close to perfect.

I saw Teddy's car parked under the stairs on my way back from the delivery. This meant that it was time to go look at all the lights in town. Elise, Mama, and I always looked forward to doing that before going to the late-night service at a country church close to where Teddy and I had gone to chop the tree. I raced up the stairs. Teddy, though, was helping Elise onto the couch, practically carrying her. She looked sick again, with the weird color in her face. *Poor Elise*, I thought. Teddy told me he could stay for a while to keep an eye on Elise and that Mama and I should go on without them. I remembered that the year before, Teddy had gone with us to see the lights, and even to church. That's when Mama decided that she liked Teddy a whole lot because he came around for the family stuff, too.

This year would be different, though, just as most things had been different since Elise had gone to the university. I knew that was just part of what happens when people grow up, but I still didn't like it. One good thing, though, was that this year, I got to see all the lights from the front seat of Mama's car. Mama seemed a little sad during some of the songs as we listened to the church choir. The year had been a hard one for her, I thought. Mama lost her Aunt Aida, and she kind of lost Elise, too, depending on how you looked at it.

"I'm glad you're here with me, Goldie," Mama whispered, as she squeezed my hand.

"Thanks, Mama. Me too," I whispered back. "Merry Christmas."

Elise was sound asleep on the couch when we returned from the late service. I went to the secret door inside our closet and pulled out what I had been working on for Elise for months. I had used Aunt Aida's cross-stitch supplies to make a heart-shaped pillow on which I had stitched a verse from *The Little Prince*.

On that night, very slowly and carefully, I tucked the pillow at the side of my sister's head. She didn't move.

Smiley slept with his head tucked into his wing in his spot on the kitchen table. When I was sure that Mama had gone to bed, I went back to our bedroom to get the gifts from me and Elise, which I arranged under the tree. The night sky was bright and clear through the big window in the living room. I stood for a moment, looking out on our little town, wondering if I would see anything special in the sky that evening.

Since Elise wasn't sleeping in her bed, I lifted her

quilt and tucked myself in.

On Christmas morning, I was the last to wake. Mama and Elise were having coffee in the kitchen when I finally came through the door.

"Merry Christmas, sleepy head!" said Elise.

"I'd say you're the sleepy head these days," said Mama, to which Elise rolled her eyes. Mama handed me the milk mug. She had already poured some coffee for me. At some point, I realized that Smiley's cage was missing from its place on the table.

"Look in the living room, Goldie," said Mama. She and Elise followed me. Smiley's cage now hung from a beautiful stand that looked as if it could have come directly from Grandpa Charlie's shop. He seemed so happy, looking out on so many more things than just the breakfast on our table.

There were more gifts under the tree. Mama loved the things that Elise and I had chosen for her, but she said her very favorite was the picture of her grown girls on Santa's lap. For me, Mama had found a brand-new shiny flute, all my own! I would no longer have to borrow one of Mr. Shankman's instruments. Elise got an envelope with money and a spiral-bound sketchbook. The best part of everything, though, was having Elise home again, just like it used to be.

On the second day of the new year, Mama insisted on taking my sister to the doctor. Elise was still not feeling well, not eating much, and sleeping more than usual. Her mood just wasn't the same. The doctor did some tests, and it turned out that there was a reason that Elise had been feeling sick. She was going to have a baby.

At first, it seemed like I was the only one that was excited about Elise's baby, so I tried to pretend that I wasn't. Elise cried, Mama cried, and Teddy and Elise had a bad phone call, so he didn't come around for a few days, at least not when I was around, which was always. I heard Mama and Elise talking a couple different times when they didn't think I was listening.

"Of course, it's Teddy's baby, Mama! How could you even ask me that?"

I really wanted to talk to Kate or to Kip. Maybe this shouldn't have happened, but it did, and so had a lot of other things that I had no control over.

"I was just your age when I had you. I just thought… well…that you would finish school and do what you wanted to do for a while, so you didn't have to…" Elise stopped Mama from finishing her thought.

"'Didn't have to what? Take care of a baby like you had to take care of me?" Elise was crying. I wanted to hug her, but they didn't know I was listening.

"No, sweetheart, that's not what I meant! I just didn't want you to have to grow up so soon. Come here… it's alright. We're all going to be okay," said Mama, and I could tell they were both crying even from behind the door in my bedroom. I wanted to be with them so badly, to be part of their circle. I thought that there was only room for the two of them.

Mama and Elise were still in the kitchen when I burst past them and out the front door without even grabbing my coat. I ran fast in my slippers, down the loose-tile apartment steps, past the gate to the shop, past Piper's Coffee Shop, and three blocks down along Follaton Road to Kate's street. I slowed my pace a few houses before Miss Marie's. Running had helped a little with the hard feelings, but I still felt like screaming, crying, and throwing up all at the same time. Still out of breath, I knocked on Kate's door. Miss Marie, carrying the pink baby on her hip, opened the door and flashed a warm smile. She was probably used to people crying and looking a mess. I liked Miss Marie, though I didn't think I would want to be her.

She called for Kate, who had been trying to help the circus boys put together a car track. "Is it time for school yet? Can it be?" asked Kate, laughing. She was probably only half joking.

Kate stopped short when she saw that it was me at the door.

"Goldie! What is it? What's wrong?" Kate always knew.

Miss Marie was already heading to where the little boys were playing. Maybe she wanted to give us some privacy, or she knew what would happen if she left them unsupervised, even for a minute.

"It's...my sister's having a baby!" I blurted.

Kate did not seem alarmed by this news. "Aw, that's so sweet! You're going to be an auntie! Aren't you excited?" she asked.

I didn't think I was supposed to be excited. I mean, everyone else had seemed upset or in a state about the news.

"Well, I guess I am excited, but only secretly, right now," I told Kate. Just then, the circus boys appeared in the hallway, one wearing only a diaper and the other wearing a Spiderman mask, cowboy boots, and nothing else.

"Or..." laughed Kate at the sight of her foster brothers, "maybe you should be scared."

We both laughed then.

"Goldie, do you think they...she...Elise will keep her baby?" asked Kate.

"Keep her baby? Why wouldn't she? What would happen to it otherwise?" I wondered.

"Well, she could have someone adopt her baby, if she didn't think she would be able to care for it. My mom had another baby when I was still really little. Things were weird with my dad. He had already left, and Mom said she never could have taken care of me and another baby too, so the baby got adopted." Kate spoke matter-of-factly. I knew she must have gotten used to this idea over time, so it probably didn't make her sad to think about it anymore.

I thought that Kate must be pretty lonely, without her mom, her dad, or her brother or sister, whatever that baby was. That's why she made such a good friend. At least she had me.

"Goldie?" Kate interrupted my thoughts to see if I had heard what she had said.

"Oh, yeah, she's going to take care of the baby," I said. I wasn't, I decided, going to say a word to Mama or Elise about anyone adopting the baby, and I hoped they didn't think of it, either.

Teddy's car passed me on the street when I was almost back to the shop. He didn't beep his horn as he normally would have, but he did wave. By the time I had made it to the gate, he had caught up to me, and we went into the building together.

"So, Goldie, how's your sister doing? And Florence?" Teddy looked a little bit nervous.

"I think they're going to be okay, Teddy," I said.

He walked through the door with me and went directly toward Elise, who was alone on the couch. Mama must have been at the shop. He gathered her up and held her for a very long time. I knew I should leave them alone. I heard Teddy tell Elise that he was so, so sorry for doubting her, that of course he trusted her and loved her more than ever, and that they would be okay. He said he promised, and I knew he meant it because he had promised me the day we went to chop down the tree that he was going to take care of her, and I believed him.

I knew he was going to take care of Elise and the baby, but I was pretty sure this wasn't how he thought things were going to be. They sat there, quietly, for a long time. I thought they looked kind of like teenagers and kind of like adults. Really, they were both.

Teddy wanted to drive Elise back to school after the break. He didn't ask me to go along this time. Elise was crying while she hugged me. "I'm sorry I wasn't all that much fun to be around, Goldie," said Elise. "You're the best little sister."

I helped her carry her bags down the back stairs. Teddy was waiting for Elise in the alley. Snow had just begun to fall. Everything looked sparkly. I could hear Teddy's loud music, and I wondered if Elise's baby was able to hear it, too. They drove off. I watched until I couldn't see the red car anymore. I felt a little jealous that Teddy got to be with Elise for the whole day. I knew they had a lot to talk about. They weren't planning to have a baby yet, when Elise was away at school and Teddy was getting ready for his first season with his college baseball team. I wondered how they really felt about the baby.

In winter, when the trees were bare, I could see through the line of old lilac bushes that had grown taller than the Quinns' house. It was evening, and Rosa was sitting on the front porch. The house was small and solid, built of brick. From where I stood, Rosa looked like a tiny doll, moving back and forth in her rocking chair. I had seen Mr. Quinn at the shop a short while earlier, so I knew that Rosa was home by herself. I wondered if she was lonely, or if she liked being alone. For a long time, Rosa moved only her feet, ever so slightly, to keep the rocker going.

The Little Prince was in the same place on our bookshelf as it had been on the day that Rosa came to see the bird. I took it from the shelf and headed down the back stairs. Before I had made it past the lilacs, I could hear Rosa's laughter. She had somehow known that I was on my way to see her.

We sat together on the Quinns's porch for a long time on that cold Sunday. I read half the book, turning pages with my gloved hands. Rosa rocked and laughed. Just before dusk, when I was thinking I should be getting home, Mr. Quinn came from behind the lilacs.

"Goldie! So nice to see you girls together." Mr. Quinn put his hand on Rosa's shoulder. Rosa didn't seem to like hugs, though she did seem to like being around certain people, especially, I thought, Mr. Quinn and me. "Rosa always likes to go to the beginning of a book, even if someone has read through a lot of it with her. You two must have been reading for a while," he said.

Mr. Quinn knew his daughter well. We had—because Rosa wanted to—started at the beginning again, where the Little Prince asks the pilot to draw him a sheep.

Mr. Quinn told me that he was hoping Elise would work for him this summer, doing landscape design, when she got home from the university. He said John-John was getting restless and wanted to move to the city. I remembered that when Elise decided to study art and design at school, Mr. Quinn bought her a beautiful set of colored pencils. I wondered if he had planned to have her work for him all along. I didn't think the Quinns knew about Elise's baby. They would find out, though, when Elise's belly started to grow.

Mama would have been home from the shop and had been wondering where I was. If Rosa and I always started at the beginning of our book, I wondered if we would ever actually read all the way through *The Little Prince*. That part didn't really matter to me, though, because I didn't think friends really cared if they finished any of their books, as long as they got to read together.

On a dreary, gray Monday in the last week of January, Kate was crying when she came to the bus stop. "Mom got in trouble again, Goldie, just when I was going to be able to have longer visits with her. I wish this didn't always have to happen. I mean, I like living with Miss Marie, but I don't really belong there. I belong with Mom." Kate cried tears that fell straight down her cheeks onto her backpack which she held in her lap. I offered her a tissue, but she had already used the sleeve of her brown sweater. I just put my hand on her knee because I didn't know what else to do.

I felt terrible for Kate. Her mom seemed to have so much trouble keeping track of herself. I wondered how she would ever be able to take care of Kate, too.

"Hey, Goldie, promise me something, will you? Will you just ask your mom about your dad already? If something happens to your mom, then who will take care of you? Well, I guess you have Elise. But she couldn't really do that all by herself...not yet. I just think you need to find out, and you need to know," said Kate.

I could tell that Kate had been thinking about this and that it was really bothering her, especially now that she was wondering who would be taking care of her. "Kate, even though you can't see your dad, are you glad you know who he is?" I asked.

"Of course, I am. I mean, I know he wasn't good to my mom, and he hasn't had a chance to be much of a dad to me, but Mom said my dad loved me. She also said that when I am older, she hoped I would somehow connect with him. I know he's out there, at least I hope he still is."

On the ride home, I promised Kate that I would ask Mama about my dad. My plan was not exactly to ask Mama directly but to ask Elise first. I figured she would have been old enough to remember some things about that time, and I could keep my promise to Kate without making Mama sad.

"Kate? I have another idea. I'm still going to do it... to ask Mama, but... I just think we should promise to take care of each other, just you and me, if one of us ever ended up alone. Seems to me like we have tamed each other, you know, like the Little Prince and his fox, and that's not something that's ever going to change," I said as I looked down at the black rubber grooves in the bus flooring.

We both sat without saying anything for a little while. I knew Kate had heard what I had said.

"So, what's going to happen, Kate? With your mom, I mean?" I asked her.

"Oh, who knows. The more she screws up her plan, the longer it's going to take for me to be able to be with her for good. For now, Sarah says I will have to wait to have visits until Mom calls her again. This has happened so much before, and Mom always promises me she is going to do better. I know she will. I know she loves me. I just wonder if it's enough..." More tears splashed onto Kate's backpack. This time, she held out her hand for my tissue.

"At least you've got me," I said.

"I'm never going to forget that," she said, as I followed her from our seat on the bus. "I've got to hurry back. Miss Marie needs my help right after school."

I waved to my best friend as she walked up the street. When I saw a letter in the mailbox, I knew it was from Kip. I felt a little bit guilty for being happy on a day that Kate was so sad.

Dear Goldie Bird,

It was a little hard to leave my family to head back to Heritage after the break. My mom and Grandpa Charlie were so sad on Christmas Day, which was exactly a year after my grandma died. I really do understand how you got so upset when you had to leave here at the end of the summer. When it was time for us to go, I got a little grouchy with Grandpa Charlie. Violet and Lark, my sisters, tried to hide me in their closet when I was supposed to be packing up the car. I think it was mostly because Grandpa Charlie wasn't sure what he wanted to do about moving. That got me worried and anxious.

Your little painting was a great surprise! Grandpa Charlie found the perfect frame for it. I thought of hanging it in the secret cave, but I decided to put it in my room just to be safe. Nobody ever made anything like that for me, Goldie Bird.

Thank you for making my sad Christmas a little better.

Love, Kip

Tucked inside the last fold of Kip's letter was a wallet-sized photo, his seventh-grade school picture. My heart skipped when I saw his face once again: olive skin, sandy hair, still messy—even for picture day—and yellow-gold sunny eyes. I missed him all over again.

With Kip's school picture still in my hand, I had fallen asleep on Elise's bed. The door buzzer startled me awake, and I wondered who would be coming by at this time. The buzzer sounded again, and another time, even before I was out into the corridor. I could see Kate's shoes, and the bottom of the brown sweater.

It was bedtime. The sun had gone down hours before. Kate had been crying again, or she was still crying.

"Goldie! I can't stay there anymore! She wanted me to watch the babies and feed them and everything while she was gone," she choked through her tears. "She doesn't care. She doesn't understand. I just want to go home!" Poor Kate. She reached out her arms toward me, and I felt her thin frame shake from her sobs as she pulled me toward her.

"Can you hide me? Can I just stay here? Please? I don't have anywhere else to go," she sobbed.

"Come on, Kate. Let's go upstairs," I said, as I led her up the old, tiled stairs, which clicked under our feet, and down the hallway to our apartment.

Mama had heard me leave when the buzzer rang. She, too, was surprised to see Kate. "Sweetheart, are you okay? What is it?" she asked from her place on the couch where she was finishing a bowl of noodle soup.

I sat on the couch, leaving a spot for Kate between Mama and me. Kate grabbed a tissue from the coffee table before joining us. She sunk onto the couch. Kate's arm pressed into mine, and I could feel her whole body trembling. Holding the locket that her mom had given her between two fingers and her thumb, Kate looked toward the floor.

"I don't matter," Kate began. "Not to Miss Marie, anyway. I had to take care of the little boys again today. She's so busy with the babies and the teenagers, it's like she forgets I'm there."

I got up to get more tissues and brought Kate a bowl of soup.

"I mean," Kate continued, "she's good to me in ways like making sure I have breakfast and school supplies and winter boots and that sort of thing." Kate looked up and moved the spoon through her soup but didn't eat any. "It's just...I need other things that she can't really give me. There's just not much left of her after she has taken care of all the kids and everything at the house."

Mama put her arm around Kate's shoulder. "Sweetheart," said Mama, "Do you feel like Miss Marie expects too much from you?"

Myles came out from the bedroom just then. He hopped on my lap, and Kate reached to pet him. His purr was so strong that I couldn't tell if Kate was still shaking.

"She got mad at me today," said Kate. "Miss Marie snapped at me earlier because the house was messy when she got back from her appointment. But the pink baby had been crying the whole time. I was trying to keep the boys from escaping and running around the neighborhood, all while I bounced and rocked the baby and carried her around until Miss Marie came back." Kate pulled the cat to her, and I saw a tear fall down her cheek into his fur.

"I just had enough, you know? Like she didn't even notice how hard I was trying. She never does. I can't take it anymore." Kate dissolved in a heap on Mama's lap, Mama who barely knew her.

I got myself some soup and handed a few more tissues to Kate. Mama moved her hand across Kate's back, and she talked some more.

"My mom has been trying so hard for me. I know she has. She's working on keeping her job and her appointments and everything. I just want to go home. I don't want to stay with Miss Marie anymore," said Kate.

"Oh, Kate, I can't imagine how much your mom misses you," said Mama. "It sounds like she is trying very hard to do what she needs to do so you can go home."

I wondered what had happened with Kate's mom in the first place, and why Kate had to live with Miss Marie, but I didn't ask.

"I know, and she said it breaks her heart that I had live with a foster family. Mom was in foster care for a long time when she was a little girl. She didn't want it to be like that for me," Kate continued. "She...Miss Marie...I know she felt bad for getting angry at me, but I just had enough. I wanted to throw things and rip the curtains down and scream at Miss Marie and the boys. Instead," she said," I just left and came here without telling anyone."

"It's good that you didn't," I said, "Rip the curtains down and scream and stuff, I mean."

Kate and Mama both laughed.

"Would it be okay with you if I called Miss Marie to let her know that you are here?" Mama asked. "She must be worried about you."

Kate nodded. She was sitting up again, holding Myles on her lap, and petting him softly.

"Mama, do you think Kate can spend the night? Please?" I asked.

Kate's eyes brightened, and she smiled, but just a little. She looked at Mama.

"I think if we let Miss Marie know that Kate's here, she will probably have a better chance of getting to stay," Mama said, and we knew that meant, "Yes!"

Mama called Miss Marie and told her that Kate was feeling sad and needed some time with her friend. Miss Marie agreed to let Kate spend the night at our apartment. Sometimes Mama really was the best. I think a tiny part of her must have understood that it was hard to be Kate, at least sometimes. Mama knew what it was like to not be able to be with her mom. She was only a little older than Kate when she went to live with Aunt Aida.

I could hear Kate crying softly on the other side of the room as she lay in my bed. Myles slept at her feet. Clover and I were tucked under Elise's blanket, where I could have fallen asleep easily if I hadn't been so worried about Kate.

"Kate? You know how I told you about sleeping back-to-back with Elise in her bed, and how it makes me feel safe when I am scared? It could help you, too, if we did that tonight," I offered. Within a few minutes, Kate's breathing had slowed to a quiet rhythm, which I could feel against my back. We slept under my sister's blanket until the morning sun came through the bedroom window.

The chrome-legged chairs seemed a hundred times heavier than they had ever been before. It was my job at the end of each day that week to put all the chairs on the desks so the janitor could clean the floor without having to worry about the chairs. Burning heat flashed in my cheeks, but the rest of me was freezing. My whole body was shaking, and my stomach hurt. My social studies teacher had no sympathy. She told me to move faster. Tears welled in my eyes, and my head pounded. Kate had left earlier that day for an appointment, so she wasn't even there to sit with me on the bus.

I wanted to lay down on the bench outside of Piper's for a while, but it was cold and starting to snow. Crossing the street, I shivered so hard that my teeth chattered. The walk to the shop seemed so long on that day.

Mama stayed with me through the night and all the next day. Mr. Quinn stayed in the shop so she could take care of me. Though I mostly slept, I woke a few times to drink water and to eat crackers and toast. Everything hurt: my head, my stomach, my throat, my eyes, and my whole body. My dreams were all mixed up. I dreamed that Elise was having a cat as a baby. I dreamed that Kip came to visit, and he had Smiley with him when I opened the door. I dreamed that Teddy and I went birch bending, only it wasn't really birch bending because we were climbing in pine trees, which were spiky and did not move like the birch trees. On the second night, my fever broke. I began to feel better. Mr. Quinn offered to stay in the shop for one more day so Mama could be with me, but she assured him that I was okay, and I would be fine by myself. If I had needed anything, I knew she was right downstairs.

I don't know what time it was when I finally felt a little hungry. Mama had already gone back to the shop after her lunch break. The sunlight coming through the window in the sitting room made my head hurt. As I pulled the curtain to soften the glare, I saw Kip walking toward the shop and the Warehouse Apartments! I was sure it was him. I wondered how he had gotten to Charlotte. He must have been coming to surprise me!

I had to go to him! I stepped into my slippers and headed for the hallway. I was dizzy and shaky, but there was a rush inside of me, too. Careful not to go near the door to Apartment #2, I hurried toward the stairs. My head was pounding. I knew I had to hurry.

One of the loose tiles from the stairs caught the edge of my slipper. I couldn't catch my balance. My feet slipped from under me. I felt the hard stairs and cold tile through my pajamas as I fell. Finally, my hip and shoulder landed hard up against the heavy door.

Through the now-cracked glass on the door to the Warehouse Apartments, I looked up to see the boy that I was so sure was Kip crossing the street toward the city lot across from the shop. It hadn't been Kip.

Mama came from the direction of the shop.

"Goldie! What happened? Are you okay?" she asked, pulling carefully at the door handle.

I felt sick again, really sick.

"I heard something, Goldie. A loud thud. The window's cracked. Are you hurt?" Mama asked.

"I don't think so, Mama," I said. I felt a little like I might throw up, but I didn't think I was bleeding or that any of my bones were broken.

Rosa's bus pulled up in front of the shop just as Mama was helping me to my feet. She must have noticed that something was different. Instead of going into the shop, she moved toward the door with one hand stretched forward. She stopped just before her hand would have touched the broken glass.

"No, Rosa, no, no..." Rosa repeated her words, rocking back and forth where she stood. I don't think she noticed me or Mama just inside the door. She turned, then, and went toward the shop, to do the things that she always did when she came from school.

Mama helped me up the stairs. She offered to stay with me, but I told her I was okay.

When Mr. Quinn found out what had happened, he replaced the glass in the door right away. Rosa clapped and laughed when she saw that the cracks weren't there anymore. It seemed like she was happy when things were back in order. He told us to avoid using the front stairs until they were repaired. By the next week, though, Mr. Quinn had called someone that came to put new tile on the stairs and in the whole hallway. Mr. Quinn told me that he wished he had done that a long time ago. I knew, though, that it had really happened because I had tried to chase after someone who wasn't even there.

I never told anyone that I thought Kip had come for me.

Dear Kip,

My sister is going to have a baby!

It took me a while to write back to Kip, maybe because I wasn't sure what to say. I told him that I thought I liked the idea of being an aunt. I also told him that it seemed like unexpected things happened a lot. Too much, maybe. I told him I fell down the stairs and broke the glass of the Warehouse Apartments door, but I didn't tell him why. I told him about reading *The Little Prince* with Rosa. I also told him about how Kate had been encouraging me to ask Mama the questions I have about my dad. I didn't have a whole lot else to tell Kip in that letter because those things seemed to take up everything. I missed Elise, and I missed Kip. I wanted time to move forward or backward. I just didn't want it to stay where it was.

Love, Goldie

Elise came home on the bus for her spring break. Mama and I picked her up outside of the home store. Elise waited inside the sliding doors until she saw Mama's car. Her face was a little bit fuller. A bulge pushed from under her sweatshirt, and I could see where the baby was growing inside of her. Her cheeks were rosy. The sparkles had returned to her eyes. She said she was starting to feel a lot better.

I saw Mama push a little tear away after she hugged Elise. "My baby...is having a baby," she said, in a voice that seemed both happy and sad at the same time.

Elise and I stayed up really late talking that first night. Somewhere deep inside of me, I kept feeling the question that Kate wanted me to ask. If I asked Elise first, I thought that might make it easier, at least on me.

"Elise, can I ask you something?"

"Anything, Goldie. What is it?" Elise had her eyes closed, but I knew she was listening.

I took a deep breath, then another. I needed to do this.

Not just for Kate, but for me, too. I made sure Clover was there under the covers with me.

"Elise," I began, "what do you remember about my dad when you were with Mama at the yellow cottage before I was born? Were you old enough to remember him, like what he looked like, or what his name was, or anything?" I knew my voice was shaky.

"Oh, God, Goldie. I didn't expect you to ask me that..." Elise whispered. "I... I was little, but you're right. I do remember some things; mostly what people told me. Mama said that the stuff about your dad was just too hard to talk about. I tried as hard as I could to just block it out of my mind, to make the images go away. Really, though, I couldn't do that, so I just tried not to think about it, and I hoped you wouldn't ask me so I wouldn't have to go against what Mama wanted. I'm so sorry, Goldie Girl. I know that wasn't fair at all, but I just secretly hoped, and kept hoping, that you didn't think about him. That was dumb, I know. How could you not? How could you not think of him?"

I could feel the tears welling up inside of me. Crying at bedtime always made my head hurt, but I couldn't help it.

"Kate thinks I should ask Mama. She thinks I have a right to know," I said. "Mama never wanted me to talk about it or ask questions or anything, but I thought a lot about what Kate said, and it's important to me to at least know who he is and to understand why he left. I mean, I'd like to know his name and if I look like him or act like him or anything."

"I know, honey, I know," said Elise. She was caught in the middle. I knew that wasn't fair to her, but it wasn't fair to me, either. Also, it wasn't fair what happened to Mama, with Elise's daddy dying and everything. "We need to talk to Mama about this, but not tonight," she said.

"Why is it so important for you to keep it a secret? Can't you just tell me about what you remember? Don't I matter?" I knew that Elise didn't want to go against what Mama wanted, but I found it all kind of unfair, even in a bigger way than when I had to leave Kip and Heritage.

"Come here, Goldie," said Elise, as she pulled up her blanket and motioned for me to come into her bed. Just like so many times before, we turned so our backs were pressing into one another. I stared out at Kate's lights, which I had decided to leave hanging even though it wasn't Christmas season anymore, and squinted my eyes to try to squeeze the tears back in. Little rainbows danced before me, as I opened my eyes and squeezed them again. Elise's back felt warm against mine. She was still for a long while, and I could hear her breathing take on a steady rhythm. I hoped she wasn't going to fall asleep because I knew I never could, not until she told me what she remembered.

"Goldie," Elise spoke my name.

"Elise," I answered.

"Goldie, do you remember hearing about Daddy's

friend, the one that was driving the car when the crash happened?" I thought this must be as hard for Elise as it was for me—maybe even harder.

I did remember hearing about that, more than one time. "Marc? You mean Marc, Daddy Davy's college friend?"

Elise nodded. "Mama visited Marc at the hospital while he was healing from his injuries," she said, seeming to guard her words carefully.

"Yeah, that's what Mama told me. I remember that. And then it was just too hard for her to see him because of what happened to Davy, right?"

Elise took a deep breath, like she was breathing for me, too. I could feel the rise and fall of her chest. I pushed harder into her back.

"Mama told the story of how your dad lived with us for a short time in the yellow cottage before he left. Goldie, that was Marc," she said gently. I didn't say anything. I couldn't. I had never put that together. Mama had never specifically told me that Marc was my father, but she certainly never told me that he wasn't.

"Goldie? Are you okay?" Elise turned toward me in the bed. She held me as I cried for a lot of things that had been stuck inside of me. She wrapped me tightly into her body so I might have almost felt her baby moving next to me. I realized, then, that I could feel her baby!

"Elise! The baby! I felt it in there!" I sat up and put

my hand on Elise's belly as she rolled to her back. Still and silent, we stayed there, on Elise's bed. When we had been quiet for so long that I thought the sun would begin to rise, I felt a tiny flutter through the palm of my hand. "There!" I said, whispering, conscious not to wake Mama, "I felt it again!"

"So, you were the first to feel my baby move! I'm so glad it was you, Goldie Girl," said Elise. "I think we should get some sleep now. It's almost morning."

We didn't talk about Marc anymore. I stayed with Elise in her bed. For that night, or what was left of it, I had my sister all to myself. My mind raced with thoughts of things I didn't know or hadn't been allowed to know, with memories that I couldn't have. I wondered why I hadn't been told the truth, or at least the details, about my father. It seemed like there were so many layers to how people loved each other, and sometimes it didn't make any sense at all.

The sun came through the window. Elise was still sleeping deeply. For just a few seconds, I put my hand on her belly to see if her baby was moving. It must still have been sleeping, too. I left the bedroom without making a sound. I needed to find Mama. I needed to know more about Marc.

I passed Smiley's cage. He watched as I poured milk into my mug. After I had my breakfast, I went downstairs to find Mama at the shop.

The cold snap had lifted. I could smell spring. Though the tiles had been repaired on the stairs shortly after my fall, I still used the back stairs every time I left the building. If I wanted to get the mail, I opened the door from the outside, took the letters, and went around to the back of the building. I'm not sure if I was afraid of falling down those stairs. I just knew I didn't want to remember all those feelings again.

Mr. Quinn was talking to Mama at the desk in the shop. I could see them through the window. The fire inside of me was burning through my arms and legs. I knew I shouldn't burst in there to talk about my dad in front of Mr. Quinn.

I heard Rosa's laughter. She had come in behind me, stopping to admire the snowdrops and the new shoots of green that poked up through the earth. I thought that I could be with Rosa for a while. With her, I would be thinking of something besides being mad at Mama. I didn't really feel like reading, though, so I hoped that Rosa didn't ask on that day. She did not.

"Smiley. Goldie. Bird. Smiley," said Rosa. I extended my hand to her. Though she did not reach for it, she followed me around the back of the building and up the stairs to the apartments, laughing louder as we got closer to #4 and, of course, the bird.

The door to where Elise slept was closed. For a long while, Rosa stood by the bird's cage, which now hung from the stand that Mama had found for me for Christmas. She followed his little paths with her eyes and laughed every so often, especially when he flew around a bit. As Rosa watched Smiley, I watched Rosa. Little things, like this bird or a little flower, made Rosa so happy, with a happiness that seemed to overtake her. That's just how she was.

Sometimes, I secretly wanted to be Rosa.

Sometimes, too, I secretly wished that Mr. Quinn were my dad. Mr. Quinn taught me a lot about flowers. If he asked me to do something or wanted to show something to me, he wouldn't just say, "Goldie, could you put this on the bench over there?" He would ask me to put whatever it was on the bench by the pink yarrow or the Josephine clematis. Mr. Quinn always had time for me, and for Rosa, too, but in a different way. He helped her make sense of things, and he knew she liked things to have order. He was good at teaching us about important things that other people might not have thought were especially important.

Rosa moved a little closer to the cage as Smiley picked seed from his cup.

I had forgotten to brush my teeth before I went down to the shop earlier that morning to look for Mama, so I left Rosa and went to the bathroom. Just after spitting my toothpaste into the sink, I turned off the water to hear a little clanking noise. Then, Rosa laughed, but not the way that she usually laughed. The laugh grew louder, as if she was gasping for breath. When I got back to the living room, Rosa was looking toward the ceiling, moving her head in an arc, watching Smiley's wild flight. Smiley! He was out of his cage, flying freely in the apartment. I screamed, which caused Rosa to scream, which caused Smiley to fly faster and more wildly. Elise came out of the bedroom looking very disturbed and confused.

Smiley flew even faster, lowering his arc this time. As he circled again, I had a bad feeling. Rosa was frozen in her position in the middle of the living room. She had stopped laughing. Elise just stood in the open doorway of our bedroom, wide-eyed, with one hand on her head and the other on her belly.

Smiley hit the window glass hard, so hard that his body dropped to the floor at the impact. Poor bird. I remembered once that I had been in the shop with Mama when I was little, and a bird flew right into the window. It was only stunned, and within a minute or so it had already flown away. I hoped this would be the case for Smiley. Elise gasped, and together we went to try to help the bird. Rosa stood, laughing again and sputtering, still frozen.

"Smiley!" Just as I picked him up, his tiny body began to quiver. This startled me. He slipped from my hands, then flew again, one more circle through the living room before flying right out the open window. I stared at the bright sky, knowing for certain that he was gone for good. I wasn't even sure if I liked this bird, but now, what I wanted most was to see him flying around his cage and to hear his little chirping sounds. I felt guilty for not really loving him enough. When she saw my tears, Rosa dropped to the floor. On her side, she began rocking, much like she had done when John-John had gotten after her for laughing. She wasn't laughing anymore.

She began calling "Mama" in a monotone voice that got louder and faster. "Mama, no, Mama..." This surprised me, because I didn't think Rosa had seen her mom in a very long time. Maybe, though, she could feel all of this in her soul, as her mother and now this little bird had each gone. "Mama, no, Goldie. Bird, no." Maybe Rosa had a deeper way of feeling, one that nobody understood until something really hard happened.

I knew Mr. Quinn had just been downstairs. I left Elise and Rosa and hurried down the back stairs, around the building, and into the shop.

"Mr. Quinn!" He turned around. "Come quick! Rosa's upset, upstairs in our apartment," I said. He grabbed his cane and followed me back from the way I had come. I didn't, on purpose, look at Mama.

Mr. Quinn was not quick, but I knew he was moving as fast as he was able in order to get to Rosa. I secretly hoped that we would enter the apartment, and everything would be back to how it was before Smiley got out of his cage.

That's not what happened, though. Rosa was still on the floor, rocking, but her cries were much softer. Mr. Quinn did his best to crouch next to her. I told him that the bird had flown out the window, but I didn't tell him that Rosa had let him out because I didn't know that for certain, and also because I thought it might break his heart.

Rosa pushed herself to her knees and stood. She took several steps toward where I stood with Elise.

"Goldie. No. Bird," she said softly, as she turned to the window.

I looked at Mr. Quinn. He nodded his head, and I went to meet Rosa at the window.

"Goldie. No. Bird," repeated Rosa.

"I know," I said, as I closed the window. "It's okay."

"Okay. Goldie," said Rosa. She laughed, then, but just a little.

Rosa left with Mr. Quinn. Elise and I went down the back stairs and around the building to the shop to tell Mama what had happened to Smiley, even though I still didn't feel much like being with her.

She felt terrible for having left the window open when she left for work. Mama said she thought that since it was such a nice day, the fresh morning air would be good for all of us. She wondered if maybe Smiley was going to fly back to Heritage. Mama said maybe he missed how things used to be.

Maybe Smiley really was a lot like me.

When Elise and I checked the mailbox on our way back to the apartment, we found Kip's letter.

Dear Goldie Bird,

I found out that my dad had not been truthful with my mom. He had kept a secret, and it was really hurtful.

It looks like I'm going to be staying in Heritage for the summer with Grandpa Charlie and then probably going home right before eighth grade. I'm looking forward to playing baseball here with my friends from school, but I think going back to Ohio will be best for my family.

Grandpa Charlie decided that he wasn't ready to give up all that he had in Heritage. He wants to keep his shop going until he really feels he is done. I'm grateful that he was honest with me and told me how he really felt. Maybe you will still be able to come back to Heritage before I leave. I hope so.

I also hope you get to have a good talk with your mom about your dad.

Love, Kip

After reading Kip's letter, I decided that I really needed to talk to Mama, even if it caused her some hurt.

I sank into the lavender bubbles. The little dollhouse people from Aunt Aida's bathtub sat on the edge of the tub. The sun came through the glass block window and sent streaks of light into the bubbles, which reflected all the colors that I liked best. As I turned off the water to avoid overflowing the tub, I could hear words between Mama and Elise.

"I didn't want to lie to her, Mama. This matters to her," said Elise. "Goldie understands more about this sort of thing than you think. Really, I'm not sorry. I'm not sorry I told her. She deserves to know."

I couldn't tell exactly what Mama was saying, but I could hear the urgency in her voice.

"It was hard for me, too, Mama, even though I was a little girl. It's going to be more painful for Goldie, though, if you don't tell her what she needs to know," said Elise.

I turned the water on again. I wasn't planning to leave the bath for a long time. Elise and Mama had stopped talking, or at least I couldn't hear them anymore. I just closed my eyes and thought about what it would be like if I was little again, taking a bath in Aunt Aida's bathtub. The water ran cold after a while, and by the time it had all drained, I was ready to get out. Dressed in clean flannel pajamas, I slowly turned the knob and opened the bathroom door.

Mama was sitting in the living room, as if she had been waiting for me. She wasn't watching television or reading or doing anything besides just sitting, at least from what I could tell. I hadn't looked at Mama all day. I wished for a place to hide, like the secret cave where nobody would know where I was, and this time, Kip wouldn't be there to tell anyone.

"Goldie," Mama's voice sounded thick. I looked at her and saw the tears. Mama's eyes were a little like Elise's but much more of a chocolate color. They were a little bit like mine. She stood and pulled me tightly to her.

"Mama, why didn't you tell me?" was all I could manage.

"I couldn't... He doesn't... He never knew. He didn't know about you when he left, Goldie," Mama said. "Marc had been Davy's best friend for a long time. When I was with him right after the accident, it seemed like part of Davy was still here, like they were the same person." Mama was shaking as she held me.

I wished that Elise was with us, too.

"I guess it was a couple of months before I started to realize what was happening," she said.

"So, you never loved Marc?" I asked.

"Goldie, baby, I did love him, but for the wrong

reasons. I loved him because he made me miss Davy a little less and because he reminded me of Davy in everything he did. Those were not the right reasons to be with someone, because you miss someone else," said Mama. "We both decided that what we were doing was unhealthy and that it would be best to just go our separate ways. He moved out of the cottage, and I never heard from him again. It was just a few weeks later that I found out I was pregnant with you, Goldie," Mama continued, wiping her cheek with her shirtsleeve.

"So, he doesn't know about me? He doesn't know I was born, Mama?" I asked.

"After the way we left things, I thought it would be best if he didn't know." Mama had a faraway look. I interrupted before she had a chance to finish what she was going to say.

"Best for who?" I asked, standing to face Mama. "For you? Because not having a dad...how could you think that was best for me? And what about him? Maybe he would have wanted me. Did you ever think of that for one second? Maybe SOMEONE wanted me," I said, as I walked away from Mama. I wanted to run out of the apartment and tell Kate what I found out. Instead, I collapsed in Elise's arms. She had been sitting on her bed, waiting for me.

Part of me felt bad for Mama, but just a little part. The rest of me felt bad for me, and for Elise, and even for Marc. Marc. I wondered...would he have loved me like

Davy loved Elise? Would he have loved me like Mama loved Elise?

We fell asleep together again, Elise and me. It was still dark when I woke from a dream that a man was walking toward me with open arms. He was calling someone's name. He came closer, and I reached my arms toward him. Just as I thought he was going to hug me, I realized that he was saying, "Elise." He walked past me, and I was left alone. I got up then, as quietly as I ever had, and crept into the closet, where I thought of Gabriella and of being a much younger girl. If this was what it meant to be growing up, I wasn't sure I was ready. I got my little notebook from inside the secret door and began writing.

Dear Kip,

Did you ever want to know something so badly, only to find that things had been much easier before you knew what you thought you wanted to know?

I told Kip about Smiley flying out the window and about Rosa. I told him that I was happy that his parents were doing better. I also told him about Marc, how he didn't even know about me, and how Mama thought that would be best. I could feel the heat on my cheeks and in my belly. I wrote that I wanted to talk to Marc, to let him know that he had a daughter and to let him decide for himself whether he wanted to step up and be my dad, and about how I was sad for Mama and mad at her at the same time.

I'm not really sad about Smiley. I'm sad for Rosa, because she loved him. She had the chance to love him before he left, and that's something that I wish I had, only not with the bird.

Love, Goldie

Ever since the incident with Kate and Miss Marie, Kate had been allowed to stay at our place whenever she needed a break. Miss Marie apologized to Kate. She said that she had no idea that what she was asking of Kate had made her so upset. She promised not to use her as a babysitter unless Kate wanted to earn money. Miss Marie said that Kate was so good with the circus boys and the pink baby, and not many people could handle them like Kate could. She could see how it was unfair to expect Kate to step in whenever she needed help. Mama said she liked it when Kate came to stay because she could keep me company and it seemed just a little bit like old times with Elise.

I shared with Kate what Elise and Mama had told me about Marc. She encouraged me and told me that I had a right to know. Things were a little weird with Mama for a while. I didn't want to talk about anything, and Mama could tell. A couple of days after Mama told me about Marc, she left a note on the kitchen table. She also left a coupon for a discounted pizza from Gas Mart.

Goldie,

I'm not very good at talking about these things. I need you to know how much I love you and how important you are to me. Even though I thought what I did was best for everyone, I now realize that it was a selfish thing. It was not fair to you, and it was not fair to Marc. If he knew you, he would love you so much. Tell me what you need me to do to help us through this. I'm so sorry. I love you.

Mama

The doorbell buzzed as I was looking in the refrigerator for something to drink. I found only a half-empty bottle of milk and an open can of diet cola. It was Kate at the door. I thought she had somehow known about Mama's note. She had come, though, to tell me something good. She had gotten a letter from her mom. She would be able to see her again soon, according to Sarah, who arranged the visits. I wondered if Kate's mom ever did anything to upset her. Then I remembered about the visits, and how sad Kate was those times when her mom messed up.

Kate read Mama's note.

"So, what are you going to do?" she asked.

"I mean, I just read the note," I said. "What does she even mean by that?"

"She's telling you that she's sorry for not telling you about Marc," Kate said, "and she is asking what would make it better. What, besides Gas Mart pizza, do you want from her?"

The answer to that seemed too clear, to me at least. "Well, Mama isn't going to like this, but I want to see my dad. At least I want him to know about me," I said to Kate.

"She knows that, Goldie. I know she does. So, I guess it's up to you guys to figure that out." She put her hand on my shoulder, just for a second. "You know, Goldie, I'm so proud of you for being brave enough to do this," she said.

Kate and I walked to Gas Mart without saying much at all. I wondered about Marc, but mostly I thought of Mama. I wondered over and over how she could think it would be that simple, that she could just pretend that I really wouldn't care how I came to be.

Mama was home when we returned with the pizza. She sat right down and started eating alongside Kate and me, not saying much of anything. Kate had convinced me to let her buy pop since I had filled her in on what was in our refrigerator at home. She chose a two-liter bottle of orange soda, which was fine with me, because Mama couldn't stand orange soda.

Elise was with Teddy, having dinner with his family, so that meant more for Kate and for me. My sister didn't like the pizza from Gas Mart, anyway. Just when I was imagining what Elise might be eating, Teddy came through the door, followed by Elise.

"You guys are back early! How was dinner?" asked Mama, pouring herself a cup of Kate's orange pop.

"Um..." started Elise, as she looked at Teddy, "It didn't go very well."

Elise went to Mama then, and they held each other tightly for a long time. I wondered if Mama understood what was hurting without Elise even saying a word. For a minute, I wished that were me and that Mama knew what was inside of me before any part of it even came out.

"I'm Teddy," said Teddy as he extended his hand to Kate.

Kate looked a little surprised that Teddy had even noticed her. She reached to meet his hand with hers. Kate had chipping metallic blue polish on her short fingernails, which I had seen her biting just before she shook Teddy's hand.

"I'm Goldie's friend, Kate," she said quietly, apologetically. Kate looked a bit like she no longer wanted to be there, eating Gas Mart pizza at the table where Smiley's cage used to be.

"Kate, I have heard the girls say such nice things about you." Teddy said. I noticed Kate's cheeks turning pink when he said that.

Elise and Mama had let go of one another. Elise had taken the fourth chair at the table.

"Ugh. Gas Mart Pizza," said Elise, getting up again and pulling the peanut butter from the cabinet. She made herself a sandwich and returned to the table where the rest of us, including Teddy, finished what had been left of the pizza without saying anything.

Mama already knew, I was sure, what Elise was going to say. When she spoke, Teddy moved behind her and put his hands on her shoulders. Maybe he thought it would be easier for her to say the hard stuff that way. Elise told Mama, and the rest of us, too, that Mr. and Mrs. Meyer hadn't taken the news about Elise and Teddy's baby very well. They were very surprised, according to Elise, and they said they didn't think their first grand baby would be the child of their youngest son. Of course, Mr. Meyer was very worried about Teddy's baseball and how he would be able to play the game and support his family.

"It's not that they don't want to be grandparents or that they don't want me to be with Elise," said Teddy, "but they just weren't expecting this right now."

"Well, was anyone, really?" Mama asked, as though she was defending them against Teddy's parents. I knew Mama would be fine with Elise having a baby; she was like that. At least, I thought she was. She had had Elise when she was near Elise's age. "Have you thought about what you might do, though, about school or anything else, either of you?" Mama asked. Mama was used to doing things on her own. I wondered if she would expect that of Elise.

Elise looked at Teddy, and Teddy told Mama that they had a lot of stuff that they needed to work out. I wondered what they meant by that, but I didn't think it was my place to even say anything about it at all.

"Mama," I began, "thanks for letting us get the pizza. Is it okay if Kate stays tonight?" Mama said that would be fine. I thought secretly that she must have been glad she wouldn't have to talk to me about the hard stuff, at least not on that night.

Kate and I fell asleep back-to-back in my bed with Myles at our feet. When I woke, the sun was just coming up. Kate and Elise were both sleeping. Elise had come in at some point during the night, quietly enough that I didn't even know. I slipped out of my bed, pulled my side of the blanket up to Kate's shoulders, and climbed into bed with my sleeping sister. I pressed my back against hers and fell asleep for the last time before Elise had to go away again.

Smiley's cage had been standing empty, left just as it was, since he had flown away. I had an idea. It was a beautiful cage, fancy and very special with the antique stand that Mama had given me. After taking the cage from the stand, I cleaned out the leftover food and bird droppings. Then, I carried the stand and cage, ever so carefully, down the back stairs. I was out of breath as I stopped to open the gate, taking a second to admire Rosa's little bulb garden. The daffodils were coming up in bunches.

Mr. Quinn was looking after the shop on that Saturday when Mama drove Elise back to school. Teddy was busy with baseball because the season was about to begin, and Elise didn't want to ride the bus. Mama let me stay home, probably to avoid talking about what we needed to talk about. I didn't want to ride all day in the car, especially not with her. Mama was a good lady. Mr. Quinn had said so. I tried to remember that. I knew it was true, though I wondered why she did some of the things that she did.

"Goldie!" Mr. Quinn brightened a little when he saw me, pulling the stand with one hand and fumbling through the door with the bird cage in the other. "Do you need help?" he asked.

"I have an idea," I said.

Mr. Quinn said it would be okay for me to go into the warehouse by myself. I filled a box with all kinds of treasures from the fairy garden supplies and returned to the table near the register where I had set the bird cage.

"Do you suppose Rosa could help me with something?" I asked. Soon, Mr. Quinn came back to the shop with his arm around Rosa.

"Goldie. Bird. No. Mama," said Rosa. She must have been thinking about what had happened with Smiley. I opened the box of fairy supplies and pulled out some moss, enough to cover the bottom of Smiley's cage. I had found a few small sections of logs which I arranged among the moss. Rosa handed me the treasures from the box, one by one, and soon we had made a bird-and-fairy garden inside the cage. We wouldn't have to worry about the fairies or birds flying out of the cage door.

"Goldie. Bird." Rosa beamed.

The cage, hanging once again from its antique stand, was a tribute to Aunt Aida, Smiley, and all other hopeful things.

Mr. Quinn helped a customer as we worked. "Goldie, you are so much like Florence, and Elise, too! How lucky we are to have you at the shop," said Mr. Quinn, as he took his time looking over all that Rosa and I had done. "You know, I would love to have you work at the shop when you are a little older. For now, though, I am going to need someone to help me with Rosa once in a while, since John-

John will be moving back to the city. Would you consider being Rosa's helper?"

I told Mr. Quinn that I would love to be a helper to Rosa, who could not take her eyes off the cage. She repeated her chant, "Goldie. Bird." This time, though, she did not seem afraid.

I checked the mailbox after leaving the shop, and there I found one more thing to make my day a bit brighter: a letter from Kip. Taking slow, careful steps on my way around the building and up the back stairs, I read the letter.

Dear Goldie,

I'm sorry for what happened with the bird, and for all of the other hard things that have been going on with you. You sound a lot more grown up in your letters now. I hope you are able to get in touch with Marc. I want to know what he's like.

When I went to Ohio for spring vacation, Grandpa Charlie met up with my dad, so they only had to drive a few hours each, instead of almost seven. Grandpa Charlie stayed in Heritage for the week to take care of his shop, so it was just me, my parents, and my sisters at home. I had lots of tea parties with Violet and Lark, and they even painted my nails. It was a really good time, like how it used to be. I think I'm looking forward to being back home for eighth grade. First, though, I'm excited to play baseball in Heritage.

And Goldie — even though we are both growing up, I don't think we'll ever be too old for birch-bending!

Love, Kip

Hearing from Kip made me wonder about Marc even more. Would he like to go on adventures? I wondered what he liked to do, if he had a job he worked, and where he lived. Mostly, though, I wondered if he would be able to make a place for me somewhere in his life.

I agreed with what Kip said about birch-bending. It seemed like Kip wasn't the only one that thought I was more grown up. Mr. Quinn wanted me to keep Rosa company, like a real job. The best part, though, was that Mr. Quinn said that I was like Mama, and Elise, too. Maybe I was like them. Maybe I belonged with them.

Gabriella and I were lab partners for the science fair. Our experiment involved music and plants, so she was allowed to come home on my bus to work in the warehouse with me. I felt a little uncomfortable without Kate in the seat next to me, but Kate said she didn't mind sitting alone on the ride home on our science experiment days. She knew I liked her best, anyway.

Our idea was to expose seedlings of the same plant to different types of music as they grew. We would see how the plants responded. With Rosa's help, we set up six tomato seedlings in the back corner of the warehouse, each in a mini greenhouse with the same lighting, feeding, and watering schedule. Five of the baby tomatoes got their own music players, each of which played a continuous stream of one type of music: classical, folk, pop, opera, and punk (Teddy's idea). The sixth plant, the "control tomato," got no music at all. We (mostly me, with Rosa as my helper, because Gabriella could only come for the first day, the last day, and one time in between) tended to the plants for the whole month of April.

I called Elise to tell her about the experiment.

"That's so cool, Goldie," said Elise. "You know, Mr. Quinn helped me with my sixth-grade science experiment, too, and I used plants just like you."

"Was it with music?" I asked.

"No, I watered the plants with different types of water," said Elise, laughing, "but I don't even remember how it worked out in the end."

I thought I would try to remember how our experiment worked out because I planned to play the music from the best tomato when I was around Elise's baby.

"Goldie," Elise spoke again, "Teddy's going to have to quit his baseball team and give up his scholarship." She was quiet for a little bit after she said that.

"Why does he have to do that?" I asked.

"He's going to have to work to save money for an apartment for us, and for the baby," said Elise.

I didn't want to think about that at all. Talking about such big stuff with Elise made me feel like it didn't much matter what type of music worked better for making tomato plants grow. Elise and Teddy were going to have to learn to take care of their baby, and they probably didn't think they would have to do that so soon. I wondered if Teddy would even still play his loud music.

After Teddy's parents had a chance to think about things, they had lots of advice for Teddy, including the idea of working full-time and saving for an apartment. I knew that playing baseball meant a lot to him, but it seemed like Elise meant even more. He could have just walked away from it all, the baby, even Elise. Mr. Meyer told him that he was sad that Teddy had to give up his baseball, but that sometimes things didn't go the way that we had expected they might. This made me think of Marc and whether he would have done things differently if he had known about me from the beginning. I wondered if Mama and Elise left the yellow cottage because Mama had wanted to start over. It wasn't, it seemed, at all like things were going to be this way for Teddy and Elise.

There weren't going to be any big secrets.

I thought about Marc every day. I hadn't talked about him any more with Mama, even though she had left me that note. It was surprising when she mentioned Marc's name one day when I stopped in the shop after school to check on the plants.

"Goldie, I want you to know I have thought over and over in my mind about how things could have been different. I should have been more open with you about your father," she said. "I don't know what I was thinking, going on like it wouldn't matter or like you wouldn't be curious at some point."

"Your bird cage is fabulous, by the way," she said.

I looked at the fairy garden bird cage—not at Mama. She continued, "It wasn't hard for me to find him, Goldie. From what I learned, it looks like he moved to the West Coast a while ago. He has a family there. He's married, and they have a boy and a girl."

She had a faraway look on her face. I wondered if Mama really knew more information or had talked to him or anything. I wanted to believe what she was telling me.

I felt a tiny flash of excitement. "So, I have a sister and a brother?" I asked.

"They would be your half siblings, yes," Mama said, "but, Goldie, they don't know about you."

Of course, they didn't. How could they, if Marc didn't know I existed? I secretly imagined the whole family waiting with balloons and flowers to greet me at the airport when I flew in to meet them for the first time.

"I'm afraid. I'm afraid to disrupt his family," said Mama.

I stood up and walked toward the front door to the shop. "You're afraid to disrupt his family? That's what I am? A disruption? Well, maybe they would want me. Did you ever think of that?"

Rosa was on the bench outside, holding *The Little Prince* on her lap. I sat next to her, but she didn't ask me to read, not that time. Sometimes, Rosa seemed to know how I was feeling when I wasn't even sure myself.

The sky had darkened while I was in the shop. A cold spring rain fell. I remembered what Grandpa David had said about the rain helping with the hard stuff. This was a good time for rain.

The science fair was held during school on a day when it was also raining. Gabriella and I measured the growth of our baby tomatoes with Rosa's help. Our conclusion was a bit disappointing. As it turned out, the type of music that we played for our plants had no measurable effect on their growth. All had grown within one-eighth inch of the tomato that was exposed to no music at all. At least this was good news for Teddy. We earned an award for creativity, though, and we had six strong young tomato plants that would soon be ready for their spring gardens. Gabriella took two for her dad's garden, we gave two to Kate for Miss Marie's garden, and the remaining two went to Rosa, who was the most excited of all to care for the tomatoes.

Part Three: Taking Flight

I turned twelve at the end of April. Mama had surprised me with a cake—chocolate with vanilla frosting—which was waiting for me on the kitchen table when I came in from school on the Friday afternoon of my birthday. I saw a white envelope with "Happy Birthday Goldie" written in Mama's handwriting. She had put twenty dollars inside. Kate and I had planned to have a sleepover, but since her mom had been doing well, she was often spending weekends at their apartment, the same one where her mom had lived for a while now. Kate's mom wasn't planning to move to Charlotte as she had once told Kate she might. She was working hard, though, to keep up with her job, the visits, and her health.

When Mama had closed the shop for the day, she took me to dinner at Burger Central. While we waited for our food, I asked her about my birthday. My actual birthday. "So, Mama, did you…were you alone when I was born?" I asked. "Because I was just thinking, wondering, how you would do that by yourself?"

"Goldie, I'm used to doing things for myself. I have had to do that for a long time. I had Elise. She was with me, even though she was pretty little. And they have people at the hospital that help you and check on you after you leave," she said.

Mama didn't need very many people. I figured that must be why she loved Elise so much because she was her daughter and her best friend, all wrapped up into one girl. And then I came along, and it wasn't just the two of them anymore.

"You know, Goldie," began Mama, "You know that I am struggling with all this stuff about Marc and everything. I want you to know how much you do matter and how much we all need you. It doesn't seem like there is an easy way through this," Mama said. She put her hand on mine for a second, but she didn't look at me. "I found his address in California. It wasn't hard to find, just a little searching. I'll give it to you," she offered quietly.

Was Mama really turning this over to me? I wasn't sure how to respond. What if I sent Marc a letter? What if his wife opened it and ripped it to pieces? What if he didn't want to know about me? I reached for Kip's stone in my pocket, just to be sure it was still there. My bracelet from Kate, too, reminded me that I could be brave through all of this.

"Maybe you should go first, Mama," I said. "You should write to him. He might remember you and open it." Mama had said she really only loved Marc because he had made her feel closer to Elise's dad. I wondered if Marc had loved Mama in a different way.

We decided that Mama would write to Marc, and she would include our address for him. Writing a letter instead of calling, she figured, would give him a little time to think about everything. She said she didn't want me to be too hopeful in case the idea of having a twelve-year-old daughter would overwhelm him. The only way to know, though, was to be honest, and we both felt it was time for that. Mama never showed me her letter, and I never asked to see it. I did, though, check the mailbox every day, and not just for letters from Kip.

After the shopping trip on that day, I came home to two surprises. Mr. Quinn and Rosa had left a clay pot with a small rosebush outside our apartment door. One red rose was already blooming, and this rose, I imagined, must have been the exact type of rose that the Little Prince had loved. Rosa would have to help me tend to my flower. There was also a message on Mama's phone. It was from Kip, who had remembered all this time, and who had called to wish me "Happy Birthday." He also said his parents gave him a phone and I was the first person he called.

Twelve, I thought, might turn out to be a pretty good year.

Elise came home from school on a Friday in early May. We slept back-to-back in her bed that first night. It seemed how things used to be.

While Mama was at work the next day, Elise and I drove all around Charlotte and a bunch of other towns nearby in Mama's car, looking for garage sales. Before we stopped home for lunch, we had already found a little cradle which Elise said would be perfect for her baby's first few months, a carrier for strapping the baby onto her when she had to do things, and a whole lot of clothes, mostly plain-looking because she didn't know what kind of baby it was going to be.

There had been lots of days when I felt like Elise wished there were someone else to look after me when Mama was working, though she never said that or ever made me feel that way. When Elise was at Mason Hill, about the age that I am now, and when I was just starting all day school, Elise would wait for my bus on the same bench that's still outside of Piper's Coffee Shop. Every time I asked, she would let me get a treat from inside the coffee shop or a single scoop cone from Benny's.

Once near the end of my kindergarten year, she took me to Benny's Scoop Shop for the second time in the same week, and on that day, I chose a peppermint ice cream cone. Elise got a chocolate soda.

Just as I leaned into the door to push it open for Elise and me, an older man was coming into the shop. He pulled hard on the door, as he hadn't seen me coming out. I was already too far forward to catch my balance, and I fell hard to the ground, at the knees of the old man. My peppermint ice cream splatted on the sidewalk.

Elise rushed to apologize to the man and to gather me up. Two dogs were already taking care of the mess on the sidewalk.

"No, dear, I am the sorry one," said the man. "It's my responsibility to yield to you coming out of the door, not the other way around. Now, let me buy the little girl more ice cream," he said to Elise, as he handed her a five-dollar bill. "And," he added, "keep the change. You know, you're going to be a great mom someday."

I hadn't really thought of that story for a long while. It seemed so silly at the time, to think that Elise would be a mom. Now, in a couple of months, she would be. I knew she would be a great one. We didn't need a little old man to tell us such a thing.

We stayed out until it was too dark to find any more garage sales. I was amazed at all the things that Elise's baby was going to need. I hadn't thought that everything would be going right into the room that I shared with Elise—and would soon share with her baby, too.

Dear Kip,

I think you and Grandpa Charlie would have had a good time with us today...

In my letter, I told Kip that I had only two weeks left of sixth grade. I had almost made it through the year that I had dreaded so much. I told Kip that Mr. Shankman had said he was so proud of how well I was doing at the flute, and Kate, too, and that we were going to get to play a duet at next week's final concert. Marcy Clown was going to have a solo, but I would never have wanted to play by myself in front of an audience, anyway. I told him that I felt like a different person than when we had first met, even though I also still felt like me inside. I hoped, I said, that he understood what I meant, and I was pretty sure that he did. Of course, I also told him all about how I had spent my day with Elise.

Please tell Grandpa Charlie that I hope we can go treasure hunting with him again sometime. Maybe we can take Elise's baby with us. Also, as much as I like writing letters back-and-forth, I hope I can get a phone someday, too, so we can call each other anytime we want!

Love, Goldie

I thought that maybe if I wrote it on paper, it might be more likely to happen, someday.

At the end of the last day of sixth grade, Kate came to the shop with me. Elise had been helping Mama with some things but was mostly working with Mr. Quinn, learning the business of landscape design. John-John had moved out of Warehouse Apartment #1 at the end of the month.

"Did John-John get a new job?" Elise asked.

"He was getting restless, "said Mr. Quinn. "I could tell. He wasn't as patient with Rosa, and he would get frustrated with me for little things. It was me that encouraged him to move to the city to enjoy being a young guy while he still could."

"John-John was worried about leaving me and Rosa," he continued. "I told him we were in good hands with you girls." Mr. Quinn smiled at Mama.

Kate was going home for the weekend, and she wanted to buy something to give to her mom. Miss Marie had given Kate money for being such a good helper. She made microwave chicken nugget dinners and read gummed-up board books to the pink baby and one of the circus boys when Miss Marie had to be at the hospital with the other circus boy because he had tried to fly like a superhero from the rail of the back deck. Kate said she didn't mind helping because she knew Miss Marie really needed her. Also, she got paid.

Elise had been working on some miniature fairy garden arrangements in wide-mouth blue canning jars that Rosa and I had found on one of the back shelves in the storage part of the warehouse. Kate chose a little jar full of moss and tiny, glittery gemstones, with two fairies hugging, tied with a strip of burlap that had been fastened into a bow. I checked my pocket, then, just to make sure that Kip's sparkly stone was still there.

I gave Kate a hug and off she went. She seemed happier than when we had first met. Usually, on the day that school ended for summer, Elise would take me to the park, which was two streets down along Follaton Road from the main block of town and just behind Piper's. We would swing for what seemed like hours. We would take turns, one sister twisting the other's chains until we could twist no more. I still remember the jarring, spinning, crazy sick feeling as the chains spun around and around until they were free from each other. We always saved the double swing for last because it was always the best part having Elise right next to me with our hands touching as we shared the middle rope. That year, though, was different. Elise was working. I would have gone to the park with Kate if she hadn't been going to see her mom.

Rosa came through the shop's door. Rosa! I knew she would love to swing. "To the flowers, to the flowers..."

came Rosa's familiar chant.

"Rosa, do you want to swing? At the park?" I asked.

Rosa froze, and her eyes widened. "Swing!" Rosa laughed, and it sounded like sunshine. "To the flowers. Swing." She went through the door to the warehouse and emerged shortly after in her garden overalls with her gloves and tool basket. She repeated her new chant a few times. I sat on the bench outside the shop and watched Rosa dig around in the flower beds for a few minutes before she took off her gloves and put them in the basket. "Goldie. Swing. Okay," said Rosa. We were definitely taming one another, I thought, as Rosa led the way to the park where we stayed on the swings until dusk. We didn't try the double swing, but I knew it wouldn't have been the same without Elise.

Elise came to bed a long time after I had been sleeping that night. She didn't know she woke me when she closed the door. We watched her, Clover and I, from a hole that had worn through one of the little flowered patches on my quilt. Elise sat on her bed and pulled off her socks, which took a while, even though they were just little white no-shows. She stood again and slipped off her skirt. She was wearing shorts. Before sitting back on the bed, which took some effort, she pulled at the band that had held her hair in a bun, high on her head. Her hair had gotten so long since she had first gone away to the university. The loose brown waves reminded me of a river with all its turns and bumps, the river where we had sent Aunt Aida to float to who knows where before she dissolved. If I looked at my sister straight on from the back, I couldn't tell that she was about to have a baby. Elise got up once again, making a little grunting noise, and plugged in Kate's lights that still hung in our room. She climbed under her covers and rolled to one side, facing away from my bed. My eyes moved to the shadowy heap of baby equipment on the other side of Elise's bed. The harder I looked at the pile, the less it looked like cradles, blankets, and toys. As the lights flashed, the circus boys seemed to appear and disappear, messing up the things and showing up randomly, sometimes fighting in one spot or another.

A soft crying sound interrupted my thoughts. I wondered if the pink baby was buried somewhere in the pile until I realized that it was Elise making the noise. It was just a soft sadness, but I knew I needed to go to her. I got into my sister's bed, turning to press my back against hers. This time, I couldn't pull my knees up as I always had; Elise was taking up so much of the bed with her big stomach that I had to hang one of my legs over the side of the bed to stay balanced. Elise's cries turned softer. Soon, her breathing matched mine.

"Thanks, Goldie," whispered Elise.

I waited in case she had just been talking in her sleep, but soon she sat up, pushing into the bed with her hand. Her spicy, flowery smell came as she lifted Aunt Aida's quilt, the one that I had taken to Kip's secret cave in Heritage. "Thanks for being here with me," she said very softly. "I'm scared, you know. This isn't how I thought things were going to be after my first year in college. I didn't think I would already be someone's mom. It's not that I don't want to, but I just don't know if I'll know how. All that baby stuff in here just makes it real."

The darkness was beginning to turn to light on the first day of summer break. "Elise?" I offered. "I'll help you. I'll help you set up the stuff, and I'll help you with the baby." I told her about the circus boys and the pink baby and how Kate had been helping me practice being an aunt. "Nobody told you how to be a sister, but you're the best. You'll know how to be a mom, too. A great one. I promise."

She turned her head to look at the pile. She pushed a tear from her cheek as she turned to me. "Come here, Goldie. See if you can feel the baby move again." I sat with her, one arm around her back, over the long swirl of her hair, and the other on her belly, until we heard Mama rattling around in the kitchen.

It was a pretty hot day for late June. Kate and I had already gone to the pool a few times since school had ended. Mama got me a pass that year because I was twelve and could go without an adult. Kate had a pass that Sarah got for her, and so did the teenagers that lived with Miss Marie. I was secretly happy that the circus boys did not have pool passes. That day, Mr. Quinn was allowing me and Kate to take Rosa to the pool. Kate still wore the brown sweater, but over her bathing suit, which was also brown. She had borrowed one of the teenagers' razors to try to shave her legs. She said she was sorry that she did it. I knew why when I saw the dozens of little cuts on Kate's yellowish legs.

We met in front of the shop and walked around the building, across the alley toward the Quinns' house. It was a small, brick ranch-style home with a deep lot that led to the woods at the edge of town, the opposite direction from the home shop and the highway where Teddy had taken me to cut the tree. Over the Quinns' rooftop, which wasn't all that high, there were a few birch trees growing at the edge of the woods. I hadn't noticed them until that day.

We heard music coming from the Quinns' house. Through the screen door, past the shadowy figure of Rosa who had been watching Kate and me as we approached the door, Mr. Quinn sat playing the piano with such emotion that I was sorry to disturb him. At the sound of Rosa's laughter, though, he stopped playing.

"I didn't know you played piano, Mr. Quinn," I said, and Kate added that it was beautiful.

"John-John always thought the music would disturb

Rosa," he said, "but it turns out Rosa really doesn't mind at all."

When Mr. Quinn turned back toward the piano, I noticed that he wasn't using his cane. I wondered if that had something to do with John-John, too.

Mama must have brought in the mail that day because upon returning from the pool, I found a letter from Kip in the middle of the kitchen table.

Dear Goldie,

You'll never guess what I am doing this summer, I mean besides playing baseball and helping Grandpa Charlie with his shop.

Nina asked me to help with her beehives this summer. Her daughter is a beekeeper in California. She convinced Nina and her husband to keep bees. Nina told me that her husband started the hives two years before he died. She said her daughter is busy with her work and family and never really comes home to help or anything, so it's a lot to manage by herself. I help her lift the boxes and do a bunch of stuff with the bees. I was nervous at first, even when I wore a bee suit. Now that I'm more used to being with the bees, it's really cool and fun.

I'm going to save some honey for you. Nina says babies are not supposed to eat honey, so you can't feed it to Elise's baby. Write back soon, Goldie Bird!

Love, Kip

I wanted to remember to tell him that I had a job, too, helping Mr. Quinn with Rosa. I knew it wasn't nearly as cool as helping with beehives, though.

Mr. Meyer was quiet during Teddy's last baseball game. Teddy decided to give up his scholarship so he could keep working to pay for an apartment for him and Elise and the baby. The Meyers told him it was the right thing to do. At least that's what Elise said, but I was pretty sure Teddy would have thought of it on his own.

It seemed like all the balls were being hit to Teddy in that game, and he was fielding every one. He was so dirty from diving to stop a ball from going to the outfield. He slid on his belly while he tossed the ball to the third baseman. When he got up to bat for the last time in the game, Elise got up from her spot on the bleachers. She moved to the backstop to watch Teddy from close up, and she had to stand at least a foot away from the screen to make room for her belly.

Mr. Meyer was cheering for Teddy as he took his spot in the batter's box. He took a base-on-balls on four pitches. When the inning ended, so did the game, and so did Teddy's baseball career, all at the same time. Mr. Meyer hugged his youngest son. "Well, I guess your little one might be my best chance for a major leaguer now," he said, and Teddy looked away.

I had hoped that the Meyers would take us all for ice cream as they had so many times before. Elise and I waited for Teddy, who was talking with his teammates, as Mr. and Mrs. Meyer walked up the hill, toward the parking lot. Maybe it was a little sad for the Meyers, especially Mr. Meyer, that there wouldn't be any more baseball for Teddy after he had gotten a scholarship to play and everything. They knew things would be different.

Elise was out of breath when we got to Teddy's car. Teddy got us some good Chinese take-out while I waited in the car with Elise. After we ate, Elise said she was just going to have a little nap before they went shopping for the rest of what they needed for the baby.

I watched Teddy, who was looking at Elise as she slept. Elise was sleeping deeply, snoring like she did during the dark part of the night when I would wake because of the noise that I had heard coming from her. Mama came in, and still she slept. Teddy told Mama to go ahead and eat the food on the table if she was hungry.

Teddy put his head in his hands.

I thought of something. "Hey, Teddy, can I take you somewhere for a little bit?" I asked, as he lifted his head to look at me. He was dusty and messy. He hadn't changed from his baseball uniform.

"I'm not sure I should leave her, Goldie," said Teddy, "but where did you want to go?"

Before I had the chance to answer, Mama called from the kitchen. "I'm here, Teddy, if she needs anything," she said. "You go with Goldie." My heart raced. I hoped this was the right thing. I led him down the back stairs, past the alley where he parked his car.

"We don't have to drive there, Teddy. I'll show you," I said, as we followed the sidewalk along the Quinns' property until it ended. We walked on the grass, through the fields, all the way to the woods. I was a little relieved that Teddy hadn't asked me where we were going because if I had told him, he may not have wanted to go. They hadn't seemed that tall, the birch trees, when I had noticed them behind the Quinns' house the day we took Rosa to the pool. Standing before them, I could tell they were much taller than the ones in Heritage. I was only wearing flip flops, so I kicked them off as I approached one of the trees.

"Ready for something?" I asked. Teddy just looked at me as I started to pull myself up one of the trees, grabbing on to a smaller nearby tree to help with my footing. I wished for a moment that Teddy was Kip and that we were in Heritage. It wasn't the same, though. There was no lagoon, and Teddy wasn't Kip. Still, he was going to love birch-bending. I just knew it.

I didn't have Kip to guide me. I could feel the heat of the Kung Pao Chicken in my belly as I pulled myself further up. Once, I stopped to look down at Teddy. "This was your idea, Goldie. Remember that," he called to me. The tree began to sway, ever so slightly. I really hoped I remembered how to do this. Holding on to the trunk of the tree with all my strength, I kicked my legs from under me and began to float toward the ground. Teddy was laughing and screaming at the same time, and he seemed like himself again. I landed on both feet, as if I had done it a million times before.

I didn't have to urge Teddy. He hoisted himself up easily into the tree. "Goldie, you are crazy! I love it!" he called, as he neared the top. He let his legs fly free, but his descent was much faster and not as graceful as mine. Teddy hit the ground hard and landed in a pile of sticks. He was laughing ridiculously, not like Rosa or the Little Prince, but the kind of laughter that makes your stomach hurt for the next two days. Maybe, I thought, this was Teddy's last turn at being a kid.

Elise and Teddy's baby was born when Kate and I were watching the city fireworks from the top of the warehouse. It was early on the Fourth of July, a Thursday morning when Elise's water broke in the bathroom. Mama said that once that happened it was time for her to go to the hospital. I didn't like hearing about any of the doctor stuff. I just wanted to know if it was a boy or a girl. I hadn't realized that it was going to take at least all day. I heard Teddy's music from the alley, and soon he came through our apartment door to help my sister down the stairs. Teddy and Elise drove away in his car, in the fast-driving style that Teddy always used no matter where he was going. Mama left just a moment later, but she came back even before she had started her car because they had all forgotten the baby's car seat. Nobody had even said "goodbye" to me.

Mama had left me some money for Gas Mart pizza in case she didn't get home in time for dinner. She also left her phone for me. She was going to use Elise's phone to keep me updated. I was happy that she didn't insist that I go to the hospital, not just because of all the doctors and blood. Kate and I had planned to have a sleepover. We hadn't been able to have many of those with Kate going to her mom's most weekends. Without Mama and Elise, we could sneak up to the roof after dark.

Mr. Quinn was going to take care of the store for the day. He also told Mama he could drive me to the hospital after the baby was born. I wasn't in a hurry for that—to see the baby—because I knew I would see it every day for the next however many years.

After rinsing my milk cup, which I had used to wash down one of the brownies that Elise had made the night before when she couldn't sleep, I headed down the back stairs and around to the shop. I had thought that Elise's brownies tasted a little like Nina's brownies, only without the thick vanilla frosting. That made me think of Kip. I wondered if he had eaten any more of Nina's brownies when he was working with her beehives.

Rosa was out in front of the shop clearing weeds from the little herb garden and snipping bunches of basil for the shop's counter. She looked so happy, outside with her tools, with her hands and knees full of dirt. Customers always asked for Rosa's herbs. She knew just the right time for harvest. She understood the flowers, just like the Little Prince.

"Little Aunt Goldie!" smiled Mr. Quinn, as I walked through the door to the store. He had been eating chocolate kisses, and he handed me the one that he had just finished unwrapping. Mr. Quinn helped me gather some potting soil and a tiny shamrock plant, some light green pebbles, and the sweetest little fairy in the whole shop, a tiny baby with a crown of baby's breath. He just watched as I filled my mug, the one that had set off my temper that day at the end of last summer, with the fixings of my miniature fairy garden. I had decided to make it special for Elise's baby.

Back in the bedroom, I put the milk mug with the little

plant on Elise's bookshelf along with Aunt Aida's garage sale copy of *The Little Prince*. I made sure the crib was all ready for the baby.

Kate and I met at the pool for a while where I fell asleep face up in the sunshine for over an hour. My body hurt when Kate finally nudged me to say that she was getting hungry. I wished I had remembered my sunscreen. The hot pizza stung my sunburned lips, but it still tasted as good as I had remembered.

At nearly eight in the evening, Mama finally called just to let me know that there was still no baby. I wanted to talk to Elise, but Mama said that she was in too much pain because she was having contractions, and her body was working hard to try to deliver the baby. That sounded awful, and I felt terrible eating chips and drinking pop with Kate while we sat around and watched a movie with all that happening to Elise.

When the sky started getting dusky, we climbed up the ladder in the yellow bathroom, tossed the quilt from my bed onto the roof, and got settled in the best spot to see the city's fireworks. I brought the harmonica that I had found in the secret closet with Gabriella when we were younger, and Kate and I took turns trying to play some of the songs that Mr. Shankman had taught us for our flutes. We were careful not to play too loudly. We didn't want anyone to know we were on the roof. We could see fireworks displays from some of the neighboring towns, but Charlotte's was the best. The reflection of the bright flashes made me feel like my head was on fire. It was hard to concentrate on watching the show when I knew that Elise was at the hospital and that things were going to be different forever. Kate was with me on top of the warehouse, but soon she would probably be home with her mom where she really did want to be. I didn't like thinking about all these changes. I just reminded myself that a lot had happened during the last year, and a lot of it was good.

Once the sky had gone dark, we stayed on the quilt for a long time. We could see puffs of smoke coming from all around, and the smell of flint filled up the air. Kate let me borrow her brown sweater because I was feeling a little chilly. The sweater smelled like campfires, french fries, and strong perfume. I didn't think she ever washed it, even though she wore it almost every day. She said the smell reminded her of her mom, and she wanted to be reminded of her all the time. It was quiet, looking out into the night. As I held my sparkly stone, I thought of that night when Kip and I sat high on the hill behind the Courtyard.

We weren't sure what time it was when Kate, too, started to get a little cold. Since I was wearing her sweater, we decided it was time to go back into the apartment. I wished we had thought of bringing a flashlight or at least leaving the bathroom light on. Kate held on to the back of her sweater, which I wore, as we made our way down the ladder. I wasn't sure how Kate thought it was helpful to keep hanging onto the sweater. It kind of made me feel a little better, though, knowing she was right there with me.

As I secured the latch on the skylight, it occurred to me that this night was the first that I had remembered spending at the apartment without Mama. Kate and I were brave enough to do this, I was pretty sure. Mama's phone made a little noise, the reminder noise that a message had come in.

"You're an auntie, Goldie!" Mama sounded happy and excited when I called her back. "Your sister had a baby boy! Everyone is doing great!" she said.

"Oh..." I wasn't sure what to say. The baby was a boy. I suddenly felt scared and disappointed. Maybe I had secretly hoped for a girl. Another circus boy...

"His name is Theodore David, after his daddy and Elise's," announced Mama. "Do you want to come see him?" she asked.

See him? It was nearly midnight. No, I didn't want to see him. Not tonight, at least, and maybe not tomorrow, I thought. "I'm tired, Mama," I said. Also, Kate and I had just come in, and we were hoping to stay up late doing other stuff.

"That's okay, Goldie. I can bring you in the morning. Elise wants me to stay here with her for a while, so you get some good rest, and you can meet your little nephew tomorrow. Tell Kate I said thanks for keeping you company," she said.

I could feel the tears brimming up to sting my sunburned cheeks. *Why do I feel like an outsider in my own family? Theodore David. What kind of name is that? It always has to be about the dads, doesn't it?* Maybe I had been thinking aloud because Kate looked at me with a raised eyebrow, one that was crooked anyway because she had tried plucking it. That went about as well as shaving her legs had gone.

"Oh, Goldie, that's a nice name. I can't wait to meet him," Kate said. "And you really are going to be the best aunt ever." She always tried to make me feel better, and she usually did.

Mama came in sometime after we had fallen asleep, but before the sun rose. I heard her singing to herself and making a little noise. I stayed super quiet in Elise's bed, pretending to be asleep, just in case Mama wanted to take me to see Elise's baby right away.

"Goldie! You should get up!" Kate was trying her best to shake me awake. My face felt stiff from the sunburn. I sat up and was a bit surprised to see that the clock said ten o'clock, which was hours later than I usually slept. Kate thought she should be getting back to Miss Marie's before too long since she would be leaving for a visit with her mom that afternoon.

After Kate, who was not afraid to use the front stairs, had gone, I made some coffee. It was mostly for Mama but also for me, even though I knew I would have to use a different mug than usual because now my special milk mug belonged to Theodore David. I thought of taking it back...but I didn't.

Hospitals always smelled the same. As I walked through the main doors with Mama, I was reminded of the time when I was a very little girl, when we had been visiting Aunt Aida. I put a piece of gravel in my nose. When I cried, the gravel went further up my nose, and nobody could get it out, not even Aunt Aida. We went to the emergency room at Heritage Hospital, and it smelled exactly like the hot dogs-bandages-coffee-disinfectant smell at Charlotte Medical Center, six hundred-forty miles away, six years later.

Elise was in a private room in a part of the hospital reserved for moms and new babies. It seemed cheery, even though there were lots of babies crying. In a room behind glass windows, three babies were lined up in clear plastic bins on wheels. They were wrapped tightly in blankets.

Two were sleeping, and one was crying. He had popped one of his arms out of his blanket. Each time he let out a wail, he would pause and then the loose arm would stiffen and start shaking. I watched this cycle three or four times, and I really wanted to go in there and stick his arm back in the blanket. I wondered if one of these babies belonged to Elise and Teddy.

"This way, Goldie," said Mama, as she pulled me toward one of the rooms on the other side of the hallway. "Are you ready to meet your nephew?" she asked.

I knew I was about to meet him, ready or not.

Teddy was holding a tiny, quiet bundle, wrapped in the same blanket as the nursery babies. Elise was sitting on the bed. She looked pale, and her eyes were dark and puffy. She wore a hospital gown. I could still see her big belly, even though the baby was already born.

Teddy held the baby—who looked more like a baked potato than a person—out to me. "Goldie, here he is!" he said proudly. "Meet Sparky. Sparky, this is your Aunt Goldie." Unlike Elise, Teddy was absolutely beaming. They had decided to call him "Sparky" because he was born on the Fourth of July. That was much better, I thought, than "Theodore David."

As he pushed his little son into my arms, I saw the joy that had brightened Teddy's eyes the day of his last baseball game, when he and I had climbed up the birch trees in the woods behind the Quinns' house. I took a deep breath and cradled the baby in my arms, just as Kate had taught me to do with the pink baby. Sparky felt lighter than the cat. His eyes opened, and he seemed to look right through me, right into my soul. I saw Elise for a second, but his eyes were more of a grayish violet, not just like hers. He had no hair, just a tiny bit of fuzz, which reflected a reddish color in the sun. I wondered if his hair would be red like Teddy's. For a second, I thought of my dad, Marc. I wondered what his hair looked like, what his eyes looked like, and if Mama saw Marc in me when she first looked at me when I was just born. I hadn't asked her to show me a picture of what he looked like but holding my nephew stirred something inside of me. I could feel it, something that called for more of a connection with my dad, with this baby, with Teddy, maybe with everyone.

Elise's baby was not like the baby that I had been watching in the nursery. He was perfectly still, intent on looking at me, or through me. One of those. I could feel his soft breathing from his body to mine. His tiny eyelashes reminded me of the inside of a flower. His ears were so small but perfectly formed, like those of a little elf. His pinkish cheeks looked like little cupcakes, frosted and perfect. Perfect. This baby was perfect.

I carried him toward the window, shielding his eyes from the bright midday sunshine. Sparky's tongue popped out from his little strawberry mouth, and I noticed a wrinkle across his nose. He closed his eyes, then, and his breathing slowed to a steady rhythm. He made me feel something, a feeling of tears getting ready to come, but tears that made me feel like there was a reason for both of us. A really good reason.

Everyone was so quiet as I held the baby. Maybe they were afraid that I would break him or drop him or something. I turned around to look at Elise to see if she wanted her baby back. It took her a few seconds to look up. She motioned for me to come sit with her, right on her stiff-looking hospital bed, where I held onto her little boy as she held me close.

I knew I had to tell Kip about all of this while those feelings were still inside of me. I ran up the back stairs without waiting for Mama and went straight to the closet to get my notebook and markers.

Dear Kip,

My sister had her baby. It's a boy...

In my letter, I told Kip about waiting for the baby to be born and about how Kate and I sat on the roof of the building to watch the fireworks. I told Kip everything that I thought he would want to know about Sparky, and I wished so hard that he could meet him because I was sure that he would love him as much as I did.

*I didn't think it would be like this. I didn't think
I would like the baby, but I really love him!*

Love, Goldie

Mama was still sleeping when I woke up on the day
that Elise and Sparky came home. I felt different after
meeting the baby. Sparky would always know where he
came from. He would know why he had violet eyes, where
his red hair came from, and why he was good—if he was—
at drawing or baseball. I wanted that, too. I mean, I knew I
had Mama's brownish hair, and I was mostly quiet around
people like she was, but I knew there had to be some things
about who I was that came from Marc. At least, I hoped
there were.

I could see Rosa from the apartment window. She had
on her sun hat, and she was pulling weeds from the front
flower gardens, the ones nearest the shop. She was pretty,
but in a really natural way. I wondered if she looked like
her mom. Rosa knew a lot about flowers like Mr. Quinn.
There must have been some things about Rosa that were
like Mrs. Quinn, too. Maybe their laugh was the same.
Maybe John-John would have gotten upset with Mrs.
Quinn if she laughed too loudly, like he had with Rosa.
Rosa seemed a bit different since John-John had left.

Maybe she didn't have as much to worry about or to be upset about without her brother telling her to be quiet or to stop laughing all the time. I wondered if she missed him. I wondered if she missed her mom.

Just then, I heard Mama's voice, which sounded a little too cheerful. Lately, Mama had been annoying me, and when she was extra happy, she was even more annoying.

"They should be home in a little over an hour!" Mama came closer as she spoke, which made me scowl.

"I want to know what he looks like. What does he look like?" I blurted.

"Well, you saw him yesterday, Goldie. Do you think he will look different today?" she asked.

"Marc. I'm talking about Marc, Mama. What does he look like? I am asking you what my dad looks like!" My heart was beating angrily inside of me as I spoke.

Mama's voice was quiet again. "Goldie, honey, I didn't expect that. I'm sorry. I thought you were talking about the baby," she said.

"I am not talking about the dumb baby," I snapped, even though I didn't think the baby was dumb at all. "I am talking about MY DAD. I want to see what he looks like. Can you show me a picture?" I asked, almost demanding.

Mama looked flustered. "I can... I will... Just not now. Elise will be home in just a little while, and I want to make sure we are all ready to welcome her and the baby! Hey, could you run down to Piper's for me and get a loaf of cheese bread? It's your sister's favorite." She handed me a five-dollar bill and turned toward her bedroom. I wondered how I could get Mama to see that I was her daughter, too, just as much as Elise was.

I left down the back stairs to join Rosa with her flowers. She would want to see me. She always did. Earlier in the summer, I had moved the potted roses that Mr. Quinn and Rosa had given me for my birthday to the back stairs landing, so I could see them whenever I passed by. Just looking at them made me feel a tiny bit better. I decided that I would think about getting Elise's bread. I stopped first in the shop to get a cup of tea. I sat on the bench where I had watched Rosa so many times before.

"Goldie. Bird." Rosa looked up briefly and let out a magical stream of laughter before turning back to her work. I watched her for a long time. Though she barely spoke to people, she knew how to communicate with flowers.

As I got up from the bench, I slipped my hand in the pocket of my shorts. My stone wasn't there. I couldn't remember the last time I had held it. It had become so automatic to have it with me. Now I didn't know where I had left it. It would turn up, I told myself. I moved my fingers to make sure Kate's bracelet was still there.

Since I was mad at Mama, not Elise, I decided to go to Piper's before going back to the apartment. I was halfway up the back stairs when Teddy's car screeched into the alley. As usual, I could hear his music blasting, even though the windows were closed. I wondered if loud music was good for babies.

"Goldie! Can you help Elise up the stairs?" he called. Teddy carried Elise's bags and the baby's carrier. Elise, who hadn't seemed to notice the cheese bread stuffed under my arm so I could use both hands to help her, walked with me behind Teddy up the stairs. Just as I was beginning to wonder what had happened to Sparky, I heard a little peep coming from the carrier. There he was, in there like a pack of gum in a purse or something. I wondered when he would sit up or start climbing around like the circus boys.

Mama had made some chicken soup for Elise to go with the cheese bread. Mama, Teddy, and I sat around the table and ate with Elise while Sparky was still in the carrier. I hurried to finish my lunch because Teddy said I could be first to hold the baby.

I sat for a very long time with Sparky on my lap on the part of the couch that had the best view out the window. The sun cast colorful sparkles and squares in a pattern down the wall, across the floor, up onto the couch, and even a little bit onto the baby's feet. He slept in my arms, fluttering his eyes every so often like a butterfly testing its wings. I felt the same warm, electric feeling that I had when I first held him in the hospital. I wanted to hold him forever.

Elise stood up after a while. I could hear her chair

slide on the kitchen floor. It always squeaked more than the others. I expected that she would come for Sparky. Instead, she went to the bedroom, and I heard the door close behind her.

"You good with him, Goldie?" Teddy asked me, as he turned to the door. "Oh..." he continued, "just take him to Elise if he seems hungry, okay? Or Florence can help you make a bottle. I'm going to go home for a bit." I was so surprised. Mama was somewhere, I knew, but how was I supposed to know if the baby was hungry? I didn't say anything, but Teddy kissed his son on his head and closed the door quietly behind him as he left the apartment.

Elise slept for a long time that afternoon. I had fallen asleep, too, for a little while with the baby still in my arms. A little sound of grunting, not really crying, woke me. I watched Sparky stretch, open his mouth to yawn, open one eye, and then close it again. He grunted again and started to fuss. I wondered if I needed to take him to Elise. She was sound asleep on her side with her quilt covering her up to her neck when I opened the door to our room. As gently and quietly as possible, I pulled the quilt down and tucked baby Sparky in beside Elise.

"Elise," I spoke, to make sure she was awake.

"Thanks, Goldie," said Elise in a quiet, tired voice. "I'll nurse him now. You're the best." Then, Elise pushed up her shirt to feed her baby right from her breast, which surprised me. I just figured Sparky would be drinking from a bottle. Elise made it look perfectly natural. I thought it was amazing that she could take care of him like that.

Sparky made some gurgling noises, and after a while, Elise pushed herself up in her bed, holding the baby over her shoulder.

"What's he doing?" I asked.

"I have to burp him during the feedings," said Elise. "If I don't, he will get a bellyache and be really uncomfortable. He could even choke. They taught me that at the hospital." There was a lot to learn about babies.

Mama was making cookies, which meant that visitors were coming. She never made cookies when it was just Elise and me, except at Christmas.

"Rosa and Mr. Quinn are here to see the baby," announced Mama, as she opened our bedroom door. Elise was just finishing the feeding, so she passed Sparky to me as she got herself together. I held Sparky over my shoulder as Elise had shown me, being so careful to support his head, and before long he had burped as loud as the junior high boys that rode my bus.

"Hey, you're going to be such a great aunt," said Elise. She took a deep breath and stood up, reaching for her little son.

Rosa stayed close behind Mr. Quinn. Something must have seemed different to her. Her eyes widened when she saw the baby in Elise's arms. Rosa laughed nervously. "Goldie. Baby," she said, which surprised me. Then, Elise passed the baby to me, and Rosa sat next to me on the couch without taking her eyes off Sparky.

Mr. Quinn asked Mama how it felt to be a grandma. A grandma! Mama was a grandma. She had just turned forty years old during the winter. I felt bad for being hard on her. I wondered if she wanted to be a grandma. Of course, she would love Elise's baby. Just because things hadn't gone that great between Mama and me didn't mean that she wouldn't want to be a grandma to Sparky.

Mama held Sparky then, and Mr. Quinn sat with her and Elise on the other couch. Mr. Quinn commented about how beautiful the baby was. Mama said that his eyes were just like Elise's when she was first born. Mama got a misty look in her eyes then. She had her hair up like Elise often wore hers, and it seemed like she could be the mother of this baby. I wondered if just for a minute, she wished she could go back to that time, when she first had Elise, and when she still had Davy. Mama had been through some hard stuff in her life. It wasn't just me. Elise, too, had lost her dad. We had a chance, though, at a lot of new things. I thought I shouldn't be so hard on Mama, even if she seemed to forget sometimes that I needed a little bit of her, too.

Sparky started to fuss, and Mama stood up with him. "I think he needs his Aunt Goldie," she said, as she tucked him in my arms once again. Like magic, he settled peacefully to sleep. Elise smiled at me. I knew that she was glad Sparky had an aunt like me.

So many people came to see the baby that day: Mr. and Mrs. Meyer, Teddy's baseball coach and some of his teammates, two of Teddy's brothers, a couple of Elise's friends, some of the greenhouse workers, Miss Marie (but not Kate because she was still with her mom), Piper from the coffee shop, and a balloon delivery guy. One of the balloons got caught on a loose nail in the door frame and popped. Poor Sparky, who had been lying on a little quilt on the rug, opened his eyes wide. His body stiffened. His tiny arms popped out from his blanket and slowly went back to his sides again. He squirmed and cried hard. I thought of the baby that I had seen in the nursery at the hospital. Elise looked at me. As I picked him up, he returned to a calmer state. Someone brought a casserole or lasagna that smelled like moth balls. We ate it for dinner, and it tasted like absolutely nothing. People loved Mama's cookies, though, which made her happy. So many people had already come to meet Sparky. I wanted him to like me best, more than anyone else.

I was hanging from a birch tree when I heard some strange snorting noises, like some sort of wild pig in the distance. The noise got more urgent, louder, and a bit more like a crying baby. Sparky's grunting had stirred me from my sleep. He was awake in the little crib beside Elise, but she was sound asleep. Elise had been so tired, really, since she was pregnant. At least, that's how it seemed to me. Maybe it was finally time for her to catch up on her sleep so that she could stop feeling so sad, and so she could be more like she used to be. Sparky's eyes widened when I picked him up, and he stopped grunting, but only momentarily, before he opened his mouth and tried burrowing in my nightgown. I thought he must have been hungry. Elise did not look like she would be waking up. I wondered if I should get Mama.

I carried Sparky to the living room. The light was still on, and Mama's shoes were not on the rug. She was not at home. Sparky continued to cry, so I knew what I had to do. Back in the bedroom, I sat on my sister's bed and pushed her little son against her. Elise mumbled something about flowers as she began to stir. I helped her get the baby set up to nurse, and she never seemed to really wake up all the way. I watched from my bed, not wanting to go back to sleep in case either of them needed something. I wasn't very tired, which was probably good, because after a little while, Sparky turned his head away from Elise. I wondered how she could sleep through this. I wondered where Mama was. I wondered why Teddy wasn't helping out. Most of all, though, I wondered what would happen to the baby if nobody helped him burp. Elise said he had to burp, or he would get a belly ache. Who wanted a belly ache?

I held my nephew over my shoulder, as carefully as before, and when he had finished burping, I laid him in his cradle. Soon I, too, fell back to sleep.

I wasn't sure how much time had passed before Sparky woke for the second time. That time, I tried waking Elise because she had told me how important it was to switch sides each time she nursed. She was aware enough to turn over, and she thanked me for bringing the baby to her, but she went back to sleep again while he nursed. I didn't mind at all. I figured that she would have gotten up eventually, if I hadn't, so it was good for her to be able to catch up on her rest.

This pattern went on through the night, with Sparky waking up hungry every two hours or so. I didn't feel tired when the sun shone through the window early the next morning. Elise was asleep in her bed, and Sparky was in his cradle. Mama, too, was still sleeping. I knew she was home because her shoes were by the door. She had always been a hard sleeper. Elise often had to wake her up on school mornings before I was old enough to get ready on my own. When I had been sick or afraid in the night as a little girl, Elise was usually the one to help me. She only called for Mama when we really needed her. Maybe Elise was more like Mama now, and it was my turn to help her.

The shop was not yet open on that morning, but I knew Rosa would be outside in the gardens. I sat with her for a while, long enough to hear her laugh a few times before Teddy pulled into the parking lot outside of the picket fence. I didn't hear his music.

"Hey, Goldie! Come with me, will you?" he shouted from his car. Teddy shoved a bunch of bags and wrappers from the front passenger seat to the floor and motioned for me to get in. The only other time I had been in that seat was when he took me to visit Elise at the university.

"I was thinking," said Teddy, "we could go get a donut or something, just you and me?" Teddy smelled good, like he had just taken a shower, and he looked well-rested. He wasn't getting up with a baby during the night.

We drove to the other side of town to City Donuts, which had the best diner-style coffee and all kinds of good donuts. Teddy said he was planning to go to the apartment, but he was thinking about donuts. When he saw me outside, he thought I might like one, too. He was right. I got three donuts: two chocolate glazed, and one with white frosting and red, white, and blue sprinkles, in honor of Sparky. Teddy only ate two donuts, both jelly-filled, like the half-donut that Nina had given me in Heritage, but he had a refill on his coffee. He thanked me for being so helpful with the baby. I told him I wasn't doing it on purpose. I just liked Sparky more than I thought I would.

"I know it's probably a drag for you to have to share your room with a baby. Even worse than with your sister," he said.

"Teddy!" He had surprised me by saying that. "I don't mind having Sparky in there at all. He just cries sometimes, but I know that's what babies are supposed to do."

"Well, thanks, Goldie," he said. "You're the best. This stuff has been pretty hard on Elise. Thanks for being such a good sister. Pretty soon I'll have enough rent money to get an apartment for Elise, Sparky, and me," he said.

I raised my eyebrows.

"Don't worry," he said. "We'll make sure there is a comfortable couch for you to sleep on!"

I remembered, then, that Kate would be coming back that day. I didn't want to miss her if she came to visit. Teddy thought we should be getting back anyway. We chose a dozen donuts, each one different, to take back to the apartment. When we drove past the shop on the way to the alley, Rosa was still in the same place, working on her flowers. When I imagined her laughter, it filled me up, even though I was pretty stuffed from those three donuts.

Teddy put the donuts on the coffee table in front of the couch where Mama and Elise sat with the baby. Elise's hair was wet. Mama was having coffee.

"You look good, sweetheart," said Teddy to Elise. "Well-rested!" He smiled at her, and I imagined Kip smiling at me like that one day.

"Teddy, he slept all through the night!" Elise spoke excitedly. "Only two days old, and he stayed asleep until morning. What a good little baby we have!" She didn't know! Elise had no idea that Sparky had been up multiple times during the night and that she had even nursed him. "Can you believe it?" said Mama. "I'm such a sound sleeper. I probably wouldn't have heard him anyway. He's just like his mama, sleeping through the night right away. Goldie, though," Mama rolled her eyes. "Sometimes I still wonder if Goldie sleeps all night. You didn't hear the baby, did you, Goldie?" Mama asked, immediately reaching for a donut and dumping the entire box onto the floor. Myles tried licking the frosting from a vanilla donut, but the rest were recovered quickly enough by Teddy and Mama.

"Well, I..." I began, but Mama was already in the kitchen refilling her coffee, and Teddy had settled next to Elise, holding the baby, who was still sleeping. They seemed like the perfect little family, and they didn't need anyone extra hanging around. Nobody had to know that I helped with the baby during the night. I figured it didn't really matter anyway.

I saved the best-looking donut, a strawberry-cream-filled chocolate one with pink sprinkles, for Kate. She would be coming back later in the day, and I knew she would want to see the baby. Everyone did.

I thought about the baby with the loose arms, the one that had cried at the hospital. I wondered if lots of people wanted to see that baby. I wondered if there had been anyone that had wanted to see me when I was a baby. Anyone that knew about me, at least.

The bell rang from downstairs. It was Teddy's parents again. I wondered if they planned to come every day. Everyone gushed about how Sparky had slept through the night and how he would be such a great baby because hardly any babies sleep that well right from the beginning.

"He's content. He's happy, like his parents," said Mrs. Meyer, as she patted Teddy on the knee. I looked at Elise, who really didn't look very content or happy right then. Her eyes were sad, and she had a faraway look on her face. She still looked tired. I really hoped it wouldn't be much longer before I got my sister back, even though I would have to share her.

I decided to go down the back stairs to get away from all of Sparky's admirers for a little bit. Kate was just coming down the alley as I was about to turn onto the sidewalk toward the front of the warehouse. We nearly crashed into each other.

"Goldie! I have so much to tell you!" She exclaimed. For the first time ever, or at least during the times that I had seen her, Kate was not wearing her brown sweater. She had on a white dress that I thought must be new. It was just fitted enough to show what little curves Kate had. She looked older, somehow, though it had just been three days since we had last been together. She wore her hair pulled back from her face with a green floral headband to hold the sections of hair that didn't quite reach the elastic band.

Then, I remembered: the brown sweater! I had left Kip's stone in Kate's sweater pocket on the night that Sparky was born. My cheeks flushed, and my heart pounded as I spoke, not even acknowledging Kate's excitement at whatever she had to tell me.

"Kate, I can't find my sparkly stone, the one from Kip! I left it in your brown sweater pocket when you let me wear it during the fireworks," I said.

"Oh, I'll check for you. It's at my mom's now, though, the sweater. She thought she should wash it for me because I couldn't remember the last time it had been washed, or even if it ever had. Hey," she continued, "do you want to go to the pool? I already have my bathing suit on under my dress."

I really hoped Kate's mom wasn't going to wash the sweater, at least not until we found the stone. I needed that stone, in case I never saw Kip again, and also in case I did.

"Oh, maybe," I said in response to her question about the pool, "after you see the baby." After all, wasn't that why she had come?

"Hey, let's just go up the front stairs, Goldie," said Kate. "Are you ever going to use them again? You know, you are not going to fall down those stairs. You can balance on a two-inch wide bench back." I wondered why she had to bring that up.

"Maybe you're right," I said, "but not today. Go ahead if you want, but I'm going up the back." Kate wasn't going to change my mind, especially when I didn't have my sparkly stone. We walked together up the alley stairs.

Kate held the baby for a little while. She said he felt like a loaf of bread compared to the pink baby, who was more like a Thanksgiving turkey. When Sparky fussed, she passed him to me right away, and he settled to sleep. I hadn't lost the baby magic, but I gave him to Elise so Kate and I could go to the pool. We shared the strawberry-cream-filled chocolate donut before we left.

When we reached the pool parking lot and I saw how many cars and bikes were parked there, I wanted to go home, even if there were too many people at the apartment. It was so hot, though, and I knew the water would feel good. Kate noticed two ladies that were just leaving their lounge chairs near the diving pool. We spread our towels. I was just getting out my sunscreen when I heard a familiar voice. It was Gabriella. She wore a pink bikini and black sunglasses. She had been walking with the boy that I remembered from the beginning of junior high, the one that she had gone with to the dance, and another boy that I didn't recognize. The boys kept going toward the gate at the diving pool. Gabriella stopped to chat.

"Hey, Goldie! Our tomatoes are doing great," she laughed. "How have you been?"

"I'm good, I guess," I said, before asking if she remembered Kate, which she did.

"We just saw the baby," said Kate, "and he is the cutest thing!"

Gabriella looked confused. "Baby? Whose baby?" she asked.

Kate looked at me. I wasn't going to say anything, so she spoke. "Goldie's sister's baby," said Kate.

Gabriella's mouth dropped open. "Elise? Elise had a

baby?" she asked. Kate looked away, toward the boys who had by then entered the diving pool.

"She had a little boy on the Fourth of July. They named him after his dad, but they call him Sparky," I said.

"He sounds cute," she said. "I just didn't think Elise… I didn't know… Is Teddy the dad?" One of the boys yelled to Gabriella just then. "Oh, I have to go," she said. "It was good to see both of you," she called, as she hurried after her friends.

"Of course, Teddy's the dad," I snapped under my breath, hoping she had heard before anyone had anything else to say about my sister.

Kate let me know how sorry she was for sharing news that wasn't really hers to tell. I assured her that it was okay. I knew everyone would find out eventually. Besides, I told her, people could say what they wanted to say about the situation. They could talk about how Elise was young, or Teddy had to give up playing baseball to take care of them or whatever. I knew it would be worth it because Sparky was the best baby.

Kate told me, then, as we climbed into the shallow part of the main pool, that Sarah had gone to court with her mom earlier that week. The judge told her that she would be able to move home sooner than they had thought. Sometimes I wondered what exactly had happened with Kate and her mom and why it wasn't happening anymore. I knew that if she had wanted to tell me, she would have.

I knew Kate was ready to go home. I just wasn't ready for her to go.

Then, Kate mentioned something that she had never really spoken about before, at least not to me: boys.

"So, I met up with some friends in the park when I was back home," she said. "My mom lets me go out if I tell her where I am going and who is going to be there. There was a new boy, Terrence. I have the biggest crush on him," she said.

"Is that even possible, to have a crush on someone that you just met?" I asked.

"I don't know, Goldie, is it?" she asked, as she pushed her hand through the water to splash me. We both laughed until our stomachs hurt.

When we got to Miss Marie's, the circus boys were at the front door, looking out the window with their open mouths smashed against the glass. They began shoving one another, each trying to be first to open the door. The bigger boy won, popping the little one to the floor in a heap. Kate walked right past them into the house, ignoring their gurgled voices as they reached for her dress and tried to say her name.

Not all little boys would be like the circus boys, I told myself as I thought of sweet Sparky on my walk back home. I missed him after being gone all afternoon. I remembered what Kate had said about going up the front steps, especially because I could get to Sparky much more quickly. I pulled open the door, pausing in front of the mailboxes. I couldn't remember if we had picked up the mail from the day before. Our box was quite full. There were several envelopes and a little brown package, along with a postcard from the gas company. "Mr. Theodore David Martell" was written on one envelope. The other two letters were addressed to Elise, and I could tell that one was from Granny Boots and Grandpa David. I could pick out Granny Boots' writing from a hundred envelopes. She had very fancy, distinguished handwriting with more swirls and curls than any other writing I had ever seen. I really couldn't read her words, but I could tell they were hers, even though I hadn't seen anything she had written in years. I had almost forgotten about Granny Boots until that envelope came.

The package was just larger than the biggest envelope, but it was thicker and heavier. Written across the middle of the envelope was the name that almost no one called me, in writing I didn't recognize: *Jane Golden Martell, 400 Main Street #4, Charlotte, Illinois.* My stomach knotted. It had come from an address in California. I knew right away who it was from.

The stairs loomed in front of me. I looked to the top of the landing. I needed to get upstairs as quickly as I could, so I could open the little package from California, which I suspected, and hoped, might change my life forever.

I didn't want anyone to know. Not yet anyway. I slipped the package into the dry pocket of my swim bag, just far down enough so nobody would know it was in there. I looked all the way up the tile stairs one more time, turned and pushed the door open, hurried around the building, and up the back steps to the apartment.

After dropping the rest of the mail on the coffee table, I headed directly to my bedroom. There were still people at the apartment, people that had come to see the baby. I didn't even stop to say "hello." I couldn't. Still dressed in my bathing suit, I went straight to the closet.

My hands were shaking. I stared at the envelope for a little while longer. I opened the secret door, just in case I needed to put the little package inside. I felt a sense of heaviness, suddenly, and fear...fear of something, as tears welled up in my eyes. What if Marc, whom I had finally found, didn't want to know about me? Inside the mailing envelope was another envelope that contained something that felt like it could be a book. Taped to that was a small white envelope, which I opened just as carefully as I had opened the first. I could barely pull out the letter—handwritten on a piece of notebook paper—as my hands were shaking so much. It had been folded to fit in the little envelope. I took a deep breath as I unfolded each section. When there were no folds left, just lines of writing, I read:

Dear Jane,

You can probably imagine my surprise at receiving Florence's letter. The time I spent with your mother seems like a lifetime ago but also just like yesterday. I have been thinking about how if I had known about you all these years, both our lives may have been very different. Now that I know I have a daughter who is nearly a teenager, and you have a father who has another family, we are going to have to figure out where to go from here. My wife May and I have been together for seven years. She works as an almond grower in an orchard here in Rumford. We have a four-year-old son, also named Marc, and a three-year-old daughter, Anna. I decided to tell May about you as soon as Florence's letter arrived. She knew about Davy and about Florence already, as they had both meant so much to me. May said that though this was going to make things different, she was happy for me that something good came out of so much sadness. I am so grateful that she sees it like that.

A giant tear rolled down my cheek and splashed right onto Marc's letter, which I set aside for a second to get myself together. More tears came as I dissolved for a little moment in sobs on the old closet floor. Nobody knew where I was. I sat up, wiped my tears—even the one that got on the letter—on the edge of my swim cover-up, and went back to reading.

Though you deserved my love from your first days, you have the love of two families now, and we will figure out what that will look like. I am sending along a book that I want you to have. It has meant a lot to me since the first time I read it. I wasn't sure why I had held onto it all these years, but now I know. I hope you will write back soon.

Love, Marc

He wrote his phone number at the bottom of the letter. I folded the letter on the same creases that Marc had made, and I tucked it back into the little white envelope, just as it was when it arrived. Now, I knew the other envelope had a book inside. I sat in that closet by myself and thought about Marc's words, words that I had longed to hear for so very long.

Sharp laughter came from outside the bedroom. Were the voices laughing at me? The book, still wrapped, felt heavy in my lap. Slowly, I breathed in through my belly, as Elise had taught me to do a long time ago when I was feeling anxious. This envelope opened easily; it had been sealed only with its small golden clasp.

Somehow, I should have known. The story of *The*

Little Prince had also meant something to Marc, to my dad. I held the hardbound copy tightly in my shaky hands, as if someone might try to take it from me. There was a small photograph tucked toward the back of the book, between pages 78-79. What I saw took my breath away.

In the picture was a man, Marc, seated on some sort of dock. I could tell because though the picture was taken from pretty close up, there was a lake or river in the background, and the sun was shining. He had the same smile as mine, with one corner going a little higher than the other, and his hair was a sandy blond, like Kip's where it looked sunny in the light. I thought, then, that this was why my hair was lighter than Mama's and Elise's. For the first time, I liked it that way. His eyes were like mirrors to mine. I had never thought my eyes were anything but a dull brown color. Though they hadn't changed, they were, indeed, the eyes of my father, whose eyes did not look dull at all. I didn't want to trade, even for Elise's violet eyes. Not anymore.

On page 78, underlined lightly in pencil, was a sentence from the text about the stars being beautiful because of a flower that nobody can see. I wondered if Marc had highlighted those words or if it had been done by someone else who had read the book. If it was Marc, and I hoped it was, maybe I understood why those words seemed important. They seemed important to me, too, right then.

More laughter exploded from the visitors. Then,

someone opened the door to the bathroom, which was right next to my bedroom. I knew I needed to get dressed before Mama came looking for me. I put Marc's picture back where he had placed it in the book, returned the book to its envelope, and made sure everything was safely hidden inside the secret door. My heart raced as I pulled on a pair of shorts and a T-shirt from my dirty laundry pile.

My hair was nearly dry by the time I left the bedroom. I wasn't sure anyone would even remember that I had been to the pool at all. Only Elise and Mama were in the living room when I came out. Teddy had taken the baby for a walk, and the guests had gone. The words between my mother and sister were different than usual. Not exactly an argument, but an intense conversation for sure. Neither said anything to me as I plopped down next to them.

"I didn't know you kept in touch," said Mama in an irritated-sounding voice that she was more likely to use with me than with Elise.

Elise sighed. "Not that often. Maybe a couple times a year, usually, until I went away to school. It's been more since then. I have talked to Granny on the phone a few times, too. I didn't think you would care, but I also didn't think I had to tell you," said Elise. "They're good to me,

Mama. And really, I'm grateful for the money. You know we could really use it right now."

"Well, that's a lot of money for them to give you, Elise," said Mama.

She walked away then, but not before she asked me what I wanted for dinner. That was very surprising because that was usually a question for Elise. Maybe when she was upset with Elise, which really hadn't happened that I could remember, I got to pick the dinner. I told her that I really didn't care, which was true because I wasn't even hungry. I didn't know exactly what was happening, but it seemed like the letter that I brought in with the mail, the one that had been addressed in Granny Boots' fancy handwriting, must have had some money inside.

I heard Mama banging around in the kitchen, shuffling papers that I assumed were the take-out menus. Then, she called someone. Soon after that, she came back to where Elise and I were. She sat next to me this time.

"You know, Mama, I think we'll use that money to help with our new place, me and Teddy," said Elise, as she looked toward the floor.

Mama stood up again, muttered something about it being "just too soon," and disappeared down the hall.

Nobody said much, not me, Elise, or Teddy, while we ate the Chinese take-out. When Sparky started to fuss, Teddy handed him over to me. I walked around the apartment with him for a little while, until he was too hungry to console. I passed him to Elise and headed straight to the secret closet to make sure that what had happened a little earlier was for real.

I read Marc's letter over a few more times and found the page in *The Little Prince* with the underlined words, and, of course, the photograph. Kate would be the first person besides me to see Marc's picture, I decided. If someone found out about Marc before I was ready for them to know, that might make the whole thing go wrong. That's what I worried about, anyway. When you get so close to something good after so long, the last thing you want is to lose it. I just couldn't take any chances. I wanted to tell Kip, too, and Elise, but not just yet.

That night, I had a hard time falling asleep. Each time I thought about Marc, I wondered how it could even be happening...that I had a dad that looked like me and who wanted to know me after all these years.

Sparky made a little snorting noise and squirmed a bit in his crib. Elise was sleeping still. She looked like a little girl. I missed how she was before all of this. I knew I would always have Elise, but not like I used to have her, and I understood that. Sparky squeaked then, and he snorted some more. He moved his head and stretched his neck to one side, opening his mouth as if he were trying to eat the air. Elise still lay silently.

I reached into his cradle and carefully scooped him up, just as I had several times the night before. He smelled so sweet, like Elise but even better. Even in the shadows, I could see the little bits of red reflected in the fuzz on his head. He nuzzled into me as I carried him the few steps to my sister.

Elise rolled to her stomach just as I was getting Sparky settled next to her. She made a sound this time. Then, she said my name as she woke.

"It's okay, Elise. I know you're tired. I'm bringing him to you so you can feed him," I said.

"You're the sweetest," she said. "You're the best. Really." She propped some pillows behind her back and began nursing Sparky. I went back to my bed. Every so often I would remember Marc's letter and photograph, and I would feel a little flicker in my heart. I imagined myself sitting next to him on that dock in the picture. Sometimes his other two kids were with us, but sometimes it was just me and Marc, and those were the times that I liked best.

Elise burped the baby and then switched to nurse him on her other side. Her head nodded up and down a few times. I knew she must have been so tired. Her eyes closed after a time, and I could see that Sparky had stopped eating. He lay there on Elise, with his mouth open and a little bit of milk running from the corner of his mouth. Worried that he might fall out of the bed, I lifted him up and held him upright until he burped. I returned him to the cradle, and this time I fell asleep easily, until I heard the baby once again. I thought about letting Elise get up for him, but I knew she would feel better much faster with my help.

A little morning light had come into the room, turning the shadows to a pinkish gray. Sparky was wet. I found out when I slid my hand under his little body. I figured it was time to learn how to change a diaper. I had watched Elise a few times, and Kate many more as she changed the pink baby. I did my best, but I guess I must have made enough noise that this time, Elise was wide awake.

"You have been getting up for me, haven't you, Goldie?" she asked.

"I knew you were tired. I wanted to do it," I replied.

"Come here," said Elise, as she reached for me with her free arm. She hugged me, and I smelled the usual spicy, flowery scent that I loved so much. "So, that first night, he didn't really sleep through the night, did he?" Elise asked, as I looked away. "I've been so tired, and I haven't been feeling like myself...I didn't even know. I'm so sorry. Why didn't you say anything, Goldie?"

"I didn't need to say anything," I answered. "What difference would it make? He's a good baby, no matter how many times he gets up in the night," I said.

"You're the greatest," she said. "Now, get some sleep, would you? I know I'll be needing you again soon!"

It crossed my mind that I should tell Elise about Marc before anyone else knew.

"Elise," I began, "I have...do you...do you think Sparky is going to like looking out at the stars?" Maybe, I decided, it wasn't the best time to tell her.

"Goldie...of course, he will," said Elise.

"I think so, too," I said, and I turned to close my eyes for a little while longer.

Mama was finishing her coffee the next morning when I came out of the bedroom. She asked me how the baby had done through the night, and I told her he was fine. I didn't really want to talk to Mama that early. I wasn't sure what I was feeling.

I wished that I had my sparkly stone. So badly, I wanted to look at Marc's picture again, to see if I still saw my own reflection in his eyes and in his smile. I looked in the cabinet for a coffee mug. Since my milk mug now belonged to the baby, I chose a cream-colored diner mug. I had no idea where it came from, and I didn't want to ask Mama.

"Goldie," said Mama, "you seem a little distant. Everything okay?"

"Yep. Fine," I offered, as I filled the mug three-quarters of the way to the top. The coffee was too hot to drink, so I just stood there for a couple of minutes with my back to Mama. Soon, though, I felt bad for being short with her.

I turned around. Mama's eyes were puffy, and she looked tired even though she had slept. Her coffee, which she had taken with cream that morning, was nearly gone.

"Mama," I asked, "are you okay?"

She covered her face in her hands for just a moment before looking at me. "It's all so fast, Goldie. I just wasn't expecting them to leave so soon," she said.

"Who's leaving?" I asked, confused. "What's fast?"

"Oh, Goldie, I don't know. I just thought I would have more time with Elise, you know, before she grew up and left me and everything. She's getting an apartment with Sparky and Teddy. Granny Boots and Grandpa David sent money for her and the baby. She wants to use it to pay for an apartment," she said, "as soon as they can find one."

I knew this but hearing it from Mama like that made it seem real. I wondered if I should tell Mama about Marc's letter, so she didn't have something else to feel bad about. Or maybe she would be happy about it. I just never knew with Mama.

"At least you'll still have me, Mama," I said, and she hugged me tightly, though I didn't know if either of us felt any better.

I couldn't think of anything else to say to Mama. I really needed somewhere to go. Outside, the warm air felt good. I took the sidewalk to where it ended, past the Quinns' house, where I noticed John-John sitting in his car. I followed the dirt path into the woods. I sat with my back against one of the birch trees for a while until I began feeling a little sleepy. I didn't think anyone would care if I took a nap. I curled up among the dirt and dried leaves. For a moment I felt like I was hiding out in Kip's secret cave. This time, nobody came to look for me. When I woke, my hip hurt from the hard ground. I had no idea what time it was. The sun was high in the sky, and it was so hot that my hair stuck to my forehead and neck. Still, though, I felt peaceful at this spot where I didn't have to worry about anything at all. I wondered if maybe when Sparky was a bit older, this could be our secret place.

The apartment was empty when I got home. I found my yellow sun dress and got a quick shower. I wanted to leave before anyone saw me. I had only worn the dress once since the summer before, when Kip had told me that I looked pretty, and I hoped that he would still think so if he saw me wearing it, or even if he ever saw me again, no matter what I was wearing. The dress fit differently now, tighter at the top than it had been the summer before. I thought it might be time to look in Elise's boxes to see if she had any bras in my size, even though I really didn't want to.

My hair had gotten longer, longer than Mama's, but not as long as Elise's. It was easy to twist it up and tie it in place on top of my head. The things that Marc had sent me were still safely tucked away in the closet. I slipped the small envelope that contained the letter inside the book, on the same page as the photo, and put everything into the drawstring bag where I kept my colored pencils, which I dumped on my bed. I hurried down the back stairs. I decided to walk along the sidewalk downtown, rather than along the edge of the streets, down Follaton Road, where I might be more noticeable. I passed Piper's, halfway afraid that Elise and Mama would be sitting in there, and kept my head turned in the direction of Benny's Scoop Shop. Ice cream sounded good, but I would have to wait until later. Once I had reached the end of that block, I turned, nearly running then, in the direction of the park, where I would get to Kate's house from the other side of her street.

Kate was sitting on the grass in front of Miss Marie's house on a blanket with the pink baby. "Goldie! Watch this!" said Kate, as she picked up the pink baby, who could stand and take steps on her own now. She put her on the grass, in a sitting position. The pink baby scrunched up her nose and lifted her feet off the grass, moving her hands in little circles. Kate laughed. "She's so freaked out by the grass!" Kate tried to get her to stand on the grass, but she kept lifting her feet.

"I have something to show you," I said, as I sat on one edge of the blanket. Kate put the pink baby back down, and she crawled right over onto my lap. Maybe she thought I would be nicer and that I wouldn't try to make her touch the grass. Kate joined us on the blanket, but the baby stayed with me.

I passed the sling bag, which smelled strongly of pencil shavings, to Kate. She looked at me, puzzled, but I wanted her to open the bag to see for herself. First, she pulled out the book. "Is this a new copy?" she asked. "It looks different from the one I was reading." Kate was waiting for me to respond. She didn't open the book. She just looked at me.

"It's from..." I started. "It's from my dad."

Kate shrieked, startling me, and making the pink baby cry.

"What did you say?" she asked.

"Marc. It's from Marc. My dad. Read the letter. There's a letter inside the book, and something else, too," I said.

Kate's brown eyes widened and welled with tears. She sat, frozen in her place on the blanket. As she read, I moved the bracelet that she had given me at Christmas up and down along my forearm. It was starting to look a bit worn with a few of the strings beginning to unravel. My heart pounded. She let out a little gasp when she saw Marc's picture.

"He's so handsome, Goldie! And he has your same eyes!" she said. The baby had stopped crying. She had crawled just to the edge of the blanket, being very careful not to touch any of the grass.

"You mean, I have his eyes," I said. I felt my cheeks getting hotter, but I didn't think it was from the sun.

Kate hugged me. She told me she was proud of me for being brave enough to find out about Marc. "I'm so happy for you. It could have gone differently, Goldie. You know that, don't you?" she asked. "I mean, what if you never found him, or he was in jail, or mean, or even dead?"

I didn't like thinking about those things, but I knew Kate was right. I felt lucky. I knew Kate must have missed having her dad in her life, the way that she probably wanted him to be. I thought she was really the brave one for encouraging me to do something that she knew would be hard for both of us. On my walk back home, I took the sidewalk at the edge of town because it didn't matter if anyone would see me. I had done what I had set out to do.

The apartment was still empty when I arrived home. That gave me time to put everything back safely inside the secret door and return my colored pencils to the bag. Just as I tucked the last pencil into the bag, I heard the door.

First, Mama and Elise came in. A few minutes later, Teddy followed with the baby. Mama and Elise had gone looking at apartments. Their voices were muffled, but the door to the bedroom was open just enough for me to hear some of what they were saying. Elise hadn't really found anything that she liked, except for one place which Mama told her she would not be able to afford. Teddy thought that he should go back with Elise to look at the place that she liked, to at least get an idea of what they should be looking for. Mama didn't think that was the best idea because she thought Teddy would try to rent the place anyway, even if they really couldn't afford it, because Elise liked it, and Teddy loved Elise. Then, Sparky started to fuss. Elise took him from his carrier so she could feed him.

It didn't seem like anyone had even missed me.

Mama returned to work the next day. Sparky had been up as usual every two or three hours during the night, and though Elise woke up with him, she seemed grateful for my help, especially when I got up to get the baby from his bed and when I helped him settle back after nursing. During those nighttime feedings, I really felt like I was doing something to help. Even though I was tired, I liked hearing Sparky's little noises in the dark.

Elise wanted me to go down to the shop to tell Mama that Teddy was coming for her and that they were taking Sparky with them to see the apartment that Elise liked. She figured that if I were the messenger, Mama wouldn't be able to try to talk her out of going because they would already be gone.

"Daisies. To the flowers. Daisies," Rosa chanted in

a giggly voice, as I passed her on the sidewalk. "Goldie. Daisies. To the flowers…"

I often wondered if Rosa was lonely, but I would remember then that she must have looked forward to the bloom of each familiar perennial at its time of year, maybe like someone looks forward to a visit from a friend. I thought of Nina, and I wondered if it was a little like that with the bees that she kept on her farm and the other seasonal things that she liked to do. Maybe it was the connection with what she loved and looked forward to that could keep her from being lonely even though her friends and family were gone.

Mr. Quinn came by. He said he had heard I was pretty good with the baby. Though he still used his cane, he didn't seem as slow or wobbly. We walked together into the shop. Mama was taking down some of the red, white, and blue decorations and replacing them with some different things from the warehouse. On that day, Mama found some heavy-looking rusty stars and some smaller, shiny silver stars to scatter around the shop. Rosa brought some of the daisies, and Mama arranged them in bouquets in different-sized mason jars.

"Florence, what would I do without you?" asked Mr. Quinn. Mama blushed as her eyes met his.

I remembered why I had gone down to the shop that morning.

"Mama," I began, hesitantly, wondering if I should

even be saying this in front of Mr. Quinn, "Elise wanted me to tell you that she was taking the baby and leaving with Teddy for a while. They're going to look at that apartment again."

I knew Mama's heart was sinking, even though I couldn't actually see it. She didn't want Elise to leave. She didn't want to let her go, not yet. She knew she was going to have to as soon as she and Teddy signed a lease on an apartment.

Mr. Quinn was first to say something. "The kids are looking for a place, Florence? Is Elise moving out?"

"They're going to get an apartment," I said, "but Mama doesn't think they can afford the one that Elise liked." I looked at Mama, who was trying so hard not to cry. "Teddy's parents want them to have their own place, so they can be their own little family."

Then, Mama did start to cry.

"I didn't know. It seems so fast, Florence," said Mr. Quinn in a gentle voice, as he moved closer to Mama. He stared out the shop window at Rosa as she poked the weeder at the base of the daisies. "Time goes so fast, doesn't it?" He reached, then, to pull Mama close to him, something I hadn't often seen him do. It seemed like neither of them really wanted to let go of the other. I wasn't sure what to do, so I started making a cup of tea.

A customer came up to the walk. Mama pulled away from Mr. Quinn and headed quickly to the warehouse.

"Oh, those flowers are so pretty!" remarked the customer, an older lady whom I recognized as having been in the store before. "Are those daisies, dear?" It seemed like she must have been speaking directly to me, as I didn't think she would call Mr. Quinn "dear."

"Yes, ma'am, they are daisies," I said, in my most polite voice. Thanks to Rosa, I knew. The lady looked all around the shop, very slowly. I let her know that she was welcome to some tea. She thanked me, but she didn't take any. After a little while, Mama came back from the warehouse, not looking a whole lot better than when she had left.

I could tell Mr. Quinn wanted to say something. He waited, though, until the lady left, once she had bought one of the mason jars full of daisies.

"You've got good help here," she said, as she winked at me and turned to leave the store. She lingered in front of the shop for just a little while longer, watching as Rosa tended to her daisies.

"Florence, I have an idea that might help all of us," Mr. Quinn said, keeping a little distance from Mama this time.

Mama lifted her head slowly.

"You know, now we have an empty apartment upstairs. The one across from yours, with the view onto Main Street," said Mr. Quinn. "John-John is all settled in his new place in the city. Do you think the kids would like to live there?"

Mama looked stunned.

"Calvin, God, Calvin...I couldn't...I never even...they couldn't begin to afford such a place. I mean, it is just as lovely as ours. It would be so perfect to have them living so close, but..." Mama took a deep breath and continued. "You have always given me such a good deal to live here. I just don't think they could do it. Not yet anyway."

"I'd never have brought it up, Florence," he began, "if I didn't think we could make it happen." Mr. Quinn walked close to the window again, this time pouring himself a cup of Earl Grey tea, to which he added a little splash of milk. He offered the cup to Mama. She shook her head. He sipped a little and returned to the counter, placing his teacup near the edge by the register.

This time, Mr. Quinn put his hand on top of Mama's. "Even before I knew John-John's heart was not in this business, I wanted to have Elise help with the landscape design jobs. You know she has that artistic eye...and I see it in Goldie, too," he said. "They get it from you, Florence, and we are lucky to have you all here. Now, though, I need Elise more than ever. I want her to take over the customer design portion of Rosa's Garden Party."

Mama listened to Mr. Quinn, and she kept her hands under his the whole time. Mr. Quinn continued, "So, if Elise is willing to help with the business, they wouldn't have to pay rent. It would be worth it to me. We can see how it all goes. I mean, I would have to start paying her a salary at some point. Do you think she would go for that? I know she just had a baby. She could start slowly."

My insides were about to boil over with excitement. I knew Elise would love this idea, and she was already really good at the things that Mr. Quinn would want her to do. And it wouldn't really be like she was leaving because she would just be moving down the hall. Mama and Mr. Quinn embraced again. Mama said she wondered how she ever might repay him for his kindness.

"My dear," he began, his dark eyes sparkling, "you have paid me many times over with your hard work. This would make me a very happy young man!" I almost thought Mr. Quinn would kiss her, but he didn't. Instead, they both laughed.

"Calvin," Mama began. "Do you want to ask her? Because here she comes!"

I thought I had heard Teddy's loud music from his car a few minutes before. Teddy and Elise, who held Sparky, must have hurried around the building from the back alley. Elise was a bit out of breath. I reached for the baby right away. He smelled like my sister.

"Mama," said Elise in a frenzy, "We need a big favor. We want to sign that lease, and we have all the money. It's just that the landlord says we are too young. He won't rent it to anyone under twenty-one, unless someone signs with us. You, we hope? Please, Mama? We won't find anything that we like any better," she pleaded.

Mr. Quinn and Mama looked at each other, and it was Mr. Quinn that brought up the idea of the warehouse apartment to Elise and Teddy.

"And you won't need anyone to sign on your behalf because there isn't going to be any rent to pay," he said after he told them that the apartment directly across from ours was available to them if they wanted it. "Elise, when you are feeling up to it, will you be ready to take over the garden design part of the business?"

"Me... What... This is all... Oh, you're the best, Mr. Quinn!" Elise looked at Teddy, and they approached him together, nearly knocking him to the floor, as Elise hugged him, and Teddy shook his hand.

So, it was settled. Teddy and Elise were moving out with the baby, but we would all still be living under the same roof. I would miss sharing my room with Elise, but now there would be a spare bed for Kate.

Over the next three weeks, everyone pitched in to help get Apartment #1 ready for its new occupants. John-John had left some furniture, which Mr. Quinn said came with the apartment. There were boxes to move, floors and walls to wash, mirrors and windows and glass to clean, a bathroom to scrub, and wood to polish all before Teddy and Elise could move in. Kate and I agreed to help with getting the apartment ready. Elise mostly stayed in our apartment with Sparky. Mama and Teddy and Mr. Quinn mostly worked, and Kate came to help whenever she could.

On the last night that we worked, as we were finishing wiping down the cabinets with soap-and-vinegar rags, Sarah came to the Warehouse Apartments looking for Kate.

My stomach dropped inside of me. I knew that everything was going to change. Kate gasped. She, too, knew what this meant. For Kate, it was what she wanted and needed. For me, it meant losing my best friend. It meant that I wouldn't have someone to sit beside me every single day on the bus or someone to encourage me to be brave.

Sarah had wanted to tell Kate in person that this would be her last day in Charlotte. She would come the next day, right after breakfast, to take her to her mom's place. She was going home.

I could tell that Kate was trying to contain her excitement. We made a plan that she would go to Miss Marie's for a while, get her stuff all packed and ready, and come back for a sleepover. Miss Marie had promised that Kate could stay at our place whenever she thought she needed to. This time, I needed her to.

Mr. and Mrs. Meyer were at our apartment when I returned from #1. They had brought pizza, but not from

Gas Mart, which was good for Elise. Piles of boxes, bags, and furniture occupied the space where, a year ago, we had stacked what was left of Aunt Aida's belongings. Elise was folding Sparky's little baby clothes; she had been washing laundry. Mama was getting the last batch of her best chocolate chip cookies out of the oven. Everyone else was eating pizza.

"Goldie, we hear you have been a great help! We are all so lucky to have you," said Mrs. Meyer. I knew she meant it. She was holding Sparky, asleep in her arms. "So, tomorrow's moving day! Are you ready to have your room to yourself?" she asked.

"I'm going to miss them," I said. I was in no mood for conversation. It wasn't just Elise and Sparky that I was going to miss. It was Kate, too. Then, the tears came. I hadn't meant to cry, not yet. Teddy put his arms around me. He promised that Elise could come back to sleep in her old bed whenever I needed her and that I could come to their apartment absolutely anytime I wanted to. He even promised to give me a key.

Then, Sparky started to cry.

"I think he needs his favorite person," said Teddy.

"I think you're right," said Mrs. Meyer, as she put the baby in my arms. As Sparky started to settle, I thought I needed him just as much as he needed me.

"Hey, Goldie, would you be able to look after the baby tomorrow while we are getting things set up in our apartment?" Teddy asked.

I nodded. Actually, there was nothing that I would rather have done.

I walked out of our apartment toward the back stairs. Victoria popped her head out of the door to Apartment #3 just as I was passing.

"Oh, hey, Goldie," she said, "you guys moving?"

"My sister is, with her baby and Teddy. Just to the front apartment," I answered, as I tried to make a fast exit.

"That Teddy," she said, "he's so handsome! Anyway, I'm glad there will be someone living there again. And I'm glad you guys aren't leaving."

"Me too," I said, as I tried to make my getaway.

"Hey, Goldie, why don't you ever go out the front door?" she asked. "I just wonder because it's closer for you..."

"I don't know," I lied. "I just don't." I ran all the way down the back steps, across the alley, up the sidewalk along the Quinns' property, towards the woods.

I heard a noise just before the sidewalk ended, like a door slamming or someone kicking something. Then, I heard Rosa.

"No. No John-John. No John-John Rosa go. No..." Her

words escalated. There was more kicking and slamming. I stopped walking towards the woods and crept slowly back onto the sidewalk, where if I peered around just at the right angle, I could see most of the driveway through one of the lilac bushes. The lilacs had long since finished flowering, and though I loved how they smelled in bloom, it was much easier to see what was happening this way.

John-John was struggling with Rosa, who did not seem to want to get in his car. Mr. Quinn was there, too. His face was flushed. I knew he couldn't bear to see Rosa upset.

"No, John-John! No. No!" Rosa persisted, as she took a swing at her brother, who was trying hard to get her into the car.

Mr. Quinn said something to John-John. Then, John-John let go of Rosa. I heard Rosa's voice again as she headed toward her father and closer to where I hid.

"No. No John-John. No Rosa go," she said, a little quieter.

"Nope, no John-John, Rosa. You can stay with Papa for now," said Mr. Quinn. Rosa laughed, and pretty soon John-John was backing down the driveway, alone in his car.

I was sad for Rosa, and Mr. Quinn, and even for John-John. Rosa didn't want to go with John-John anymore. John-John didn't want to stay in Charlotte anymore. Mr. Quinn just wanted his kids to be happy. Change is a hard thing.

As I got closer to the woods, I realized that there was

something that I really needed to do with Kate. She had never done birch-bending. If she had to leave me, I wanted her to have a chance before she was gone.

It was already dusky by the time I reached Miss Marie's house. One of the circus boys was alone on the front porch, fully clothed and eating a bomb pop which was dripping down in red and blue all over the front of his white shirt. He almost never wore clothes. I could hear the other boy crying from inside the house.

Kate heard me as I was getting ready to ring the bell. She had only a little bag to bring for the night, but I could see a stack of some boxes and a few garbage bags as she opened the screen door. It seemed a little sad that her things were in garbage bags instead of a suitcase, but I figured Kate didn't really care how they were packed because she was finally going home.

The outside circus boy followed us. When we reached the sidewalk, he stopped walking, but he began breaking little bits from what was left of his bomb pop and throwing the drippy, sticky blobs at Kate and me. He somehow knew that he had to stay on Miss Marie's property, so though he kept trying, he never actually hit us with anything. I wondered if I would ever see that circus boy again. I hoped not.

We took a little detour into town before we went back to the apartment. I hadn't been to the Candy Counter since Elise left for school. The rows of glass jars held licorice wheels, hard candy sours, lemon drops, Mary Janes, chocolate stars, and my favorite rock candy sticks. The whole place smelled like happiness and like being with Elise. Kate and I made our selections just before the shop closed for the day.

When we came up the back stairs to the apartment, I could hear Teddy's music from the other end of the building. Our apartment was quiet, only Mama was in the kitchen, cleaning up from her baking. Kate went to the bathroom right away, and Mama called for me.

"Hey, Goldie, I wanted to tell you that I found a picture of Marc, from the day Davy and I got married. Do you want to see it?" she asked, offering her full attention, which I hadn't had in a while.

"Oh, yeah, but no rush, Mama," I said. "I already have one."

I left Mama in the kitchen without either of us saying anything else because Kate came out of the bathroom. I didn't look back to see Mama's reaction. Before it was too dark, we had to get back to the woods.

I was getting used to seeing Kate without her brown

sweater. She had gone home for the weekend two more times since the Fourth of July, but she hadn't brought it back with her, nor had she brought back the sparkly stone. She said her mom didn't find it in the laundry. I couldn't be mad at Kate or her mom, though, because it was me that left it in the sweater pocket in the first place.

A misty rain had begun to fall as we entered the woods and arrived at the birch trees. Kate looked at me, then up to the top of the tree that Teddy had climbed, then at me again. I started up the tree as quickly as I could. The rough, peeling bark was slippery from the rain, but that didn't stop me from climbing pretty far up. I let go with my feet, and the familiar feeling of excitement and fear carried me to the ground where my bare feet met the leaves, dirt, and bark.

"Okay! Ready?" I asked Kate.

She shook her head. I looked at her tall, thin frame. Her legs were already covered in bruises. Kate's hands trembled as she stretched to grab onto the trunk. Her toes curled to hold firm to her flip flops. She looked up high into the tree, then back at me. She shook her head again.

"No, Goldie, I don't think I can do this," she said.

"It's okay, Kate. You are already so brave," I said. I put my hand on her back and led her out of the woods.

"Another time, I promise," Kate said. The summer rain was falling harder. I hoped with everything I had that there would be another time.

"Hey, I think we can still make it to the ice cream place before it closes," I said. We ran in the rain and we did make it, but just by a few minutes. I bought Kate a banana split with some of the money that Mr. Quinn had paid me for helping with Rosa. I got a double cone with scoops of pink bubble gum and rocky road. Since it was closing time, we ate our ice cream on the bench outside of Piper's. It was still raining, just not as hard. By the time I had finished, the mess on my arm and down my elbow was as bad as that of the circus boy with his bomb pop. Kate didn't even need to wipe her mouth.

The rain had stopped. I didn't want to go home in case Mama was going to ask me about what I said about Marc's picture. I knew we needed to talk about it, but this was my last night with Kate. In that moment, that was what mattered most to me.

We walked up Main Street and turned in the direction of the park, which had closed hours before. As I flew high above the trees on the swing, I thought of the time that I had gone to dinner with Mama at Nina's farm and took her cat on the swing with me. After swinging for a while, my stomach was sick. I jumped off and sat in the grass for a bit, watching Kate fly up and down. She had told me once that when she was with me, she felt like she was still a little kid, and she liked it. At Miss Marie's, she was a helper, but she was also on her own with a lot of things. At her mom's, she said she felt nearly grown up. Her mom asked her for help and guidance, and she was in charge of a lot of things. She said she liked that, too, because she loved being with her mom. I knew, though, that Kate was going to somehow be different the next time I saw her.

"Goldie," asked Kate, as she jumped off her swing and joined me in the wet grass, "do you remember when we first sat together on the bus in the beginning of the school year?"

"Of course, I do!" I said.

"It doesn't seem like that long ago, but don't you think we're different than we were at the beginning of last year?" she asked.

I was looking up at the sky. The clouds were beginning to clear, and the moonlight's reflection made swirls of magic in the sky. Every so often, some stars came into view. I didn't answer Kate's question. We both already knew the answer.

"Kate, you know the words from *The Little Prince* that were highlighted in Marc's book? I think that's how it's going to be for us, too," I said.

"I know just what you mean, Goldie. Even if we don't see each other very much, we're still each other's best person, and the stars will remind us of that," she said, closing her eyes for a bit. I pulled her up and we both got on the double swing, just for a little while. The whole time I could feel her arm against mine as we held the middle rope.

We didn't know what time it was anymore when we decided to walk back to the apartment. It was peaceful along the edge of town. Once we got close to the woods, we heard some snapping sounds and some creepy animal noises. We ran, careful not to make too much noise, all the way to the alley without looking back.

The door to our apartment was unlocked. Someone, it seemed, had remembered me. Kate stumbled over Teddy's shoe, which wasn't usually at the entry. According to the clock, it was 2:47 am. I gasped when I entered my bedroom. Teddy was sound asleep on my bed, on top of the covers, still wearing the clothes from the day before, except for his shoes. I knew I was going to have to share my bed with Kate, but I hoped we wouldn't have to share it with Teddy, too.

Sparky was sleeping away in his cradle. Elise turned over in her bed and woke.

"Oh, Goldie, I thought you were sleeping at Kate's!" she said. I had forgotten that it would be our last night sharing a room, but it was also my last night with Kate, so we all got mixed up.

"It's okay. We can sleep on the couch," I said. As I opened the closet to get the extra blankets, I thought of getting Marc's picture from inside the secret door. I wanted to hide it, and the letter and the book, away from Mama for keeping him from me for so long. As I looked up at the high shelves in the closet, something occurred to me. There were two sleeping bags on the tallest shelf. I climbed up onto the shelf and pulled them down. Mine, for Kate, and Elise's, for me. They smelled musty and a bit like the last campfire that we had, but I could still detect a little bit of Elise's spicy-flowery smell on hers.

"Hey, Elise, don't tell Mama. We're going to sleep on the roof tonight," I announced. Teddy was still sleeping in the same position.

"You're what?" she asked. "Oh, never mind. Just be careful, and don't get in trouble." There was one time that she and Teddy did get in trouble for sneaking up there.

"Goldie?" called Kate from the doorway, "Don't forget a flashlight this time."

We managed to climb up the ladder and out onto the roof without making much noise at all. We had to be super slow about shutting the skylight, though, so it didn't slam when we closed it. On top of the Warehouse Apartments, we were even closer to the night sky. The stars shone brightly, and I felt as if I were among them. I was tired, but I knew I wouldn't sleep.

The town of Charlotte was quiet. Every so often, Kate thought of something that she wanted to say to me, or I, to her. She asked me questions, mostly about Kip. She wondered if I loved him because she thought I did. She made me promise to save the letters that he wrote so she could read every word the next time we saw each other. I asked her about Terrence, mostly because she had asked about Kip. I also asked about her dad because I really wondered. I wondered if talking about Marc made her miss him more, but she said she didn't think so, but even if it did, she was so happy for me that I had found him.

While we were up there, we heard some noises. Kate would shine the light, and it would usually be nothing. Once, a bird landed on the ledge, and we could actually hear the flapping of its wings in the calm of the very early morning. A car alarm went off at some point. Kate grabbed the flashlight and, starting at one corner where the edge of the roof met the ledge, traced the lines to make sure that we were the only ones up there. Something sparkled back at her when she shone the flashlight on a small patch of the rooftop behind the skylight. She held the flashlight there, and I could hear as she took a deep breath. What seemed like the boniest part of Kate's elbow stabbed suddenly, sharply into my ribs.

"Look!" she exclaimed. "Could that be your stone from Kip?" We had been huddled together on top of the sleeping bags. The night air was still very warm, but neither of us wanted to be far from the other up there, on top of the Warehouse Apartments, where we were not supposed to be anyway. She stood up, pulling me with her.

There, in a pile with a few rocks and a handful of

gravel, was the sparkly stone from Heritage. It must have fallen from Kate's sweater pocket on the Fourth of July! Even in the darkness, it was more sparkly and prettier than I had remembered. Kate handed me the stone, which I slipped immediately into the pocket of my shorts.

"Now, don't ever let go of that, Goldie. Let it remind you of our adventures, too, along with all of the ones you had with Kip," said Kate.

We curled up together in our spot on the roof. With Kate's arm around me and the stone pressing sharply into my hip from its place in my pocket, we finally drifted off to sleep under the stars, which were, indeed, beautiful.

"Goldie!" A muffled voice called my name. There was loud pounding coming from below me. Before I realized that it was Teddy and that he was banging from inside the skylight, I was dreaming that Marc had come for me.

I pushed Kate's arm from across my neck and shook her awake. She asked what time it was, and I said I didn't know. The sun was beating on the black roof of the building. It was already so humid.

"Goldie! You awake?" Teddy banged at the skylight again just as I reached to open it. "Oh, hey, you almost knocked me off this ladder. Not such an early bird this morning, are you?" Teddy laughed.

Kate, still trying to wake up from our not-very-restful sleep on top of the Warehouse Apartments, followed me down the ladder.

"Elise just finished feeding the baby," said Teddy. "He's all ready for you. Just bring him to our place when he gets hungry. Thanks, Goldie. You're the best." He left before I had a chance to respond and before Kate had even made it to the bottom of the ladder. Sparky lay sleeping in the cradle.

I looked around the room. Most of Elise's things were already gone. Her bed was still there, but she had taken her blanket, the quilt that Aunt Aida's friend had made when Mama's mama died, and her pillow. The little corner that I had set up for Sparky was empty. I wondered if Elise had kept the milk mug with the little plants and the copy of *The Little Prince*. I hoped so.

Her section of the closet was also bare. She probably hadn't had time to look inside the secret door to find Marc's letter or anything. She never kept anything in there, anyway. Then, I remembered the harmonica, tucked away inside the secret door with Marc's picture and letter. I had thought of giving it to Kate, so she would still be able to play music even though she had to give her flute back to Mr. Shankman. Kate, I knew, needed the harmonica more than I did. When she played it, I hoped she would think of our time together, so she would never forget me. The harmonica barely fit in my pocket, stuffed in my shorts with the sparkly stone.

"Goldie! It's almost ten! Sarah's going to come for me soon..." Kate burst from the bathroom. "Goldie... I'm going home! I'M GOING HOME NOW!!!" She nearly knocked me over as she jumped up and down.

"Shh...you're going to wake Sparky!" I said, though I wouldn't have minded if she did.

We walked together through the kitchen, where I stopped briefly to offer Kate some toast and jelly. She didn't want any, though. She said she had to go. She turned and walked to the door. I popped two pieces of bread in the toaster because I was starting to feel hungry, and then I ran through the living room to catch her before she left.

"Hey...here..." I said, as I slipped the harmonica into Kate's hands. She looked down at the dull metal harmonica, covered in both of our fingerprints, and probably Gabriella's, too. Her brown eyes welled with tears.

"This is the best gift anyone has ever given me," she said, as she wrapped her long arms around me. "I love you, Goldie Bird. Goodbye."

We promised to write to one another, just like me and Kip. She was hoping her mom would get her a phone soon. Kate told me that as soon as she got her driver's license, she would come to Charlotte, and we would have another adventure. That seemed like a really long while, but then I thought of the words from *The Little Prince*, and it didn't seem quite so far away. My toast, which I had already forgotten, popped as I walked back through the kitchen to my bedroom. Sparky still slept peacefully. From the window next to my bed, I watched Kate as she walked down Follaton Road. Her thin frame got smaller and smaller as she got farther from me, nearer to where she was going. At one point, I saw her pull out the harmonica, and I wondered what song she played as she faded into the distance.

There was a hollow feeling inside of me as I returned to the kitchen for my breakfast. I watched the empty plate slide into the bubbly dishwater, disappearing as did so many things in my life. Sparky's pig noises disrupted my thoughts. I lifted him from the cradle and held him in the window. He watched me as I looked out onto the town, wondering what would be next.

Boxes were everywhere in Apartment #1. I could barely get through the doorway with Sparky in my arms. Elise was sleeping on the couch that John-John had left. Teddy took Sparky from me. Already, I could tell that the two looked alike. I wondered if people would have said that about Marc and me.

"Goldie," said Teddy, "you know, we could never do

this without you. This stuff is hard for Elise, and for me, too. You are making it easier. So, thank you."

I looked at Elise, who did not look as sad when she was sleeping. She had to feed Sparky, though, so I knew we had to wake her.

While Elise took care of the baby, Teddy pulled the stroller from the mound of baby things in the living room. It would be easier, he told me, to take it down the stairs before we put Sparky in. Teddy turned toward the front of the building. This took me by surprise.

"Hey, could we...could you take that out the back way, please?" I asked, as my heart jumped in my chest.

"What?" asked Teddy.

"I think we'll go through the alley. It would just be easier to go out the back," I explained.

"Anything for you, Goldie," smiled Teddy.

They told me to be careful with the baby and to come back if we needed anything. Elise gave me her phone and said to call if we needed anything. I gathered my tiny nephew as we started on our first adventure.

Sparky looked like he did not yet belong in the stroller. He was so small. Even with a blanket tucked on each side of his body, he only took up a little section of the stroller. We rolled along Follaton Road for a while before I was feeling so sorry for him looking so lost among those blankets that I scooped him up and held him in one arm as I pushed the stroller with the other. I remembered what

Teddy and Elise had said about being careful, so I used one of the blankets to protect the baby from the sun.

It had been about an hour and a half since Kate had gone. I knew Sarah would have picked her up to take her to her mom's by then. Walking by Miss Marie's house would have made me sad. I passed her block and went along to the next block, where I turned to take the long way to the baseball fields.

The fields at the high school were empty. It was close to noon, so I knew that the players would be coming soon for summer ball practice. We wouldn't need much time. After taking a few minutes to look around and to breathe in the familiar baseball smell, I left the stroller and my flip flops near the dugout. I hoped that Sparky would be ready for this. He was three weeks old, and I thought it was time.

I looked to the top of the bleachers, up to the highest rail, where I would sneak to balance when Elise didn't know. There was a lump in my throat, probably because I was trying to swallow all the thoughts about not having Kate around anymore, or maybe because I wasn't sure if I should really be doing this with Elise's baby.

It was easy getting up to the third, and even the fourth long, metal seat. Sparky was light in my arms and still kind of sleeping. His grayish-violet eyes opened from time to time, but it didn't really seem like he was looking at anything in particular. I felt like crying. The last time I had been at the field was for Teddy's last game before Sparky was even born. I missed baseball. I couldn't imagine how Teddy must have been feeling to know that he had to give up playing, mostly because of the little, tiny guy that I held so tightly just then. Someday, though, I knew that Teddy would take Sparky here, and he would teach him how to play the game that had meant so much to him.

A cloud cover gave a break from the sun, but the bleachers were hot under my bare feet. The fifth row was the top. My throat ached. It was hard to hold back the tears, so I didn't. Nobody would see me there, I reasoned, unless the summer ball players showed up, but I doubted they would even notice me. We were high above the field. I showed Sparky where his daddy stood to play shortstop, and I told him a little about pitching and catching—what I knew about them, anyway. I told him everything else that I could think of about baseball. I turned toward the very top rail, but something kept me from climbing any higher. Teddy and Elise had told me to be careful, and I was pretty sure balancing with their baby on the top rail of the bleachers was not what they had in mind.

I let the tears fall for Kate, for Kip, for Elise, for Marc, and even for Mama, and for knowing that I really wasn't a little girl anymore and balancing on the bleacher rail would be a bad idea. Then, Sparky made a little pig noise, so I knew he would be hungry before too long. I carried him, just like before, and pushed the stroller along the sidewalk toward town. As I gripped the bar of the stroller, I noticed that Kate's bracelet was no longer on my wrist. Somewhere, sometime, it had fallen away, as so many other things seemed to have done.

A car horn startled me, and as I turned around, I saw Teddy's car.

"Goldie! I'll give you a ride," he called from the window as he pulled up close to the curb. The loud music coming from Teddy's car made my feet vibrate.

I hadn't really wanted a ride. I liked walking with the baby. Still, I approached the car and strapped Sparky into his car seat while Teddy folded the stroller which we really hadn't even needed. He must have noticed my tear-stained face. "You okay?" he asked, turning the volume down on the stereo.

Looking down at my sparkly blue toenail polish, fresh from the night before, I nodded.

"It seemed like it might rain. I wanted to make sure you were alright," he said. "And I'm glad you didn't take him all the way up there."

"Huh?" I asked, keeping my head down.

"All the way up on that top bar on the bleachers. The way you always liked to balance. I'm glad you stopped at the last bench," said Teddy.

"You saw me? At the games?" I was confused.

"Of course, I saw you at the games. And I saw you

today, with Sparky," he said.

I still felt the knot in my throat as I looked at Teddy. "I wanted to. I wanted to take him up there, but I was afraid. When it was just me, it was different," I said.

"Yep," said Teddy, "It's different now..." His voice trailed away.

We just sat there for a minute. Sparky made a little pig noise every so often. "You really miss him, don't you?" Teddy asked.

"Who?" I wondered.

"The boy from Heritage. What was his name again?" Teddy asked. I hadn't talked too much about Kip to Teddy, so it surprised me that he would even remember.

"Kip. Yeah, I do," I said. "Seems like lots of people I care about go away."

"You know," he said, "Heritage isn't really that far away, Goldie. I think we should take a road trip sometime. We could show Sparky some of his history," he laughed. "You've been amazing, helping Elise and Sparky, and me. It's the least we could do."

My eyes widened. The thought of going back to Heritage seemed surreal. I knew, though, that soon Kip would be leaving. Still, it made me feel happy just thinking that Teddy would do that for me. Maybe if I asked, he would take me to Ohio instead. It was closer, anyway.

"Promise?" I asked. And he promised.

"Goldie, promise me you won't take him birch-bending. At least, not yet, okay?" We both laughed. I was feeling lots better.

More pig noises came from the back seat, and Teddy pulled away from the curb and began the short drive back to the Warehouse Apartments. Thankfully, he parked in the alley, and we took the back stairs.

Apartment #1 was already beginning to smell like Elise. In the couple of hours that I had been gone with the baby, Teddy and Elise had worked hard to get boxes unpacked and things put away. I looked up at the high ceilings which were just like ours. The light came in from the big windows, bright even with the clouds in the sky, just like it did in our place. It was the same, but it was different, because it was theirs. They thanked me for taking the baby, and Elise said I would be welcome to sleep on the couch anytime.

I left the apartment and closed the door behind me. I really wanted to go back and tell Elise and Teddy about Marc, but I didn't.

The mail carrier was just leaving out the front door when I left Elise's place. When I walked through the hall, I could smell something baking. A driving rain had begun by the time I made it down the back stairs. I really hoped all the hard stuff might get washed away once and for all. I ran around to the front of the building and opened the heavy glass door to the landing. Through the tiny window on mailbox #4, I could see a white envelope, addressed to

"Goldie Bird Martell" in red ink, and I knew right away that it was from Kip.

"Oh, hey, Goldie," I heard Mama's voice just when I was about to open Kip's letter. "Mr. Quinn is in the shop for a while this afternoon. Would you like to go to Piper's with me?" she asked.

I really didn't, I thought, as I stuffed Kip's letter into the pocket of my shorts.

Mama and I went down the back stairs together. As the rain slowed, the wind picked up. I could smell the mint and basil from the herb garden as we walked near the fence. The shower had softened the hard, late summer ground in the flower beds outside the shop. Rosa was sitting on the bench. She ignored Mama, as she often did.

"Goldie! Bird!" she called out, not looking at me.

I waved to Rosa, calling her name, and kept walking with Mama.

"I like Rosa," I told Mama. "She's my friend. She teaches me a lot about flowers and things like that."

We picked a table near the window, the same one where I had sat with Elise the day she threw up in the bathroom. Piper asked how Elise was doing and how the baby was, and she said to be sure to stop at the counter before we left because she wanted to send another loaf of cheese bread home with us. Mama and I ordered lattes, Mama's plain, and mine with vanilla syrup, and we each got lemon shortbread. I liked Piper's lemon shortbread even more than Elise liked her cheese bread.

I hadn't thought about why Mama would want to take me for coffee until we sat down. She got quiet and didn't look at me. That meant that she had something to say. She reached into her back pocket and pulled out a photograph, placing it on the table before me. She took a deep breath but still didn't look at me. I knew before she spoke what she was going to say.

"Goldie, that's Marc in the photo," she said in a quiet, shaky voice that made me feel sad. This was so hard for her. "He's standing next to Davy and me. This was from the day we went to the courthouse to get married," she said. When she looked up briefly, I could see the tears lined up, waiting to fall.

I took the picture from Mama. My hand trembled, but I said nothing.

"Marc was Davy's college roommate," Mama continued. "He stayed upstate in the college town after Davy and I moved to Charlotte, when Davy got his job. Marc had been visiting for the weekend when the accident happened," she said quietly. "We would get together when we could. We had such a strong friendship, the three of us," said Mama.

My head was spinning. I really wished that Elise had

been sitting beside me, eating her cheese bread, and just making it easier to hear all this stuff, even if she said nothing at all. I remembered, then, that I hadn't even told Elise about Marc's letter.

I stared at the photograph. Mama looked exactly like Elise, especially because it was hard to tell what color her eyes were in this photo. She must have been about Elise's age. Davy had both of his arms around her, and her hands held tightly to his wrists. Mama had on a flowy white cotton dress and brown sandals. She wore a garland crown in her hair, which was tied up on top of her head the way she often still wore it, and the way Elise often wore hers. Davy was handsome. His hair was brown, darker than Mama's. I had seen pictures of him before. Marc, who looked just the same as in the picture that he had sent but with a little shorter hair, was hugging both of them. In this picture, too, he had that smile where one side of his mouth went a little higher, just like mine. They all looked so happy. I was sure that they had been.

"It was so hard and confusing when the accident happened. Davy was gone and Marc was recovering. Elise was a little girl, and, well, everything was just too much," said Mama. She looked down at the crumbs that were left from her lemon shortbread. She wiped a tear from the side of her face.

"Mama..." I managed.

"Goldie, I know I shouldn't make excuses. Remember

when I told you my friend from Heritage made me remember how I used to be and that it was just nice to have seen him? Things should have been different with Marc. I wish it could have been more like it was with my friend, like how we could just enjoy each other's company. With Marc, everything was mixed up, and we both knew that, or we thought we did. So, we just parted ways," she said.

I looked at the picture again. I saw so much of myself when I looked at Marc.

"It was hard not to contact him, to honor the decision that we had made together," she continued, "but it wasn't hard to find him when you asked me to. He answered my message right away. I hope he contacts you. Goldie, you shouldn't have had to ask me to...." Mama's voice trailed off, and I saw her wipe another tear from the same cheek. She stopped talking.

I wondered how long we had been sitting at Piper's. Mama hadn't finished her coffee. I hoped nobody was listening to what Mama had been saying. I thought of something then that hadn't occurred to me before. Not once could I remember having heard Mama talk about her own father, and I had never asked, or even wondered. I thought then that that was part of why none of this was easy.

"Mama, I have his picture. He sent it to me along with a letter," I said. I didn't mention the book. Mama was holding her coffee cup, but I could tell she wasn't drinking from it. I didn't know if I should say anything else. Maybe I didn't want to share Marc with her. I wanted what tiny part I finally had to be all mine.

Mama put her cup on the table and reached for my hand. "We went through a lot. I wanted to protect you, Goldie," she said. "I'm sorry."

"I know, Mama," I said. I squeezed her hand so she could really feel that I meant it.

"You deserve to be part of this," she said. "I'm really happy he sent you the letter."

I wasn't exactly sure about everything that Mama had said, but I started to feel like we were going to be okay together, her and me. I slid the photograph back toward her. She picked it up without letting go of my hand.

"We need each other, Goldie," she said quietly. I squeezed her hand one more time.

"I should be going back to the shop, sweetie," said Mama, as she picked at the last few bits of her shortbread. She had never called me "sweetie" before. That was what she had always called Elise.

"Should I get Elise's cheese bread?" I asked, pushing my chair from the table.

"Your sister would love that," said Mama, as she stood to leave. "I love you, Goldie, and I'm sorry," she said. And I could feel the love from her heart to mine.

Mama went back to work. As I was leaving the shop with Elise's cheese bread, there was Gabriella, sitting on the bench outside. I could see the straps from her pink bikini that she wore under her t-shirt, tied at the back of her neck.

"Hey, Goldie! Your mom told me you were inside. Want to go to the pool?" she asked.

We walked together up the back stairs and into our apartment. As I was changing into my bathing suit, I remembered Kip's letter, which was still sticking out of the pocket of my shorts. I would have to wait for a little while longer to open it. I tucked it safely inside the secret door alongside Marc's letter, just in case.

I thought of all the times I had walked up Follaton Road with Kate. I was glad to still have someone to walk with me, even if it wasn't the same.

"Goldie, you should join the dance team with me," Gabriella said. "The tryouts are during the first week of school, and I know you'll get picked because there is nobody that is able to balance up high as well as you!"

I didn't tell her that I would rather stay home and do nothing, or at least join the band again. I didn't tell her, because even though the dance team seemed awful, I loved that she wanted me to be part of it with her.

"I'll think it over," I told her, even though I knew I didn't need to.

Gabriella's dad picked her up from the pool just before more storms rolled in. His car had a Christmas tree smell, like John-John Quinn. He insisted on dropping me off at the Warehouse Apartments so I wouldn't have to walk home in the rain. I had only met her dad a few times before, but he asked that I call him "Leo." He said it made him feel like a young guy, which made me laugh and made Gabriella roll her eyes.

"See you soon, Goldie," Gabriella said, as I closed the door to Leo's car. I waved to them and thought that maybe Gabriella and I would still be friends even if our names didn't start with the same letter. They had dropped me off in the alley, and I hurried up the back stairs. As I passed Victoria and Robin's door, I could tell the baking smell was coming from their apartment.

When I opened Kip's letters, even after nearly a year, my hands still shook, and my heart pounded in my chest like the very first time. I sat on the floor in the musty smelling closet, still in my bathing suit, and read Kip's letter.

Dear Goldie,

I can't believe you're an aunt!

I really love working with the bees with Nina. One or two times every week, as long as the weather is right, I ride my bike to her farm after school to help her. She makes me dinner. Sometimes she gives me her good brownies to take home.

We're getting ready to harvest honey for the second time this season. This honey will have a different taste than the earlier harvest since the sources for nectar are different. Isn't that so cool? I think I might want to get my own bees someday, or at least work with them for my job like Nina's daughter, May, the one who works with bees in the almond groves in California.

Baseball was amazing! I'm going to play fall baseball in Heritage. I'm not moving back to Ohio after all—not yet. The city offered to buy Grandpa Charlie's building. Since he had been considering closing the store at some point, he decided to accept what they offered. He's going to take his time to close his business.

My parents thought it would be great for me to stay in Heritage for eighth grade to help Grandpa Charlie. Then we would both move back home. I think it's a good plan for everyone.

Promise that you will come to Heritage, Goldie. I want to show you the hives. It will be amazing to see you again.

Love, Kip

I thought that sounded like a great plan, especially because Teddy was going to take me to Heritage. He had promised.

My heart skipped a beat, then, as I read Kip's words again: a girl named May...almond groves...California.... My head began to spin.

The electricity feeling was back, running up and down my legs. Without even changing from my bathing suit, I gathered my letter from Kip and the one from Marc, along with Marc's photo, and crossed the hall to Elise's apartment just as a rumble of thunder shook the building. Teddy answered the door. He had chocolate around his mouth and in his teeth.

"I need Elise," I begged, pushing past him. "It's really important!"

Elise came out from the bedroom. She knew. She always knew when I needed her.

"Elise!" I was shaking.

"What is it, Goldie?" she asked. "Wait, just a second." Elise disappeared into the kitchen, returning with a plate of brownies. She sat on the couch and pulled me next to her, offering me a brownie. She was already on her second. I put my hand up to refuse. I knew I couldn't eat just then.

"Do you know Nina's kids? Or her grandkids or anything?" I asked, almost frantic. "Did you ever meet her daughter, May?"

"Goldie, what…. Are you okay? I mean, no, I have never seen any of them. I've never even been in Nina's house. I don't remember her even talking about her kids. Why? I mean, I only saw Aida like once a year, not even, but I don't remember ever hearing about Nina's kids…" she said. "Why, Goldie?"

I couldn't speak.

"God, those brownies…" Teddy piped as he took two more from the now half-empty plate. I wondered if they were eating the brownies that the girls down the hall had made.

"Could…I mean, could he have married Nina's daughter?" I managed to ask.

"Goldie, what…who? What are you talking about?" Elise reached for another brownie.

"It's just that…I wonder if Ni—" I was afraid to say anything more. I handed Elise the letters and gave the photo to Teddy, so he would have something to do besides eat all the brownies.

I walked into the bedroom where Sparky was sleeping. I wished he could stay little like that, so quiet and calm. Hard things would happen to him, because hard things happened to everyone. Good things would also happen to him. Good things had already begun to happen to Sparky because he had a mom and a dad who loved him and an aunt who was going to make sure he had the best adventures.

Teddy was sitting with Elise when I returned. The letters fell as she opened her arms for me. Teddy wrapped his strong arms tightly around both of us, just as Marc had wrapped his arms around Mama and Davy in the picture that Mama had shown me.

"So, Goldie, you think that Marc somehow ended up in California with Nina's daughter?" asked Elise, "…and you think Nina…you think Nina is your grandmother, or step-grandmother, I guess?" Her violet eyes sparkled with wonder.

I didn't think. *I knew.* I reached for the last brownie on the plate. I could think of only one other person's brownies that had ever tasted better.

"I guess we'll have another reason to take that trip to Heritage," said Teddy. I hoped so much that he was right.

That night, I slept on Teddy and Elise's couch, and I dreamed that I was with Kip, high atop the hill behind the Courtyard, watching the sparkly violet sunset.

I carried Sparky into the woods. He liked looking up at the birch trees. We walked for a long time before he fell asleep. I kept on for a bit, deeper into the woods, until I found a stump that looked like a good resting spot. For late August, it already seemed a bit cool. In just a week, I would start seventh grade. I was going to have to decide if I would join the dance team with Gabriella or stick with the band, which I mostly liked because of Kate. I remembered Marcy Clown, the other flute player, the one who had the twitching eye. I liked her. I figured Gabriella would understand if I chose band.

Sparky slept in my arms as I thought about how the next day would mark exactly one year since I had met Kip. I was grateful for the sunsets, the laughing, the ice cream, the birch bending, but most of all for the way Kip made me feel important, like I meant something to him. I had a sparkly stone to remind me of that every day. One day, I knew I would gather the courage to write to Marc and even ask him about Nina. As I stood, the filtered light flashed across Sparky's perfect little face, waking him from his sleep. His eyes opened.

"That's the sun. And those are birch trees," I told him. "You and me, Sparky, we are going to climb up one of those birch trees someday, and I will have the best surprise for you," I promised. Then, Sparky's eyes lit up. His tiny mouth opened, and out came the most beautiful, sweetest laugh I had ever heard. It could have come from the Little Prince himself!

I stopped at the shop to see if Mama was still there.

Elise had been meeting with Mr. Quinn to talk through some of the details about what her job was going to be. Mama thought she might be staying just a little late that evening to finish some things. It was actually Elise, though, who was locking up the store when I got there.

"Hey, Mr. Quinn was hoping that you could stay with Rosa for a little while tonight," said Elise, as she took Sparky from me. "He and Mama are going to get some dinner."

I handed Elise her phone, which she had given me to take just in case Sparky needed something. I wondered if I should tell her that I heard the baby laugh. I didn't, because I knew she would want him to laugh for her for the first time. It would be our little secret. Sparky's and mine. The first of many.

"And Goldie," began Elise, as I turned toward the door, "did you know that Sparky smiles now?"

"Aw, that's so cute," I said. I did know that because, though I knew you could smile without laughing, I knew you couldn't laugh without smiling.

Rosa was sitting on the front steps holding a book when I reached the Quinns' house. She lifted her head but did not look at me. "Goldie. Goldie Bird." She stood, taking my hand. Rosa laughed then and continued to pull me through the living room and into the kitchen where I was surprised to see Mama and Mr. Quinn standing close to one another.

"Goldie. Bird! Smiley!" Rosa exclaimed, jumping up and down this time. On the counter in the kitchen was a small bird cage. In the cage was a tiny yellow canary.

"She calls it 'Goldie Bird Smiley,' Goldie," said Mr. Quinn. "She named him after you, and after your bird, I guess. Seems like quite an honor."

I smiled at Mr. Quinn. He had gotten Rosa a bird.

"Goldie, read!" said Rosa then, handing me the book that she had carried inside. It was *The Little Prince*. I had decided to leave the copy from our bookshelf with Rosa since I had one from Marc. The torn strip of paper still marked the page where we had left off the last time, which was the same place we left off every time because Rosa always wanted to start at the beginning. We went back out to the porch where I opened the book to the beginning.

Rosa laughed and pushed my hand. "No, Goldie," she said, as I began to read. "Goldie. Read." Then, Rosa took the book from my hand. She turned the pages, briefly studying each one. I noticed some lavender sprigs poking out from the pocket of her overalls. When she reached the page where we had left off the time before, the spot marked by the paper strip, she handed me the book and pointed to the last word we had read previously. "Goldie, read. Please read," she said. I heard Sparky's laughter and also that of the Little Prince along with Rosa's as I thought of how we had tamed each other.

We had read only a few pages when Mama and Mr. Quinn left to go to dinner. I wondered if they were going to Burger Central, how long they would be gone, and what they would talk about. At some point, as they walked further up the road, Mr. Quinn wrapped his arm gently around Mama's shoulder.

Dear Kip,

I'm glad you're staying with Grandpa Charlie for a while longer. Maybe things happen to help us along a little bit when we are trying to decide what to do...

I told him all about what I had been thinking, about Marc and Nina, and how small the world seemed, kind of like the Little Prince's planet, about how I had always wished to have a grandma, and how I figured out that just maybe I did have one all along...unless...well, I wasn't going to think about that.

I'm ready for school, and for whatever else is going to happen this year.

Love, Goldie

I held my breath as my foot hit the first step on the staircase that led to the front of the building. Though I was fearful, I kept going. I tucked Kip's letter into the "outgoing mail" slot under the mailboxes and pushed open the heavy door to the morning sunshine, careful not to touch the glass that had been replaced after my fall. Something caught my eye as I approached the bus stop. Perched on the back of the bench outside the coffee shop was a tiny goldfinch, ready to take flight. I boarded the bus for my first day of seventh grade, claiming the same seat that Kate and I had shared the last year. Though I was by myself in the seat, I didn't really feel alone. As the bus pulled away from the curb, I leaned into the window and watched the little goldfinch fly off toward the sun.

The End

...or maybe just the beginning, depending on the direction of the sun...

Author the Author

Patty Ihm is a writer, former early intervention therapist, and teacher living in Illinois on a farmette where she

 is a mother to many; three biological, six adopted, and 18 children she and her husband have offered their home to as foster parents—some for a day and some to stay forever. She is also the author of *Isn't That Enough? Musings of Motherhood and the Meaning of Life*, a memoir published by Our Galaxy Publishing in 2022, and *Ode to a Boy*, a self-published work dedicated to her now grown sons.

Fueled on coffee and the soul-cleansing therapy of the written word, Patty tends to thirty-something chickens, a mix of hens and roosters, nine bee hives, and a thriving garden. In the quiet parts of the day (and sometimes amidst the chaos of life), Patty finds pockets of time to write and share her experiences with others.

To learn more about Patty and her books, visit her website:

www.pattyihm.com

Our Galaxy Publishing is a service-based platform for aspiring authors to get the tools and resources they need to write, edit, publish, and market their books and build their author platforms. Our mission is to promote an entrepreneurial mindset around becoming a published writer, educating and supporting women-identifying people about the publishing landscape and how to move through the ever-changing industry and literary world.

We're putting the power back in the writer's hands with a team of experts who empower authors to take creative control of their experience. Our array of services spans from writing and publishing assistance to strategic planning and marketing, ensuring authors have everything they need to succeed regardless of their publishing path.

Join our expedition: www.ourgalaxypublishing.com
Follow us on Instagram: @ourgalaxypublishing
Follow us on Facebook: @ourgalaxyco